Finding

Harmony

by Boda Wise

To my friend Rhonda from Janet a.k.a. Boda Wise 7/18/2019 BE WELL :)

First edition, April 2011

Copyright © 2011 by Boda Wise

Boda Wise
Finding Harmony, First Edition, 276 pages
   ISBN-13: 978-1461089803
   ISBN-10: 1461089808

Printed in U.S.A.

Dedicated to the one who knows me more than I know myself,
to my beloved friends around the world who share my real life and
my virtual life, to the musicians who inspire me, and to all
who love stories of faith, hope and redemption.

Shall I go walk the wood so wild,

Wand'ring, wand'ring here and there,

As I was once full sore beguiled,

Alas! for love! I die with woe.

Wearily blows the winter wind,

Wand'ring, wand'ring here and there,

My heart is like a stricken hind,

Alas! for love I die with woe.

— The Woods So Wild (a traditional song)

ಬ *1* ೞ

At a time in early spring when Jack Brewster would otherwise have been idly following warmer climates across southern states, he found himself parking his well-weathered green van along the curb of an old, familiar neighborhood in Portland, Oregon. With emotions jumbled in a tumult of distress, nostalgia and melancholy, he hesitated, poised to switch off the ignition, as a deep uneasiness overtook him and he fought a sudden, strong urge to put his foot to the accelerator and retrace the short route back to the interstate highway. Turning his eyes toward the house, he gathered his courage and shut off the engine.

Graffiti assaulted the outer walls and the detached garage in hastily sprayed layers — evidence of cryptic skirmishes in a territorial turf war between rebels hungering for control. For Jack, its message screamed that the peaceful neighborhood of his distant memory was overrun with anger, and no longer existed. He was entering a long-avoided battle zone, exposing the obscure markings sprayed across his soul to claim him during the war against his youth — a war which had never been won, but one from which he'd put himself at a safe distance more than two decades earlier.

Rationalizing that time had passed and ended that turmoil, his shaking hand told him otherwise as he lifted the latch and pushed the van door open, forcefully, as if a hundred devils held it closed. While time may have altered the battle zone, his war still waged. As he strode toward the porch from the curb and halted on the front lawn, a lingering scan of the area punctuated that reality. Weather-beaten houses on junk-strewn lots dotted the street, visually mocking an equal number of tidy homes that begged for order amidst apathy and neglect. Turning his gaze back to the property he now owned, he was surprised to notice its freshly mowed lawn and neatly trimmed shrubs, which made no sense whatsoever.

It had been several months since the notification of his uncle's death had caught up with him in Austin, Texas, the most recent stop in his itinerant life as a musician. By the time he'd received the lawyer's package, there had been nothing to do but sign the paperwork via notary and secure the keys. Impersonal formalities had marked the unceremonious end of the last member of his family in a manner that, with respect to Jack's wandering life and aimless detachment, invoked an uncomfortable awareness that his own death would be equally as unceremonious. But it would now be complicated by material possesions, with no heir for claim.

That his uncle had made Jack sole beneficiary was understandable, since there was no one else in his family line and their relationship had been as close to father and son as any secondary relatives could become. The bond they'd shared throughout the early years of Jack's life had been deep and strong, filled with incredible music, influencing his direction, shaping his character and defining his manhood, much supported and enriched by the tender kindnesses of his nurturing aunt.

Jack's ties to his Uncle Dan and Aunt Eva had gradually tapered off during the years of constant travel that framed his adult life, eventually dwindling to a few odd phone calls and greeting cards, often received long after any associated event had passed. A mutual, unspoken fence had grown slowly across their painful memories, to be crossed rarely, if only to keep the best memories of loving each other alive. His last call to his Uncle Dan had occurred a little less than a year before, the week after his Aunt Eva had been laid to rest. It was the first time he'd known his uncle to cry, yet he'd still not perceived the true depth of pain that had evoked the tears.

Until now.

Jack's scheduled performances had prevented him from attending his aunt's funeral. He'd made sincere plans to visit his uncle as soon as he could clear his calendar of obligations and bookings, but the plans had been sketchy and the timing too late, much to his profound regret. All that now remained was the material and empty shell of their lives — possessions gracing a broad-porch Victorian style home in an aging northern section of the city.

The estate included a sizable financial portfolio accumulated from years of frugal living and wise investments, along with the home and its contents, the mortgage having been settled long before with wages his Uncle Dan had earned as a master carpenter. Jack's inheritance, when added to the money he'd personally saved and invested in his minimalist existence, had offered him the unexpected opportunity to live a quiet and easy life of early retirement; yet, what would have been a reassuring comfort for most people had plagued him enormously as he'd at last cleared his schedule to make the long journey he'd dreaded taking.

Jack was forty-two years old, with no person or city to lay claim to as his own. His camper van, and an endless stream of small rooms, cheap motels and short-term rentals, had been his experience for so long that he was distressingly unsure of his ability to ever put down permanent roots, though a small but persistent part of him had begun wanting desperately to try. The wandering life, so familiar to him, had now been abruptly halted by circumstance and pain, and he was confused by the strange mix of emptiness, fear and comfort he felt. Strong memories flooded back, unguarded and overwhelming, unfettered and uncontrollable. It was a situation he was ill prepared to handle, and his sense of loss ran deep as he stood motionless on the front lawn, lost in a vortex of feelings, as if rooted to the landscape during his long moment of internal wrestling.

His feet carried him unwillingly toward the entrance. It surely wasn't the first time he'd approached the front steps of this home while juggling a disjointed array of unresolved emotions. A subtle smile of inner foolishness softened his face as he caught himself standing hesitantly at the door, dimly aware that his thumb hovered over the doorbell.

No one is here to answer, Jack.

Fingers fumbled with keys as he rationalized that today he wasn't here seeking refuge. Still, as he unlocked the door, his hand trembled and a dull pain knotted his stomach. Stepping inside the entryway to the hollow creak of aging hinges, he began from old habit to fabricate a casual story to explain his unannounced visit, half expecting his aunt and uncle to rush into the living room to greet him with welcoming smiles and unquestioning acceptance of his latest reason for being here. A disturbing silence answered his mindlessly whispered hello. The lingering aromas of Aunt Eva's baking and Uncle Dan's pipe were gone, replaced by a musty combination of dust, age and stagnant air.

It had ceased to be a home. It was now just a house, no longer deserving of the title of "home" in the welcoming sense of that word. Despite his adept comfort and vagrant ease in living a solitary lifestyle, Jack had never before felt so alone.

❧ 2 ☙

Fingers flew with precision and strength across the strings as his lips made perceptible counting motions to the beat of his guitar riff. Practice was his daily homework — his after-school routine for as long as he could remember. The discipline was self-imposed by an inner motivation that had little or nothing to do with musician worship or being cool. He had no idea what had sparked his passion for rock guitar. He only knew that his thirst to play music was insatiable.

The fury of his powerful music was for his ears only, played just below an ear-piercing level through a headset, distorted sounds slickly delivered by a small device that applied his favorite creative effects. It spared his mother from disruptive racket on her day off work. Today he'd caged himself in his room, his mind half on his playing, his thoughts unable to rest, filled with guilt in wishing she was scheduled to work.

At seventeen, Nick Weber was a young man living in two separate worlds. In one, he was a strong student with a kind and likable personality, pacing toward his final free summer before entering his senior year of high school. In this world, his neighbors and teachers all described him as a great kid with a lot of potential, and the good son of a single mother.

Nick's other world was much darker, swayed by older friends with few ambitions, whose primary pastimes were getting high, feeding their sexuality and playing loud, driving rock music, though not necessarily in any order. It was no secret amongst his peers and fellow students that Nick frequently dwelt in this other world.

His darker side of life had grown slowly over time, beginning with associations he'd developed in grade school that had centered around his good friend, Brandon Jakes, and their common interest in playing music. Two years older than Nick, Brandon was a renegade leader with few boundaries, who possessed a rare ability to charm his way through any situation. His strong presence and handsome, athletic looks were magnetic to peers and adults alike, and he got away with pretty much anything and everything he did. Brandon's smooth-talking perfection stood in stark contrast to Nick's olive-skinned, post-pubescent, boyish awkwardness which was not unusually captivating or winsome but held the promise for a handsome and confident manhood. Also unlike Brandon, he bore an underlying respect for the consequences which his actions might bring upon himself and others.

Despite their core differences, Nick was solidly in Brandon's inner circle of buddies, and he found himself liking the peer status that came with it. Nick's mother, Kate, had never particularly cared for Brandon and had never been charmed by him in the way that most people seemed to be. Had she known of the true corruptive influence that Brandon had imposed on her son over the years of their friendship, it would have shocked and crushed her.

Brandon had dropped out of school in his senior year, having the kind of family who didn't care much one way or the other. Since then he'd relied on his street smarts and friendships with neighborhood drug dealers to settle into a workable way of getting by in life, living with two roommates, who were also musicians, in a rental house just a few blocks from Nick's home — a place which had come to be known as "The Hanger". It was there that Nick could frequently be found, without the knowledge or permission of his mother, especially on the many days that she worked a twelve-hour nursing shift at the local hospital.

Nick's singular motivation for being at The Hanger was to play hard rock music. He lived for metal and traveled everywhere with his electric guitar, as though it were an additional arm. He was ready to jam at a moment's notice, and the group that gathered at The Hanger was always ready to join in. Nick's music mentors were the legendary lead guitarists of early rock — Jimmy Hendrix, Jimmy Page, Eric Clapton, Alvin Lee, Dave Gilmour, and Eddie Van Halen topped the list. He'd tirelessly studied their work and had incorporated his own ideas and techniques to develop an agile and unique style that got the attention of all who listened.

The Hanger's dining room area had become a permanent space for playing music, complete with electronic drums, sound equipment and a variety of electric guitars. Like a shrine, the walls were plastered with posters, concert notices and rock memorabilia. The atmosphere drew a steady stream of drop-in rockers as a mecca for the music and related activities, which had become a highly profitable venture to its residents. The promise of the band Nick and his friends had begun to form now drew him closer than ever to that social scene. His desire to be there ran circles around his life at home and school.

The Hanger was a party in continuous motion. People came and went, all familiar faces and all seeking to score, to hang out, or to do both. Scoring at The Hanger was meant in the broadest sense of the word, in terms of both sex and illegal substances. One of the popular upstairs rooms in the old, two-story house had earned the nickname of the "bump room". Nick had glanced into it once or twice when it was empty, but had otherwise never entered. It was furnished with a few mattresses, pillows and rugs;

a small, square table in the corner offering various drug paraphernalia; and had a sign over the door that automatically lit when the door closed.

The sign's message pronounced the room's main purpose: [No Clothes --- Anything Goes]. Most of the young people who visited The Hanger had, at one time or another, participated in bump room activities — usually privately, but sometimes in small groups. Despite the ribbing he often got from Brandon for his refusal to take part in the things he knew went on in there, Nick had opted to stay out of the room completely.

It was widely acknowledged at The Hanger that Nick was an exceptionally good musician, and it was his talent which had earned him acceptance amongst a group of kids that, in all other ways, were far more reprobate in nature than he'd ever been. Having rarely drunk more than two beers in a day and never having used any drug stronger than pot, he chose to do either of these only on very rare occasions.

The same could not be said for his cohorts, but they overlooked his reluctance to join in, counting it as a weird artistic need for clarity. His exceptional ability to play the music they loved made him a highly regarded peer. To the local rockers, Nick was a minor legend yet, while they worshiped his skills, they would never have understood or accepted his true reason for abstaining from the sex and drugs they lusted for — that he didn't want to disappoint his mother. As uncool as it was, he respected and loved her, and thus mostly avoided doing what he knew would break her heart.

Nick's two worlds suspended him in a strange conflict within his soul — the desire to excel in life and become what he knew would make his mother proud, and the need for his identity as a gifted rock musician to be proven and praised amongst the strong majority of partying kids that ruled the neighborhood and craved metal. The result was his inability to live in either world with any degree of comfort about himself.

ℬ 3 ℭ

Jack's first week in the house was mainly focused on the cleaning and clearing of living spaces. At once he had gone from a small cache of possessions that easily fit into his van, made up of clothes, musical instruments and sound equipment, to the ownership of an entire life's worth of material collecting, requiring him to sift through shelves filled with books he'd never read, cupboards stocked with items he'd never purchased, and closets stuffed with clothes still fragrant with his aunt's and uncle's scents. With the physical activity came an emotional toll that drained him each day to a point of exhaustion, yet addicted him in a strange way to the process, as if the purging and organizing of familiar items long forgotten were the means to catharsis.

That Uncle Dan had died only a few short months after Aunt Eva's passing had been a testimony to their deep love for one another. His uncle hadn't changed anything in the home, nor had he removed any of his wife's toiletries or personal items, leaving them, seemingly, as a continuous connection to his deepest affections, until his broken heart had taken him to her at last.

Jack had seldom stayed at his uncle's house for more than a few days at a time, yet it had offered the closest thing to a normal way of life than anything else he'd known—now bringing strong, deeply buried feelings to the surface. As he sorted and assessed their belongings, the process of discovery and decision-making was stirringly wrenching and filled with all the best and worst remembrances of his youth. At times he'd wept.

Uncle Dan was his mother's much older brother and, as such, he'd taken on the difficult role of dealing with the aftermath of her irresponsible and destructive choices. Sometimes that was as simple as having Jack stay overnight. Other times it had required buying groceries, gasoline, school clothes or supplies. Twice it had meant securing a bail bond to get Jack's mother out of jail.

Sifting through his uncle's belongings brought on waves of long forgotten longing to know his father, a nameless man whom his mother had never married nor spoken of. Throughout Jack's younger years, his mother's revolving selection of men had ranged from the pathetically insecure to the cruelly abusive. She had changed men as often as some women change purses, opting for something new whenever her flirtations caught the interest of a man with more money or better looks. Those seemed to be her primary factors in choice. In her younger days, finding new prospects happened quite frequently, since her beauty was undeniably stunning. The men she'd attracted were never much interested in Jack's presence on the scene, so they were always willing to drive him over to visit his Uncle Dan for the day — and the night — or for several nights. Not a single one had been fatherly.

Men who didn't choose on their own to leave his mother within the first week or two on the scene were always ousted against their will at some point. On the rare occasions when she'd paused significantly between relationships, his mother had been spontaneously fun and quite nice to be with. Jack had enjoyed those fleeting times immensely, always hoping that they indicated a change in the compass of her attentions. But when a new man inevitably entered her life, she was consumed by the relationship and Jack was left, once again, in the margins of her next chapter, barely a side note in her saga.

Neither his uncle nor his aunt had contributed to any of the hard things that Jack had faced in the chaotic young life he'd been forced to live, and they were ever the providers of the solace and stability he'd needed. Were it not for them, he wondered if he'd have survived his early days. Even when his own choices caused him suffering, from a lack of wisdom and direction, they had never failed him in their love and support. Unable to have children of their own, Jack's visits were always welcomed and treasured, and their home had been his best refuge.

Had it not been for the money and perks that his mother received from state agencies on behalf of her son, she might have allowed him to live permanently with her brother and his wife. Were it not for Jack, Uncle Dan and Aunt Eva might not have been willing to do all that they had done for his mother. He wasn't sure on either count. As it was, Jack had spent countless nights in the spare room of their home, prompted to be there voluntarily in his teens by drunken arguments, overtly sexual activities and abusive episodes that came to characterize his mother's life as she aged.

It was that same small spare room in the house he'd inherited which Jack had now chosen to remain as his bedroom. He'd felt the need to dedicate the much larger bedroom that his uncle and aunt had shared to the possesions that represented their lifelong loving devotion. Like a museum, that room now began to hold a growing number of pictures and treasures from their life spent together. It was his way of honoring them — by preserving a place of remembrance that he didn't feel privileged or worthy to be stepping into, nor idly using. At least, those were the thoughts behind his choice.

After all, what do I know of devotion and love?

❦ 4 ❧

Nick entered through the unlocked side door of The Hanger and dropped his backpack full of textbooks beside a chair in the den. Brandon's roommates, Benny Stuart and Diggs Delamondo, sat alertly and aggressively on a worn, stained sofa, each playing the same online war game, keyboards clicking to rapid finger fire on their laptop computers, which competed for space on the small coffee table with the empty take-out cartons from a Chinese lunch. They greeted him tersely without looking up, the sounds of the battle mixed with occasional shouts and curses from Diggs. Benny was obviously ruling the game.

None of The Hanger's residents held regular jobs. Benny was the oldest who, at twenty-three years of age, was the middleman for most of the drug action that supported The Hanger's activities and the neighborhood needs. Brandon, at nineteen, was Benny's main legs on the street, and Diggs, at eighteen, was the only one of the group who managed to make his rent legally, creating jewelry, t-shirts, leather guitar straps and artistic drug paraphernalia, all of which he sold on the internet.

A loud groan from Diggs ended his gaming, as his hands flew up in a gesture of defeat. "*Shit*, Benny, how'd you do that? That's enough. No more." After exiting the game and shutting down his computer, he turned to Nick and said, "Hey, dude, where's your ax?"

"I came right from school. Figured I could use one of Brandon's guitars." Music at The Hanger was an open-ended event, where equipment was readily shared.

"Sure. He may not be home anytime soon, man, unless he gets real lucky one way or the other." Diggs flashed a grin at Benny, who didn't look up from his game but offered a fiendish chuckle. Diggs added, "The rent's due tomorrow and he's short a hundred bucks. Benny won't let him slide." The two of them moved into the dining room where all the instruments were kept, set up and ready to jam.

"So, Brandon's selling at the school?" Nick asked.

"Maybe before. Now he's probably at the park, man, unless he scored big. He's got a different kind of hustle there." Diggs answered while taking a seat at the electronic drums, turning on the amplifier and adjusting sound levels by playing a few rolls.

"He's selling at the park? That's pretty stupid."

"What he sells at the park gets him a lot more money, man, and it's all his to keep. When he's real short, it's his best gig. That's when he earns his initials, but he gets pissed when we call him that for short," Diggs chortled. "C'mon, man, break out that Ibanez, and let's do some Zeppelin."

Nick grabbed the guitar and began to plug in and tune up, silently taking in what Diggs was hinting at. Brandon's initials were B.J. After playing a few warm up licks, he asked, "Is that for real, about Brandon?"

"No lie. He hates owning it, but he makes fast money from guys who dig finishing their workouts at the park with a little extra action in the johns. His looks make it work. Look, man, don't tell him I told you. He'd flip out." Diggs seemed serious, but Nick didn't want to believe it, nor could he understand something that major being thrown out as such a casual remark. He'd known Brandon since grade school and had never seen any hint of that activity from him. As handsome as Brandon was, he had girls waiting in line for him, and he loved it and took maximum advantage of them. Nick wasn't sure why this side of Brandon would disturb him, but it did. With an inward shudder, Nick shrugged off the new and disquieting thoughts and adjusted the amplifier settings, getting ready to play.

The music took over the moment as he pulled his favorite guitar pick from his pocket and began his best Jimmy Page riffs from Led Zeppelin's *Whole Lotta Love*. Diggs wailed out the lyrics to the driving tempo he set on the drums. Somewhere in the midst of the song Benny ended his online game and joined them in the dining room, picking up his bass guitar. It was Nick's turn to rule as he worked the solo break into an intricate lead progression. They continued without a pause, moving directly into songs by Metallica, Breakdown and King Crimson, opting that day to play older, classic rock in their jamming. Besides the classics, their growing repertoire included alternative metal with extreme riffs by bands like Primus, Tool, Nine Inch Nails, Disciple, Alice in Chains and Papa Roach, along with a number of originals that were written by Nick.

An hour or so later, Brandon entered through the front door.

"Hey, Nicky, how's the Tune Man?" he remarked. "You sure make that old Ibanez smoke." He grabbed his favorite guitar and joined the group. Nick soaked in the praise. Brandon's backup guitar skills now filled in the holes behind Nick's powerful lead lines as the four of them worked through an entire song set.

"Way to wail, Nick!" Benny remarked, when at last they took a break. "You've got the licks *down*." He lit a cigarette and went into the kitchen to grab a beer. Nick watched Brandon follow him there and hand him a rolled up baggie and a folded wad of money. However he'd done it, he had obviously managed to produce his share of the rent.

When Benny returned to again pick up his bass, he said, "Hey Nick, know anyone interested in some Red Mercedes? I know it ain't your thing, but it's quality E."

Nick shook his head and adjusted the amplifier's settings for more reverb. "Nah, not offhand." Whatever was left in the baggie Benny got back, he figured that it wasn't his concern. He preferred keeping his head clear and his thoughts focused on the music.

෨ 5 ෬

Sam Johnson sat alone at his kitchen table, as usual, having prayed his prayers and finished his bowl of oatmeal. His talk with God had been long that morning, and filled with remembrances and emotions that had been dormant for several months.

He missed his good friend and neighbor, Dan Brewster, with the grieving heart of a man who had lived long enough to see his deepest relationships parted by death. Dan and his wife, Eva, had supported Sam through difficult times after he'd lost his beloved Lucille more than ten years earlier. At Eva's insistence, he'd been a regular guest at their dinner table from that day on. When Eva had passed away, Sam's friendship with Dan had deepened, as Dan struggled to cope with his own loss. Despite Sam's support, the will to live had quickly ebbed from his good friend, who could no longer find meaning in everyday life. Even Dan's fiddle music, so much a part of him, couldn't bring him peace or enable him to express his sorrow. Sam watched helplessly while Dan steadily slipped away in grief and despair.

Despite his faith in God, which was the strength by which he lived his simple life, Sam had felt a disturbing new emptiness in his own existence. Still, it was the times of change that kept him looking forward. Autumn. Spring. Dusk. Dawn. He reasoned that natural, inevitable events of transition somehow carried with them a sense of hope. Life had its seasons, and each offered the ability to see familiar things from a new perspective. He clung to that reasoning.

Throughout his life, Sam had been a hard-working, humorous and straightforward individual, striving to overcome the senseless and cruel prejudices that black Americans regularly encountered in the early decades of the 1900's. Unable to afford an education beyond elementary school, he'd moved to the northwest from Mississippi and turned a part-time job with the railroad into a lifelong career that allowed him to marry and buy the home that he'd lived in for most of his life. His musical talent and innate kindness toward others had awarded him a level of sincere acceptance in the neighborhood, which was hard-won in those days. Dan Brewster had stood up for Sam against adversity on many occasions over the years, and their brotherhood had solidly bonded out of mutual respect, shared musicianship, and the unusual misfortune that neither of their marriages was blessed with the ability to have children. Through it all, Sam had read his bible and talked early each morning with God in the most natural way — as a son speaks with the father he trusts and loves.

One of the things that Sam had admired most about Dan was his response toward his family situation. Sam and Lucille had moved into the neighborhood shortly after Dan's father had passed away, when Dan was twenty-two and his sister, Elizabeth, was a precocious and sweet eight-year-old. Dan was working as a carpenter's apprentice back then, living on his own. He'd moved back home to help his widowed mother, Anna, keep their family home from repossession. She had taken on work as a clothing store's seamstress. With both of them gone in the daytime, Elizabeth (then called Beth) stayed with the neighbors next door, Lenny and Maggie. Their lives were content and stable for a few years. During that time Dan and Sam had met and discovered their mutual love for playing music. Gradually their musical porch gatherings had grown to include Lenny, who played upright bass, and a variety of drop-in neighborhood musicians who came upon their impromptu but regular events and joined in.

Beth was twelve when she first became rebellious and moody. Her bright smile and silly humor slowly faded as her studies at school noticeably declined. She ran away from home a few times, and her antics began to move into promiscuities which were reported by the school and bantered about the neighborhood through talk at the local cafe. Dan had been heartbroken to see the change in her, and it had been the topic of many deep discussions with Sam, as he'd struggled to make sense of it. He'd felt a great degree of guilt, being unable at that time to earn enough money to allow his mother to stay at home. Beth was obstinate and unreachable in any attempt to reason with her about the changes.

When Beth's behaviors had resulted in pregnancy at age fifteen, it was no real surprise. Dan and his mother had spent their hard-earned savings to send her to a special home in California, a place that would take her in throughout the pregnancy and place the child in an adoptive home after the birth. It was an action that was still somewhat common in those days, yet it had devastated their mother. Anna died of a heart attack while Beth was away, and Dan was left to maintain the home and cope with the situation. He wrote numerous letters to Beth which were seldom answered, and then only with brief solicitations and idle chat. Had he not met and married his beloved Eva, Sam felt certain that Dan's life would have been marked with hopeless despair.

After Beth's baby was born and adopted out to a family, she didn't return immediately to Portland. At age eighteen, when she finally came back, there were two surprises. One was that she was pregnant once again, with a son whom she named John but called Jack. The other was that she had changed her nickname to Liz. She'd grown to be an incredibly beautiful woman who easily attracted men and, if anything, her salacious behavior had only worsened during her time away. Liz stayed with Dan until shortly after Jack was born, then she'd taken up with a middle aged real estate broker with whom she and Jack lived for a little over a year. She'd never again returned to her childhood home, preferring to live off the attentions of a long array of lovers.

Despite the course of his sister's life, the shining outcome of the situation for Dan was Jack. His nephew was an intelligent, funny and delightful youngster who was devoted to his uncle. The fact that he possessed an unusual gift for music made their relationship all the more special. In every way Jack was like a son to Dan, and Sam had also been allowed to share in that relationship, in the role of a proud uncle and music mentor.

It had been difficult for Sam to observe the hurtful things that had regularly surrounded Jack's home life but, to his credit, Jack had handled most of them with unusual maturity. He'd focused his growing years toward the things that Dan and Sam both represented to him — decency and musical dedication. The sorrow for them, in playing that role, was being unable to avert the damaging events that had assaulted Jack's understanding of relationships. As his youth gave way to an endlessly wandering life, the aftermath of the situation was evident. He seemed unable to take root anywhere, with anyone.

It was a pleasant surprise for Sam when he'd recently observed that Jack had arrived at his uncle's home once again. Seeing that familiar green van parked beside the house for the last week or so, a flicker of light had shone onto his empty, lonesome days. A transition time. It had been many years since they'd spoken, and Sam wasn't sure if their friendship had withstood the test of time. He also wondered if his heart could endure yet another parting, and so he'd hesitated to walk around the corner to say hello, and had left the yard work for Jack to take over.

Jack might not have come to the neighborhood to stay. His years of wandering certainly made that a strong probability. Dan's old home, so rich in the good memories of bygone days, might soon be sold to owners who cared nothing for its history or its special place in the neighborhood.

Sam had made this new turn of events the main concern of his daily prayers.

ℰ𝒪 6 𝒞ℬ

Kate sat in the break room at the hospital in the very early hours of the morning, sipping a cup of coffee and resting her feet. The Progressive Care Unit had been short-staffed for several months, and a recent series of assigned twelve hour shifts were beginning to take their toll on her.

Most of all, she hated the limited time that her nursing job was allowing her to be at home with her son, Nick. He was a big help to her in handling things around the house, but she was concerned about the amount of unsupervised time he'd spent in recent months. For so many kids around their neighborhood, living in single-parent families, the story was much the same — mothers worked long hours to make ends meet, which meant their teenagers were largely on their own. Most of Nick's friends didn't share his drive to be responsible with their activities and school work. Kate was proud of the fact that he maintained a high grade point average, but she also knew that his passion for hard rock music took priority over almost anything else in his life. He often came home smelling of cigarette smoke and, while she didn't think he'd taken up the habit himself, her concerns about what might be happening during her son's idle time weighed heavily on her mind.

She'd never expected to raise him alone.

Kate reflected on her own youth, remembering the hardship of being raised by a single mother and, eventually, a stepfather whose verbally abusive influence in their lives had inflicted more damage than it had done good. It was a situation she'd tried hard to avoid in bringing up a family of her own. She'd married her high school sweetheart, Nate, when she was twenty. By then he'd finished college and entered the military, and she'd completed an associate degree in nursing. Nick was born a year later during her husband's unexpected deployment to the Gulf War in Iraq. Nate was killed in action a few months into his service there, having never held his son. It had been the most devastatingly defining period of Kate's life, crippling both her faith in God and her strong conviction that happiness in life resulted from carefully planned outcomes.

Her thoughts were interrupted when Sue Danner entered the break room, poured herself a cup of coffee, and sat down opposite Kate. "We finally had to restrain the guy in thirty-two. He kept pulling out his catheter. His wife'll probably freak when she sees him tied up later. She's been harder to deal with than he has."

"Just another day in paradise." Kate answered. "How are you holding up?" The question spanned more than the shift they were working. Sue was a long-time associate and friend of Kate's whose husband had recently been injured in an accident on his construction job, keeping him from working and cutting back their income, despite workman's comp. The ordeal had only added to Sue's stress and made her long work shifts especially difficult.

"Taking one step after another, hoping nothing trips me up. That's the only way to get through all this, isn't it? How about you? These long days been screwing up your love life?" Sue winked as she spoke, knowing that Kate's world was entirely devoid of any such thing.

"What's a love life?" Kate answered in kind. "Anyway, the only thing I miss in my bed nowadays is me comfortably sleeping in it." They both chuckled. The hospital's staff "rest areas" were notoriously bad for getting any actual rest, making their twelve hour shifts especially hard to endure.

"We need to get together soon for a good day of window shopping and an extravagant lunch. It seems like the only thrill either of us is likely to enjoy these days."

"You're on." The idea sounded good to Kate. Neither of them were avid shoppers but they both enjoyed spending a sunny day browsing the shops and dining along Twenty-Third Street.

"You know my schedule, hon. Just let me know when you can break away to do it."

Kate nodded, stood up and went to the sink to wash her hands. "Time to return to healing the masses." With a wave she left, steeling herself for the next three hours.

ℬ 7 ℭ

In Nick's life there was only one thing that competed with his love for music. Her name was Jenny Dunn. Since grade school she'd held the deepest place that any girl could hold in a young man's heart, even though his relationship with her had always been only as a friend. Long blond hair and sapphire blue eyes framed a very pretty face that made her the crush of nearly every guy Nick knew, but her academic record and strong moral compass kept her at arms length from them all. Jenny simply knew where she was going, without conceit and with deep conviction. To Nick, that made her desirable in the most distractive way.

Jenny stepped out of the local coffee shop one Saturday morning, while Nick was locking his bike to a nearby fence. His mother had sent him on an early morning errand for stamps and a gallon of milk. His heart leaped when he saw her stopping to sip her drink.

"Hi, Jenny. Seeking some caffeine, I see?" He racked his brain for something clever that might spark a longer conversation.

"I was up half the night working on my final paper for English Lit. I figured I'd grab a latte and a scone before starting back into it this morning. How are you doing, Nick?" Jenny flashed him her fabulous smile and his mental quest for small talk went into meltdown.

"Uh — good. I'm good. You?"

"Procrastinating mostly. It's too nice a day to think about sitting at the computer."

"I can help you waste some time if you want to walk in the park a little." Nick cringed inwardly, hoping he hadn't stepped out too far on a limb.

"That sounds nice. What about your bike?"

"It's fine where it is. I need to come back for some stuff later, so it's fine where it is. No problem. It's fine." *Nice going, Nick. Keep repeating mindless words to prove beyond doubt that you're an imbecile.*

Jenny laughed. "Well, I guess 'it's fine where it is', then. Hold on a second." Jenny went back inside the coffee shop while Nick stood at the door, feeling like an idiot and renewing his attempt to think of more intelligent things to talk about. She returned with a small white bag. "I got some broken biscuits and stale bread to feed the ducks."

Nick loved that she'd thought kindly about the ducks. In fact, he loved everything about Jenny. As they walked toward the park he was thrilled to be beside her, feeling lucky that the morning had brought them together, proud to be in her circle, imagining what it would be like to be strolling as boyfriend and girlfriend, wishing he could take her hand in his. He inquired about her English paper and asked if she was looking forward to being out of school, but they soon ran out of small talk and walked on for two blocks in a long but not uncomfortable silence.

"How's your music going, Nick?" Jenny asked, breaking their conversational pause.

"Great. We've got enough song sets going that we may be able to play at some parties soon."

"We? Are you in a band now?"

"Sort of. We don't have a name yet, but I'm getting a group

together with Brandon Jakes and his roommates." Nick hoped his being in a band with Brandon made him look good to her.

When Jenny frowned and simply said, "Oh," Nick winced, realizing she wasn't impressed with his choice of band-mates.

"They're okay. I just play music with them."

They'd reached the park and found an empty bench under a tree, in front of the small pond. Immediately the park's resident ducks started swimming across the pond toward them, having been trained by experience to favor bench sitters carrying bags.

"They're so cute!" Jenny exclaimed as she threw food to them, trying to give all an equal chance. The large white ducks seemed to bully the smaller mallards regardless of her efforts. She offered some of the crumbs for Nick to throw but he declined, preferring to watch her enjoy the moment. The bag was soon empty and the ducks swam away one by one.

Jenny seemed concerned as she returned to the subject of his music. "Why Brandon, Nick? Aren't there are other people who play instruments?"

"He's got a lot of the equipment we need. He also has a strong voice for the lead vocals and seems to be able to draw an audience. Of course, the crowd has a lot of girls in it — his looks and all. I take it you don't like him much?"

"I don't like what he's all about. He was always getting in trouble in school whenever he bothered to show up. And he always got out of it somehow. Since then he just keeps sliding downhill. You know more than I the kind of things he's been getting into lately." Nick suspected she meant drugs and sex.

"I thought all the girls went ga-ga over his looks. You don't?"

"Sure, he looks good, but I wouldn't want anything to do with a guy like that. Not ever."

Suddenly Nick was ashamed of his ability to overlook the

things that Brandon's life revolved around. People he knew were so captivated by Brandon that Nick hadn't realized that his popularity had limits. Jenny seemed to be repulsed by him.

"I guess I'd never given it much thought," he said.

"You're such a nice guy, Nick. I'd hate to see him get you in trouble. He could, you know. He doesn't care about anything or anyone but himself."

"You may be wrong about him, Jenny. He's been a good friend to me." Nick felt strange defending Brandon against Jenny's remarks. He hated being against her in any way.

"If he has, Nick, you can be sure it's because your talent does something for him. Maybe you don't see that." Jenny got up from the bench. "I have to get back to work on my paper."

He wasn't sure what to say and so he said nothing. The silence that again fell between them now lay like a brick on Nick's chest, as they began walking back. His emotions were in turmoil. When they reached the street that her home was on, Jenny parted his company saying, "See you around, Nick. Be sure to take care of yourself."

Nick said his goodbyes to her. He had no clue at that moment how right Jenny was about Brandon, or how terrible it was going to be to find it out.

ℬ 8 ℭ

Jack had always enjoyed the covered porch that wrapped around two sides of the house, facing both streets of the corner on which it sat. His fondest boyhood memories were of the music that was shared there, rain or shine. When Uncle Dan had raised his bow and fiddle on warm summer weekends, it had seldom taken more than the first two songs before an impromptu group of musicians and listeners started gathering on the porch to enjoy good music and good company. Food and drink appeared from around the neighborhood, and from Aunt Eva's kitchen.

Uncle Dan's friend, Sam, who lived across the alley, could always be counted on to sidle in with his guitar or dobro. Laid-Back Lenny would arrive from next door with his upright bass. At times there were more than a dozen players on hand, adding a variety of stringed, wind and percussion instruments to the circle, and sharing new songs they'd learned or written. Jack had honed his own guitar skills and musicianship during those days, playing old-time bluegrass favorites like *Arkansas Traveler*, *Man of Constant Sorrow*, *Hesitation Blues* and *Red Haired Boy*. Music became a way for him to retreat from the world for a time, to a place where joy and sorrow could mingle together and speak to the individual soul. He played with all his heart, and his improvisations were moving and powerful.

It seemed quite natural that the fond memories of those times and the recent warm days would once again woo him onto the porch with his guitar, hoping to find solace there, as he had so often in the past. The hard work of the past two weeks had made his living spaces quite comfortable and eased some of the pain in his heart, yet he hadn't taken much time out to keep his fingers nimble and in shape to play his guitar. He limbered them up that evening, playing instrumental riffs as the sun was setting. The emotions that had moved in him over the last few weeks, nebulous and unresolved, worked their way from his heart to his fingertips, bypassing his brain altogether, making sense and connections where previously there had been none. He sat with his eyes closed, rocking lightly in a lover's dance with his guitar, blocking out the world around him and playing from his soul. So intense was his inward focus that he imagined gentle harmonies softly blending with his melodies, joining their freeform flow in subtle and beautiful ways that were meant to be together and could never be made to live apart. As the last note's sound faded into silence, he was startled by a deep voice.

"Yo' Uncle Dan would o' been proud, son." Jack opened his eyes and blinked to focus them in the dim twilight. A figure was seated across from him holding a well-worn Gibson guitar. It was old Sam. Jack grinned.

Without speaking a word, both men shifted their positions and carefully set their guitars aside, then stood to shake hands. Their gesture turned into a long and hardy hug. The sorrow over Uncle Dan's death and the long years of Jack's absence were all communicated in that brief moment, welling up wordless tears of shared understandings.

Sam was in his late seventies now, facing his own personal twilight. The sound of music rising up from the house across the alley had once again stirred him from the lonely confines of his home, guitar in hand. It had been many years since Uncle Dan's fiddle had filled the neighborhood with song, yet Jack saw a light in Sam's eyes as bright as those days. His silvery white hair, weathered, black skin and tall, wiry and slightly stooped frame were merely a mask tonight, hiding the spirit of a much younger man for whom music was the blood of life. There was no mistaking his innate ability to move silently into Jack's song, with a sweetness that completely blended the sound of two guitars, as if the notes could not be separated without a sense of loss. Such was the nature of pure harmony.

Not much was spoken. There would soon be a time for words, but that night was a time for shared song and unspoken memories. Jack lit the lantern that hung from the porch beam, sat down with his guitar, and moved with Sam back into a timeless place where young and old are equally rewarded.

* * *

It was just after ten o'clock at night when Kate pulled up to the stop sign near her home. She was surprised to see two men playing music by lamplight on the porch of the corner house. Neither of them looked familiar, and she wondered what had become of the elderly couple that had once lived there. To her remembrance there hadn't been a sign that the home's ownership had changed hands, though there hadn't been much activity there at all for as long as she could recall. The sudden appearance of these musicians was a curious development.

The black man appeared to be much older than his companion, yet they both seemed familiar friends. With her car window down to enjoy the pleasant night air, she listened to the soft, melodic sounds as she passed by slowly toward her home, which was a few houses down and across the street. She noted that their music was remarkably good.

Kate arrived home to find that Nick had already gone to bed for the night, leaving her a note that dinner awaited her in the refrigerator. It was such a sweet gesture that he often made meals for her during her later work shifts. Many mothers had heartbreaking stories of their teenagers' reckless and selfish misbehaviors, and she felt enormously blessed to have such a considerate and responsible son.

Perhaps it was merely his own natural inclination toward kindness, which he certainly had, but Kate also felt the difference may have come from the way she'd always included him in talks and plans for their future. She'd tried hard to make him feel that he was an important part of the success they made of their lives together, opting in his earliest years to be an extremely strict parent, then loosening up her restrictions as Nick's sense of responsibility matured. In contrast, most other parents she knew allowed their toddlers and tots tremendous freedom of will with no responsibilities whatsoever, trying as they got older to then begin applying rules and requirements in their lives. That approach seemed to meet with a stubborn opposition that she had mostly avoided with Nick. It wasn't obvious where she'd learned that strategy. Certainly not from her own mother, who had radically exercised free will and loose responsibilities throughout her entire life.

Kate had always tried to be the parent she'd wanted to have, treating Nick like an adult-in-progress, applying life's lessons in a purposeful way. Now that they were completely on their own, with no living relations as a part of their lives, she depended on Nick's maturity to make things work. Still, she often wondered if she'd been able to impart the kind of influence that his father might have given him over the years — the wisdom of how to be a good man in a very tough world.

Thinking of Nate always left Kate with a strange mix of feelings that she couldn't resolve. She'd been remembering him a lot lately. The absence of partnership and intimacy wasn't always easy to ignore, and the seventeen years since he had been permanently separated from her life had not erased the memory of his love, his kiss, his strength. Once again she cursed his decision to enlist, hating the senselessness of war, grieving that the time had been so brief for their love to live, cutting short their immensely deep and passionate feelings. It was a love she had never come close to finding again, and she wondered if that part of her had died with him, causing her to pour herself into motherhood and its very different but very powerful force, to fill the hole in her existence.

Joke as she might with Sue, her singleness had begun to close in on her at a rate proportional to her son's approach to adulthood. The responsibility she nurtured and cherished in Nick might soon move him away to start his independence. And what then?

She chose to drop her thoughts for the moment and opened the refrigerator to find the dinner that awaited.

ಬ 9 ಜ

Jack was making slow progress on the house. The main floor had been the initial focus of his efforts. Once his attention had shifted to the upper floor and basement, it became evident that the accumulation of furniture and goods, stuffed into every available space, dated back to long before his uncle's inheritance of the home from Jack's grandmother. The salvage attitude of his grandmother, raised in the generation that endured the 1930's depression era, had clearly ruled over any thought of discarding items. It seemed that his uncle and aunt had only added to the initial amassing over time.

Photographs he'd found from the early days of his uncle's and mother's lives revealed that the house had historically been an example of vintage splendor. Built-in shelving that was now painted bone white had, in years past, matched the doors and moldings in a rich mahogany finish. Oak floors, now covered with old shag carpeting, had at one time graced the home throughout in natural wood beauty, with tapestries and woven rugs to add warmth and style. He wondered how his uncle, a finish carpenter, had ever allowed the surfaces of such beautiful wood to remain covered and painted.

Somewhere in the midst of Jack's efforts to clean and organize, he began to ponder the idea of restoring the house to its original grandeur. He had no illusions about how difficult the job would be, but he knew that the time taken would be rewarding. It would also serve to erase the current look of the home from his bittersweet memories of time spent there. The influence of Uncle Dan's lessons in carpentry during his youth had rewarded him over the years with a skilled trade. Miscellaneous carpentry jobs had supported him when the music business got tough, which it occasionally had.

Applying his knowledge to the restoration of the home seemed an appropriate tribute to the skills that had been passed down to him, and a way to focus on a project that connected him to his uncle once again. Underlying Jack's thinking was also the idea that, in the event he was unable to endure a life lived in one place, the restoration of the home would pay for itself.

The fine spring weather that the northwest was experiencing had offset some of Jack's indoor work efforts by enticing him outdoors to plant a garden. It was something he'd never done but had wanted to try since the days when his aunt had tended to her vegetables and herbs in the backyard, enlisting Jack's help with the weeding and harvesting. Many a salad on Aunt Eva's table had been topped with fresh peppers, cucumbers, tomatoes, basil and onions from their work in the garden. It was the only place he'd ever experienced the feel and smell of good garden soil, and known the satisfaction of watching things grow.

It took three days for Jack to clear a small garden plot under the bay window of the kitchen's breakfast nook. He'd chosen that spot as the sunniest area, which was also close to a raised spigot that could easily accommodate a fixed garden sprayer. The ground had been hardened from years without tilling, and it had taken several soakings and a good pickax to break it up.

On the last day, when he'd finished preparing the soil, Jack rewarded his hard work with a free afternoon on the front porch, exercising his work-stiffened fingers by playing jigs and reels from the British Isles. That style of music had seemed appropriate in keeping the tone of the day earthy and upbeat. Jack was so engrossed in the intricate tunes that he didn't notice the young man who had ridden up the walkway on his bike to watch him play from the edge of the porch steps. On his back the boy carried a black electric guitar case, its straps crossing over his shoulders like a backpack.

Jack looked up from the ending of a song and saw that he'd been quietly and intensely observed by the lanky lad with dark brown hair. "Nice playing. What style of music is that?" the boy asked, parking his bike and walking up the steps.

"Thanks." Jack replied. "I'm playing some of the old folk tunes from England and Ireland." He paused, balancing the guitar on his knee. He recognized the teen as the one who lived across the street and a few houses down. Pointing at the guitar case, he added, "You play?"

"Yeah, but not that kind of music. I don't think I've ever heard those songs before, but I sure like your fingerpicking style. It's incredible."

"Thanks. They're not the songs you'd hear everyday on the radio." Jack smiled at him and offered him a handshake. "My name is Jack Brewster, by the way."

"Nick Weber." Nick shook hands then laid down his guitar bag. "I live just down the street. Do you mind if I look at your guitar?"

"Not at all. It's an old Martin small-body cutaway. It's been with me a whole lotta years."

Nick pulled up a chair and very carefully took the guitar from Jack. "I've only had an electric. This is really different — the action is higher. The strings don't bend as easily." Nick tried playing some of his lead lines, but found the guitar's wider fretboard to be a challenge. "How did you play all that fingering on this? It's a lot tougher to play than mine."

"Not tougher, just different. It wasn't designed for the style of music you're trying to play. I take it you enjoy rock?"

"It's the best. I mean, I like what you did, too, but mostly I play classic hard rock and metal. I love it." Nick seemed to respect Jack as a fellow musician, even if he didn't understand or perform his style of music.

"Nothing wrong with that. The important thing is to play what you feel, and feel what you play." Jack pointed again to Nick's guitar case. "Mind if I have a look?"

"No, go ahead." He handed Jack the bag.

Carefully, Jack unzipped the case and pulled out a white-on-red Fender Stratocaster. "Really nice Strat," Jack remarked as Nick beamed with pride. The guitar was expensive and high quality, and it was obvious to Jack that it was the most important thing Nick had ever owned.

Jack pulled a flatpick from his pocket and began to play a small series of basic rock leads, being careful to keep his riffs much simpler than those Nick had played. He didn't want to compete with this young man's abilities needlessly, especially since he'd displayed a great deal of talent. "It's sweet." Jack offered his approval of the guitar.

"So are you renting this house? I didn't see anyone move out, but you're new. There used to be some old people living here."

Jack laughed softly. "They were my aunt and uncle. She died last year and he died in February. I inherited the house. I used to come here a lot when I was your age. Now I'm tackling cleaning the place up."

"Sorry I called 'em old people."

"No problem. They were. My uncle played the fiddle like you've seldom heard. In fact, my love for music grew right here on this porch years ago. It's why I come out here to play now."

"I heard you playing out here the other night. It sounded great. At first I thought it was a stereo, but after you lit the lantern I saw you on the porch with some other guy. You must play together a lot. Sure sounds like it."

"That's Sam. He was my uncle's good friend and he lives across the back alley from here. We hadn't played together for a lotta years until that night. When I was a kid we used to jam with all the other musicians who gathered here. He's played guitar and dobro longer than you and I put together have been alive. He's really good."

"What's a dobro?"

"It's a resonator guitar that you play on your lap by sliding a steel bar along the strings. It makes a beautiful, soulful undercurrent of sound within a song. You see them played mostly in traditional blues and bluegrass bands. It gets its sound from a metal resonator built into it. The thing looks like someone attached a hubcap to a guitar, but Sam can make it sing so mournful and sweet." Jack spoke the last words with reverence.

"Yeah, I think I've seen those instruments sometimes on Austin City Limits."

"Probably so."

Nick rose up and swapped Jack's guitar back for his, putting his back in its case. "Wish I could stay and talk more but people are expecting me. I gotta jet. Maybe another time?"

"You ought to come by next time you hear us jamming out here. I suspect that'll be fairly often now that the weather is warming up. You need to meet Sam and hear his style, being a musician and all. He'd be eager to meet you, I'm sure." Jack liked the gentle soul this boy seemed to have, and felt kindred to his love for music.

"I will. I'd like to join in, but I don't think my Strat would cut it for that kind of jam."

"I have a few other acoustic guitars — we could break one out that would suit you fine. I hope to see you, Nick."

"You will. Thanks for letting me try out your guitar." Nick strode down the porch steps and hopped onto his bike to leave. "Nice meeting you, Jack." As the boy rode away Jack steadied his guitar and settled back into his music.

ℰ 10 ℭ

The local neighborhood cafe, Tony's Place, had been in its street corner location, and had looked just the same, for as long as Jack could remember. It was attached to a small convenience market that sold the best ice cream cones in town. Both were run by the same owner. The building must have been painted inside and out in all those years, but it always seemed to be in the same ageless state of wear. There was something solid and comforting in the continuity of its existence amidst the endless change going on everywhere else in the city. Local residents who shared the feeling were the regular customers that kept it alive.

If you wanted to find out what was happening or being sold within a three mile radius, Tony's Place was a reliable source of information. The latest news and gossip could be found over a good home-cooked meal and a cup of coffee at the cafe, which was open for breakfast and lunch every day of the week. Notices and items for sale were posted either on the cork board beside the front door of the market or the wooden utility pole that stood on the corner.

The original owner, Tony, had long since passed away, but members of his extended family had run the place over the years, taking it over as a tradition and a steady source of income and work for their close knit Italian family. They'd each kept the name in remembrance of Tony.

The current owner of Tony's Place was a small, matriarchal woman in her late sixties named Ruby. She was a mother hen, serving wisdom and advice as free side dishes to her customers in the cafe, usually with her index finger wiggling straight up in the air for emphasis.

Jack experienced this on one of his first visits to Tony's in many years. He'd ordered breakfast from a young woman named Angela, who'd poured his coffee. It was Ruby who'd served him the meal, remembering him (much to his surprise) from days gone by. "Your Uncle Dan was a good man," she stated in her strong Italian accent as she set his plate in front of him, "and he always worried about you wandering all over the way you do." Her finger rose as she stood over him to declare her concerns with sincere warmth. "You should only stay put. You're a nice looking boy. You should make your uncle happy, God rest his soul. This is a good place to do that."

Jack grinned boyishly, rubbed his neatly trimmed beard, and simply answered, "Yes m'am."

"Watch out. Ruby's looking to marry off her daughter, Sophie," said a stocky old patron who sat at the counter finishing his breakfast. He wore a plaid shirt and faded jeans held up by well-worn suspenders. It seemed to be a standard uniform for half of the men who dined there.

"You mind your business and eat your food, Bert." Ruby warned with a false sternness. "My Sophie, she's a good girl. She has herself a sweetheart, you know, and she's a beautiful girl. You gonna make this boy think he no want to come here." She turned back to Jack. "You no listen to these men here. You listen to your Aunt Ruby."

Bert laughed and held up his cup for a refill of coffee. "He won't want to come back because the service is so bad. My cup's been empty for half my meal, Ruby."

"Your cup's been empty for half your life, you old fool." Ruby walked over to pour his refill, then returned to the kitchen.

"Why do I keep coming back?" Bert said to Jack. "If I wanted abuse I could stay home with the missus. But she watches her morning shows and I come here to take it in the ribs, ya know?" Jack grinned and saluted Bert with his coffee mug from across the room.

Evidently, the ritual "abuse" of patrons suited more than a few of the locals, and Jack had immediately become one of them as a breakfast regular at Tony's Place, where people fondly remembered Uncle Dan as one of the best men around — and one of the best fly fishermen. To be an owner of one of Dan's Damsels, his specialty custom nymph that was the best trout fly in anyone's tackle box, was an honor amongst the patrons there. Those who had never met Jack nevertheless knew who he was. Uncle Dan had spoken of him like a son, which made him an instant local, held in high esteem. He liked the feeling.

❧ *11* ❧

Frequent practice sessions held at The Hanger had produced a strong set of songs for the band, and the music was getting tight. Neighborhood teens who regularly came by to hang out and listen were becoming avid fans. While Brandon remained the primary focus of their adoration, as lead singer and band spokesman, Nick found that his own popularity had kicked into a higher gear. People he barely knew now went out of their way to say hello and seek his attention. While it felt good, gnawing at the back of his mind was an acute awareness that the two most important people in his life weren't amongst those who supported the band.

One Friday evening his mother called home to tell him that the hospital was extremely short-staffed, and the night supervisor had asked her to extend her swing shift to a double shift. Though he'd expressed his disappointment to her, Nick was secretly thrilled. As soon as he hung up the phone he biked over to The Hanger, hoping to start an open-ended jam session that would likely run into the wee hours of the morning.

As he arrived he met up with Benny, who was walking from his car carrying a pony keg. "Hey, Nick! We were hoping you'd show up with your ax. Good wavelengths, dude. You down for a kick-ass night?"

"You for real? This guitar's so hot it's gonna burn a hole through my shirt." He opened the door to find the place in full swing, being greeted with as much enthusiasm as was the beer — and maybe more. About a dozen drop-ins had already formed the growing impromptu party.

"Nick—*y!*" Brandon's broad grin and slap on the back made him feel important in the moment. "You showed up. Good man!" Nick's buddies purposely avoided phoning him at home, since his mother strongly disapproved of them and knew nothing about Nick's visits to The Hanger. They were cautious not to arouse her curiosity; they knew that Nick spent every minute he could with them. Keeping his visits clandestine had also been the main reason Nick had never pushed his mother for a cell phone.

"Dude, we need to talk about things," Brandon turned to him with intent. "Our gig's getting serious, man, so we need to make some serious plans. With your mom's bullshit and you bein' in school, there's a lotta crap in the way, ya know what I mean?"

"Whatever." Nick's reply was curt. He hated to hear his mother's caring for him being reduced to bullshit, but knew that Brandon didn't have the capacity to understand their relationship. "I'm here when I can be. A couple more weeks and school'll be out for the summer. I'll have more time for practice."

A guy that looked to be in his thirties, with stringy, black hair and an unkempt beard, interrupted their conversation. His faded, sleeveless, AC-DC t-shirt showed off his heavily tattooed arms. He handed Brandon a freshly lit joint. "This herb is dank. Go for it." Adopting a devilish grin and bobbing eyebrows, he added in a deeper voice, "It'll inspire ya." After Brandon had taken a hit, the man said, "You guys can start playin' anytime now. We need some good mood here. The radio's been playin' a buncha shit."

"We'll get to it, man," Brandon answered, "but we got things we gotta do here first." With a joking jab and a nod to the man, he added, "Benny's tapping the keg. Go pour yourself a beer — and put some money in the jar this time, you freeloading bastard." He took another hit off the joint and offered it to Nick, who shook his head. They watched the AC-DC stoner head

48

toward the keg in the kitchen. On the way he stopped to sweet talk a young girl wearing a skimpy halter top and cut-off jeans. She seemed totally enamored with his tattoos. He traced her breast with his fingertips under the pretense of showing her where she might like a tattoo for herself. Nick frowned, knowing the man was just an older lech copping a feel. Brandon chuckled, then steered Nick toward a quiet place for them to talk without interruptions.

"Who *is* that guy?" Nick asked.

"Just some dude Benny knows. He's crashed on the couch here a few times. He's kind of a pain in the ass, but Benny wants us to put up with him. I dunno. Probably some sort of connection."

"He seems a little old to be hanging out here."

"What the hell, he's a rocker. He's here to listen. Get used to a broader audience, Nicky. It's a big world and people like what we do."

"Right. Anyway, I need to get my guitar out and get tuned up." Nick started to walk away.

"Hold up, dude. Why don't ya chill a little and help me smoke this doob while we talk."

"Talk about what?" Nick stopped and turned to face Brandon once again without looking up. He ignored the joint being handed to him, swung the guitar case off his back and began to unzip the bag.

"Nick—*y!* Don't cop an attitude. Like I was saying, we've got plans to make. There's money to be had for a good rockin' band, and that's what we're getting to be. Benny's been in touch with the owners of some clubs around town. Shit, man, we ain't even got a fuckin' *name*, yet! We've gotta talk about this, dude."

"I'm only seventeen. How the hell am I gonna play at a club

that serves alcohol?"

"Well, you'll be eighteen at the end of the year. Then you can legally be in a club to play as long as they hire you to do live music on the stage and you don't drink there. Before that, well, we're lookin' at lining up some house gigs — keggers and shit like that. And Benny thinks he may be able to get a few smaller club owners to shine-on their need for ID from you." Brandon was obviously stoked from these new developments.

"No lie? I thought you had to be twenty-one to play at a bar." Nick's attitude was changing. His future in music was suddenly getting brighter.

Brandon smiled and turned on the charm. "Nope. We got the scoop straight from the books. Dude, if musicians had to wait until twenty-one to start playing gigs they'd never get a start. The places we play would probably have to serve food, but just about every bar does that anyway. The way you play, man, we're gonna be booked solid in no time."

Benny strode up to them about that time and Brandon passed him the joint, which now needed to be re-lit. He chimed in, "True story, Nick. Been checking with a few places and took along some of the cuts I recorded during practices, with two of our originals. They like it. They like it a *lot*. They're talking serious gigs with us."

Nick's face beamed. "The hell, you say! That's great!"

"Yep. So we've gotta get official, come up with a good name for the group, get together some promo stuff. We've been talkin' through some of it, but we need you here to help get it going. We need you to commit yourself. That is, if you're down for it?" Benny's last remark was a challenge, not a question. When it came right down to it, he ran the show at The Hanger and he was all about business, whether selling the legitimate or the illegitimate.

"It's my dream. Even when I can't be here, I practice."

Brandon and Benny exchanged glances, then Benny said, "We know you do, Nick. We can hear it. But we need to be together on this. We all need to jam together. We can't just be hanging out here waiting for you to show up."

"What else can I do, man?" Nick was getting defensive. He saw that the two of them (and maybe Diggs, as well), had been hatching plans to capitalize on his talent. He knew that without him, they would be just another mediocre band trying to get a gig anywhere they could.

Brandon answered. "You could move in here, dude."

"Are you nuts? You know I can't do that!"

"We'd all let you ride on the rent until the band starts making money," Benny interjected, "and that won't take long once things get going."

"You forget, dude, I'm only seventeen."

"Diggs was only seventeen when he moved here."

"Yeah, but Diggs didn't live with my mother. She'd never let me leave before I was eighteen, and if I tried to do it without her permission, she'd have the cops here so fast you wouldn't have time to blink."

At the mention of police, Benny's eyes clouded over. There was a heavy silence as Nick's words settled into their thoughts. Finally, Benny spoke. "Yeah, well we can't be having that, now *can* we? A nice boy like you doesn't want to hurt his mommy."

"*Fuck* you, Benny!"

"Hey, hey, *hey* now!" Brandon jumped into the tension, holding his hands up briefly between the two. "Let's not get personal, guys. What we all wanna do here is figure out how to make this work. We've got a great band on the rise. No doubts. Nick's right, Benny. His mom is pretty uptight about what he does. We don't want her causin' any fuckin' trouble. A few months down the road, when Nicky turns eighteen, there ain't a shittin' thing she can do when he moves out. Until then, we just gotta take what we can get and find other ways to make things happen."

"You're forgetting, Brandon. I've still gotta finish school next year. I've been thinking of college, too." Nick was calmer, but was still perturbed that his life was being so cavalierly plotted out for him.

"C'mon, Nick. What the hell do you need college for? Music is gonna be your life, dawg. Music. You don't need *any* more school, man. You' *got* what you need already!"

"You mean I've got what *you* need, right?"

"Hey, don't fly that shit here! We *all* need each other to get where we know we all wanna go. Yeah Nick, you're an amazing guitarist and a decent singer. But you know as well as I do that you can't do much without good backup. We're a band with or without you, dude, but together — together we' got the stuff that can go far." The Brandon blarney was pumping full force, but Nick saw the threads of truth in it.

Nick had been putting off thinking of these things because his deepest motivation for playing music was simply the fun of playing music. He was getting uncomfortable with this new vein of demanded expectations being exposed. It was obvious that the fundamental incentives for Benny and Brandon were not oriented to music, but to money and connections. Whether they admitted it to him or not, Nick knew he was an essential ingredient to include in their recipe for success. He also knew that his own ability to promote himself was very limited. Making connections with people was what Benny and Brandon excelled at. It was their lack of discretion and morality about doing it that worried him.

"I know, man, I know." Nick had decided to ease the current tensions as much as he felt comfortable. "I still have a lotta thinking to do about all this. But you know I'm committed to music — and I know you're doing what it takes to get things going. I appreciate that, man, and I plan to do my part. We don't need to make any decisions tonight, but I promise I'll think a lot about it and we'll talk again, soon. Okay?"

Benny and Brandon both relaxed noticeably. They each exchanged handshakes of brotherhood with Nick, then Benny said, "The offer is standing, Nick. You can move in anytime you feel it's right. Meantime, be here when you can."

Nick grinned. "Like tonight, man. I've got the whole night. Let's get rockin'! And I do believe I'll have me a beer, first." As he turned to put his guitar down and move toward the keg, Benny reached into his shirt pocket for his lighter. It promised to be a good night.

❀ *12* ❧

Jack and Sam sat on the porch late one afternoon, drinking iced tea and sharing stories and songs. Sam's mood was rather melancholy, his songs reflecting the sentiments born from a long life of hardship and loss. His worn and leathery face, shadowed with the silvery gray stubble of an old man weary of daily shaving, gave him a look reminiscent of the many life-worn and crusty blues musicians Jack had encountered in his travels to the Deep South. Sam seemed at that moment to be a man waiting to be called to his eternal rest, biding his remaining time with soulful music.

"At my age, Jack, the life I seen and knowed jus' don't fit with what's happenin' nowadays. Things move way too fast, and folks who stand too slow ain't nothin' mo' than speed bumps fo' the rest." Sam had spent most of his life working for the railroad and had retired with a comfortable pension. Earlier in the day Jack had helped him navigate a new online health care system that was slowly replacing the paper-based process Sam had been using for seventeen years to handle his claims. The difficulty in being forced to deal with web-based procedures for the first time had been rough on Sam, leaving him feeling inadequate and archaic. "We ain't meant fo' things t' be this way. Folks can get used t' it, fo' sho', but it whittles they soul away without them even knowin' it. We deal with so many machines that we never hardly need t' say howdy to no one. We fo'get how. We jus' ain't designed like that, ya know? It stops us from bein' friendly no mo'. It ain't right. It ain't good fo' a body."

"There's a lot of truth in what you say, Sam. But there's no going back. You just let me help you through it, okay?" It was a lot for Jack to promise, considering his own limitations with internet-based systems. He was concerned that this man, once so vital in the days of Jack's youth, was feeling such a loss of control and dignity. It was a symptom of the years to come for those on the sidelines of the world's massive transitions.

Sam nodded and began to pour the pains of his soul through the wistful strains of the blues he played. It was a thing that no machine could ever replace — the soul of the song. They blended their instruments to express the mutual angst of their inevitable life changes.

Jack was surprised and glad to see Nick appear at the porch steps, with a smile on his face. Jack introduced him to Sam as a young man with a spirit and talent for music. Sam's smile was genuine as he welcomed Nick to join in on the jam. Seeing that he'd arrived empty handed, Jack invited Nick into the house to choose a guitar to play and grab a glass of iced tea. In a short while they were settled into a small music circle on the porch.

"I don't know much about the kind of music you're doing," Nick apologized as he sat, ready to play, "so let me know if I'm screwing things up too bad for you."

"Never you mind about that, boy." Sam said as he moved into a brighter attitude of wisdom and mentoring. "Ain't nobody here ain't been right where yo' at this minute. I remember the days Jack sat there, jus' like that, and said it jus' like you said it. That's how ya start, son — it's how *ever'one* starts. Ya jus' let what ya know nat'ral shine right through." Sam was once again in his element.

They started with a few easy bluegrass tunes that allowed Nick to get a feel for the tempo and simple chord structures.

He played backup with ease, then performed musical breaks that showed a highly developed ear.

Jack and Sam both expressed sincere praise for Nick's ability to hear what was happening and play right into it. When Sam launched into blues songs, Nick was right at home, since the fundamentals for rock and blues are the same. He played with gusto and confidence.

Jack grinned at Sam. Nick was a natural. Even better was what Jack saw when Sam winked back at him. His old eyes glowed strong and bright once again.

ℬ *13* ℭ

The neighborhood had certainly changed since the days when Jack had roamed its streets, but it hadn't deteriorated completely. The homes were older but well built, and many long-term residents still remained. Those who'd left and chosen to keep their properties as unsupervised investment rentals were largely responsible for the increase in crime and decrease in upkeep that plagued this part of town. He'd seen the same thing in city after city in his lifetime of travels. It was easy to see the places where respect for life and law had cheapened from a lack of caring, brought on mostly by poverty, drugs, weakening family ties and marginalizing social standards.

The recent stretch of sunny days had lasted just long enough for Jack to paint the exterior of the house and garage, before hiding itself once again behind the late spring rains that now soaked the earth. It had felt good to roll a new look over the markings and profanities that had covered the porch walls and garage for several years. He felt certain that the graffiti would return again, now that he'd created a fresh and tempting canvas. Some of the tags and pieces had actually been quite good, displaying a creativity that might reward the artist nicely if channeled in a direction other than vandalism.

Jack had shaken his head and chuckled more than once as he'd daubed new paint over the defaced exterior. It wasn't the first time he'd put a fresh painted look on this home. In fact, it had been an early spring season about twenty five years before when he'd tackled the same job as a form of punishment. That was the year his budding defiance had reared an ugly head against one of his mother's lovers.

The man, named Bruce, was an insurance broker who wore a gold ring on nearly every finger of both hands, and a gold chain dangling across a hairy chest, sporting the open-shirted, plastic look so popular with the older "hip" men of those days. Bruce was all talk, and Jack had him pegged from the start as a suave charmer who loved to dangle Jack's mother like an arm ornament at social events. He'd bought expensive outfits for her to wear, as if she were a living Barbie doll. It was all about creating envy using the look and feel of success as an illusion to cover the reality of his insignificant mediocrity. Once, while alone with him, Jack had confronted Bruce about one of his grandiose fabrications. In answer, he'd been introduced to all eight gold rings, acting like brass knuckles into his gut. He'd known from past experience that the incident wasn't going to be random or unrepeated.

Bruce drove a Mercedes sports convertible and had a habit of leaving his car keys on the table when visiting. Jack never truly regretted heisting the car late one afternoon while Bruce was indisposed in his mother's bedroom. He'd taken a long, fun joy ride before pushing the vehicle over an embankment that rolled it straight into Johnson Creek. The four stitches he'd received that day came much later, when Bruce had confronted him, but his mother had kicked the man out of their house just the same, and a very pleasant month had passed before she took up with an investment counselor from Beaverton.

It was the talk he'd had with Uncle Dan after the incident that had offered him a harder lesson of shame. His uncle had acknowledged that the anger causing Jack to react was very real and appropriate, but had sternly pointed out that Jack's way of handling things hadn't cost Bruce anything, since he was an insurance man, yet it could easily have changed Jack's life for the worse in any number of ways, had things gone differently or charges been pressed. Uncle Dan had been deeply disappointed by Jack's poor judgment. He'd stuck a brush in Jack's hand and told him to think things through as he painted the house.

The carjacking was the last malicious act that Jack had ever pulled on anyone for any reason. Now, so many years later as he tackled the same painting chore, it dawned on him that his uncle had only taught him how not to handle his anger. In the absence of a better alternative, Jack had chosen retreat as his next best option.

The true result of this choice was becoming alarmingly clear for the first time in his life. His own personal emphasis on detachment and solitary living had come at a very high price — the absence of community. He was beginning to understand the need people have always had to seek the solidarity of groups and gangs. The desire to belong was very real and ran deep. When family and social structures failed to provide a strong sense of membership in a community, people usually found a place to belong anywhere they could, no matter what the cost of the ticket to join. Jack was slowly awakening to the fact that his role as a loner was nothing more than being an individual who had given up on belonging anywhere at all in the fear that he couldn't. He now faced the biggest challenge of his life — finding the courage to even try. It seemed that everywhere he turned, that message was being delivered to him in unmistakable ways.

This new realization rang true one evening while sharing music with Sam, the regular activity that they had now come to call their "porch jams". Sam took a small break and set down his dobro.

"You put a whole lot o' feelin' in the things ya play, Jack.

You ever gonna fit that into yo' real life?" Sam wasn't one to make idle chatter, and Jack sensed he was taking him somewhere with intention.

"I'm not sure what you mean, Sam." Jack tried not to sound like he was evading the direction Sam was headed when, in fact, he was.

"Hear me out, son. I don't mean t' judge where ya been o' what ya done. I know mo' than most what set ya t' yo' ways. As a boy, you was always sensitive, and ya got dumped on the side a lot. It made ya go deep. You play music with yo' whole soul, and that's the God's honest truth. Mo' than I ever seen. Y'always did. But ya don't seem t' embrace life, son. Ya never have — kinda like ya done stood on the outside lookin' in. You been livin' here a little while now, but mostly ya got the lookuva a man who wants t' run. Am I feelin' that right?" Sam's question didn't come from the idea that he might be wrong. He had Jack pegged, and the words were hard to hear. Silence awaited Jack's answer.

"Yes, Sam. You see it. A way of life like mine doesn't turn on a dime. There are days when I feel like I'm an actor in a role where I don't know my lines. Times like that always told me that the road was calling. That just doesn't change overnight. But I still want the change, if that's what you mean to ask." It was the first time in Jack's life that he'd reasoned about his style of living with someone who cared about the outcome.

"I can see yo' point, Jack." Sam spoke as he reached for his dobro once again. "Just remember that they's a need fo' rehearsal and a time fo' the show. It's a hard time when it's show time. The nerves always come the night o' the show, but they ain't much use in stayin' in rehearsal all yo' life. You'll get used t' things by and by. Stay and be in the show, Jack." As usual, Sam's simple wisdom fit the context of music and hit home. Their songs started again and Jack was calmed a bit in the midst of his storm.

☙ *14* ❧

Kate arrived home one night after her swing shift to find Nick sitting in the living room with his guitar. His small amplifier was turned down low and she was surprised to hear him picking out the melody to *Tennessee Waltz*. It was a side of his musical interests she'd never before seen. He stopped his playing to greet her as she came through the doorway from the kitchen.

"Don't stop playing, son. I love that song." She kissed him on the forehead and put down her backpack to sit across from him on the sofa.

"You know this tune?" It was his turn to be surprised.

"Sure. It's a traditional song. It's not what I expected to hear coming from your guitar, but it's lovely. You have an amazing ear for music, Nick. To just sit and learn a song like that without sheet music or a recording — you make it look so easy."

"It's a cool tune. I had some help, though. There's a guy who moved in across the street that's been showing me how to play stuff like this. I always thought these kind of songs were simple and lame, but I dunno. This one has some great chord changes, and it sure isn't simple."

"The man that lives in the corner house?" Kate's question came from more than just idle curiosity. The man who lived there had suddenly appeared from nowhere, and she knew nothing about him, other than the fact that he was an accomplished guitarist.

"Yeah. His name is Jack. He invited me to come jam anytime, so I've been going over there after school now and then. He's really good! He's been a professional musician all his life." Nick's admiration for Jack's musicianship obviously ran deep. She could hear it in his voice. She'd never seen him express such eagerness for any style of music other than hard rock. Even though the kind of music he was now taking an interest in was more acceptable to her than heavy metal, she was concerned about the kind of influence a middle-aged man might be imposing on Nick. In her mind, professional musicians tended to lead loose lifestyles with even looser morals. Kate felt uneasy about the association.

"How did you meet him?"

"I rode up on my bike one day to listen. He was out on the porch doing some really tight fingerstyle stuff. We showed off our guitars and talked a little. He seemed pretty cool and I couldn't do the kind of stuff he was playing. That made me want to learn about it." It made sense to her that new and difficult styles would appeal to Nick. He worked relentlessly to improve his abilities.

"Did he rent the home from the elderly couple? I don't see them there anymore."

"Those folks were his aunt and uncle. They both died recently, I guess, and left the house to Jack. He said he's here to clear it out and fix it up. It sounds like he's lived out of his van mostly, until now." Nick didn't realize how much this last statement alarmed Kate. She knew Nick's desire to be a musician was extremely strong. A wayward drifter was not the kind of role model she cared to have persuading her son's future.

"What sort of man is he? Was he homeless?"

"Nah, nothing like that, mom. He's a really nice guy. He seems to have money and he's working hard to get the place fixed up. There's a really old black man named Sam that lives on the next street over. He's known Jack all his life and he's pretty cool, too. They play music together and want me to join in whenever I can." Nick seemed to sense Kate's discomfort about Jack. "He's a good guy, mom. Honest. There's nothing to worry about. The music we play over there is fun."

"Well — don't make yourself a pest, son. I don't want you going there all the time."

"I won't, mom. But you should go meet him sometime. You'll see that he's okay."

Kate intended to do just that.

"Okay, Nick. For now you can play music on the porch with these men. Now, did you happen to leave me any supper?"

Nick jumped up to head for the kitchen. "I didn't get a chance to even make myself supper. You sit, and I'll make us soup and a sandwich."

"Thanks, my good son." Kate lounged back into the chair she was sitting in and put her aching feet up on the nearby ottoman. After a long, hard day at work, she wasn't in a mood to disagree with anything.

⧽ *15* ⧼

Jack's breakfast jaunts to Tony's Place were now, more often than not, accompanied by old Sam, who had fast become his most trusted friend. Sam was a beloved part of the local scene at Tony's, respected by all for his gentle spirit and simple wisdom. The familiarity and routine of the neighborhood's pace was growing on Jack, but there remained a vague restlessness that he couldn't seem to shake, and a feeling that somehow the life he was beginning to enjoy was merely a temporary phase that he wouldn't be able to sustain. He never had in the past.

One morning Nick joined them for breakfast at Tony's, excited to talk about his growing affinity for acoustic music and feeling the camaraderie that several recent porch jams had begun to develop amongst the trio. The generational gaps between each of them were bridged by their common love for the music they shared.

Nick saw the life Jack had led on the road as a source of inspiration and the symbol of merit for a good musician. Like most people, he felt the true measure of success in a musician's career was in the size of the audience and the distance traveled to play performance gigs.

"My best work has always centered around songs where the music and the meaning of the lyrics come together to say something that hits deep, whether the song is mine or somebody else's. They aren't always the popular songs, but they still strike a chord in the heart." Jack was describing how he'd selected and expanded his repertoire of songs over time. "Then there are the songs you learn just because, no matter where you go, musicians are playing them and folks want to hear them."

"You've traveled all over the country, haven't you, Jack?" Isn't it way cool to do that?" Nick's question was filled with the sense of adventure that Jack's lifestyle brought to a teenager's restlessness.

"I've been a lot of places, yes." Jack answered. "The thing about traveling that comes home over time is that wherever you go people are the same at the core and every locality has its share of promise and problems."

"That's the God's honest truth, Nick. I seen that in my railroad days, too." Sam added. "It seems t' be thataway so's folks ever'where have the same chance o' gettin' the good with the bad. Life is all 'bout learnin' how and what t' choose, ya know? You can do that anywheres equal-like. The good Lord done designed it thataway fo' us all, so's the true heart gets its testin'. You can be sho' o' that — the testin' is gonna happen, indeed."

"But you saw lots of things and went wherever you felt like going, right Jack?" Nick was holding fast to seeing the adventurous side, and Sam's comment had rock-skipped across his focus.

"You go where the gig money and the weather take you. Along the way you meet people, but you don't get a chance to really get to know them. I never wanted the big audiences or the controlled career, so to me that meant staying freeform and always being on the move. I used to have a booking agent, but over time I made enough connections of my own to keep me busy and moving around. I always felt that traveling meant your music and the audiences never got stale, even for small gigs."

Jack reflected deeply over the meaning of his words and his life as he continued. "Once I met a guy in Phoenix who'd played at the same small venue for over fifteen years. Same gig over and over. He was an amazing musician and played a lot of different instruments, with the kind of talent that invites record contracts and gets your name plastered everywhere you look. I asked him why he chose to stay in the same small place all those years. I'll never forget his answer: '*Whether your music speaks to hundreds or to millions doesn't matter. I make enough money to live a nice, simple life and I know the people who love the music I play. I know them by name. They come in and I say hello. Now their kids know me, too. What more do I need than that?*' He made me think, Nick. He made me think hard about my own shapeless life."

Nick took his story in stride, but Jack could see that he wasn't comprehending the value behind the reasoning. For a young person starting out, the experience that supported it wasn't there, and the idea of finding fortune and praise doing something you really loved ruled over the need for stability and a sense of community. The importance of those things always seemed to come later in life.

Would I have listened had somebody said this to me long ago at his age?

Sam's thoughtful look toward Jack was piercing. Jack realized what Sam was seeing and hearing behind his words — the revelation that his inner battle was unraveling him. He fought the sudden, urgent cry for retreat in that moment. It cut him down to the bone.

⥡ *16* ⥢

The sound of the doorbell brought Jack up from the basement, where he'd been making a broad assessment of its contents and structure. Looking at his watch he saw that it was too early in the morning for a visit from Sam.

He opened the door to a very attractive woman with dark, medium length hair and vivid green eyes. She appeared to be in her early thirties and something about her seemed familiar. His fingers automatically combed through his thick, recently trimmed hair and he dusted off the front of his shirt in a hurried attempt to clean away any basement cobwebs and look presentable.

"You must be Jack?" she said, more as a statement than a question. "I'm Kate Weber." He knew he'd looked puzzled, as she added, "Nick's mother."

"Ah, yes! Weber." He started to offer a handshake then hastily stopped midway to wipe his hand on his jeans before extending it once again. "Sorry. I've been down in the basement looking things over and I'm probably a mess." She returned the handshake regardless.

"I didn't mean to disturb your work. I just wanted to come over and introduce myself. I understand my son has been spending a fair amount of time at your home." Her tone seemed a bit stiff and cautious, as if the meaning of her words were meant to probe for information.

"Yes, he has. Once he found out that playing music was a regular activity around here he became a welcome addition to it.

Won't you please come in?"

Kate stepped inside and looked around. Jack saw that her visit was one of motherly concern as she appeared to be assessing the kind of lifestyle he lived. She fixed her eyes for a short time on the guitars and instrument cases in the corner of the room.

"Please excuse the pockets of chaos around here. This home belonged to my uncle who passed away last February. I inherited the house and everything in it, and it's been quite a chore trying to get things organized."

"I'm sorry to hear about your uncle. I'd wondered why we never saw a rent or sale sign before you moved in."

"Well, probate took a little time. Can I offer you some coffee?" Jack was beginning to wonder if he was passing her approval tests.

"That would be nice, thank you. I hope you don't mind my being here now. I could come at another time."

"Not at all. This is a great time. I imagine you're here to check out why a middle-aged guy who just moved into the neighborhood is suddenly hanging around with your son. I don't blame you at all for that — it's the sign of being a good mother."

As if I'd know what that really means.

His words seemed to relax her slightly. "Thank you. Yes, I've been a bit concerned, as you said. It would be nice for us to sit and chat for a few minutes."

"Absolutely. We can sit in the breakfast nook."

Kate nodded. Jack led her into the kitchen, poured two cups of coffee, then placed cream and sugar on table as well. He was glad that the kitchen was clean and the sink empty. She seemed to notice as they sat down across from each other at the table.

"Can I call you Kate?" Jack asked.

"Please do."

"Thanks. Kate, I should probably tell you briefly about myself. That may help put your mind a little more at ease." He cleared his throat and sipped his coffee. As he did, he gazed at her lovely eyes and face. She'd looked familiar to him because Nick had her same features and hair color. Jack was suddenly aware that he wanted to earn her approval in more ways than just being a safe friend with whom Nick could play music.

"I grew up in this neighborhood, visiting my Uncle Dan and Aunt Eva a lot. I was like a son to them since they'd had no kids of their own. The front porch was a place where musicians gathered all summer long. Uncle Dan was a fiddler who got things going. A lot of great music happened here back when I was Nick's age." He took a sip from his coffee mug and settled back into the seat. "I went on to be a traveling musician in life and never settled down — but I don't do drugs and I don't smoke."

Kate relaxed in her seat and gazed back at Jack. "I know my son well enough to understand how your music experience brought him here. It looks like your life on the road has been sidelined, then?"

"When Uncle Dan died and left me the house, I took the opportunity to return and see if I could learn to settle in. Music is just a natural part of that. Nick seems to get a lot out of playing songs on the porch with me and old Sam from across the back alley." Jack paused, then said. "I hope you'll see that this is a good place for Nick to be. He's a great kid and we really enjoy his music. He's extraordinarily talented."

Kate took in Jack's succinct summary and smiled at him. "It'll take a little time to feel completely comfortable about it. No offense to you, just a mother's caution. I know how much he loves music and how good he is at it. And I can see that your style of instrumentation doesn't lend itself to loud rock, tattoos and body piercing."

Jack laughed. "Nah, we're pretty tame in life and music here. You're welcome to come over and listen to us anytime."

"Nick would hate it if I did." It was Kate's turn to laugh. She sipped her coffee again and paused to think before going on. "For now, perhaps you can simply keep the music on the porch where I can hear it from afar?" It was a nice way for her to say she'd like him to keep Nick's participation in plain view.

"Well, that's easy. That's where it tends to happen anyway. But I think you might be surprised about Nick's feelings toward your listening to what we do here. You should give it a try sometime. I'm sure Sam would like to meet you as well. He thinks the world of Nick, and his playing is remarkable to see."

"I'll think about that." Kate finished her coffee. "I know Nick loves music more than anything. He carries his guitar like a prosthesis that helps him walk but I'm not usually invited in to listen when he plays. I never know how much space to give that, but I see him keeping up his grades and helping around the house. It's hard to know when to stop being a mother and let your son grow up for himself. I try very hard to mother him without smothering him."

Jack was glad to see that Nick had a good home life where he was loved very much. He liked Kate and saw a lot of her mannerisms in Nick. "Does Nick's father take much interest in his music?" Nick had never talked much about his home life.

"His father died in the Gulf War when Nick was an infant. Nate would have enjoyed the way his son takes to music — he'd played piano as a hobby and was quite good. That must be where Nick gets his gift for music since, Lord knows, I have no musical talent whatsoever." Jack enjoyed watching Kate talk. Her voice was expressive and her eyes were dazzling.

"I'm very sorry to hear about your loss. You've done a great job raising Nick. He's a terrific young man."

"He is." With that, Kate rose from the table. "I've taken up enough of your time this morning, Jack. I only intended to visit briefly and I need to think about getting ready for work. Thanks for letting me drop in unexpectedly. It seems maybe Nick has found a nice place to sharpen his musical skills and has made some good friends in the process." She headed toward the front door. Jack was sorry to see her leave so soon.

"Consider yourself welcome here anytime, Kate. It's an open invitation, music or not. But I think you'd enjoy hearing it, and I know that Nick would want that, even if he did protest on the surface. But I don't think he would. A boy wants his mother to be proud of him." Jack followed her to the door, said goodbye, then watched her walk back to her home from his porch. An odd feeling of envy overcame him in that moment. Nick was a very fortunate young man to be loved so much by his mother — by this woman.

ℰℴ *17* ℭℬ

School had finally ended and summer had arrived. Jack, Sam and Nick were quickly building a strong repertoire of songs together, and their porch jams were becoming a regular afternoon routine that Nick looked forward to as much as he'd ever enjoyed being with the band. In fact, the porch music had begun to take up a lot of the day's time that would otherwise have been spent at The Hanger. Sam primarily played his dobro when the three of them gathered, adding an amazing warmth to their sessions, and his ability to choose when and how to fill the spaces in the musical background was the subtle mark of his impressive musicianship.

As it turned out, the first one to come see Nick play music on Jack's porch was not his mother, but Jenny. Nick was playing with his back to the street and he didn't see her move slowly up the walkway. She was careful not to disrupt the song that they were working on. As it ended, Jack looked up and smiled at the lovely young lady who was taking such an interest in the music. "Hello. We welcome all listeners here," he said, waving her toward the porch. Nick turned to see whom Jack was addressing.

It was evident to Jack from the smile that split Nick's face in half that he already knew the girl. "Hi, Jenny!" Nick's voice brimmed with delight. "C'mon up and meet my friends."

"I thought it looked like you up there, Nick. That was really great." As she climbed the steps she gave them a smile that lit up the day. Turning her attention toward Jack and Sam, she said,

"Hi, I'm Nick's friend, Jenny," and held up her palm in a hello gesture that was both confident and sweet.

Jack was charmed and saw Sam grin from ear to ear as he answered, "Jenny, it's good t' know ya. This here is Jack Brewster — it's his porch we's on — and I'm Sam Johnson. Right pleased ya could stop in. Ever'body's welcome, but a friend o' Nick's is a special treat, indeed."

Jack jumped up to scoot a chair into place for Jenny. "Can I bring you some iced tea?"

"Yes, thanks. I don't want to interrupt your music. It sounded so good I just wanted to listen."

"It's nice to hear that. Nick really brings a lot into it; he's been a welcome addition to our little group." As Jack went in to get the tea he saw Nick beaming. He paused at the door. "Lemon? Sugar?"

"Sugar, thanks." she said, then looked back at Nick. "This is cool. I'll bet you have a lot of fun here."

"It's a blast. I learn a lot from these guys."

Turning toward Sam, Jenny asked, "What kind of an instrument is that?" Sam showed off his dobro for a few minutes, demonstrating how it sounded and was played. Meanwhile, Jack had returned with Jenny's iced tea.

"I don't know much about playing music," she remarked to Sam, "I just play the stereo. Nick is really good, though. I've always known that. It's funny to see him without an electric guitar."

"Nick's what ya call a nat'ral. He done came in here and jus' picked up the music like he was born t' it. I 'spect we'll see him go places." Sam's pride in Nick was only outshone by his desire to make him look good for Jenny.

"Okay, okay — stop talking about me like I'm not here. I can only take in so much honey before I start to get sick." Nick bemoaned, embarrassed by their conspicuous flatteries.

Jack had sat down once again and picked up his guitar. "Gentlemen, I do believe the lady came here to listen to our songs, not our jabber. Shall we?"

Their music was especially smooth. Nick played his heart and soul for Jenny's benefit, with even more sensitivity than usual. It was clear to Jack that this pretty girl was more to Nick than just the friend she'd claimed him to be, though he doubted she knew that.

Whatever Jenny's feelings were for Nick, she'd certainly proven herself to be supportive of their trio that afternoon. Her praise was generous and sincere, and she stayed to listen much longer than would have merely been polite. Jack and Sam were enchanted with her intelligent and direct manner and humor, and both were happy to make Nick shine in his moment like the bright star they knew him to be. The two great loves of Nick's life came together that day in a way that they both felt privileged to see.

‍❧ *18* ☙

Brandon looked up as Nick walked into the living room of The Hanger in the late afternoon. A loose scattering of CDs surrounded the chair in which he sat, and his guitar was laying face up in his lap, in the process of being restrung. Another guitar sat propped against the arm of the chair. Nick set his own guitar down and plopped himself onto the sofa.

"Hey, Nicky, where you been hangin' lately? I thought you were waiting for school to end so we could practice more. You missed a killer party last night. We freakin' *jammed*!" Brandon tightened the tuner on his guitar while plucking out a sound. It modulated between low and high pitches as the new string began to stretch into place. "Shit, I hate putting new strings on. Broke two of 'em last night — we were fuckin' wailing. Dude, you shoulda *been* here!"

"If you changed your strings more than once a year they wouldn't break so easily. They'd stay in tune, too." Nick spent a small fortune on new strings, changing them every other week or so. As much as he played, they lost their tone quickly. They did for Brandon as well, but he was less concerned with the quality of his music and more concerned about how good he looked in front of an audience.

"Why are you always pitching me shit for that? Jeez, you sound like a preacher. Anyway, what the hell good does it do to have new strings if you never show up to play? Everybody's been asking where you are." Nick had a feeling that Brandon's disappointment was more about him not being there to make the rest of the group look good. Without Nick's leads, the very little time that Brandon spent practicing to actually improve was all too apparent.

"I had other things going on," Nick said emphatically.

"Sure you did. I'll bet you were off somewhere feeding your crush. When are you gonna get wise that Jenny's legs are locked at the knees?"

"Are you ever gonna get your mind out of the gutter, you jerk? And no, that wasn't what I had going on." Brandon's comment had irritated Nick. He wished that he'd never said anything about his feelings for Jenny. For Brandon, the only reason girls existed was to stoke his insatiable desire for sex. Those who didn't put out weren't worth the time of his day.

"Just bringing you back to reality, Nicky. There's a dozen girls we know who'd shag you in a heartbeat. Why the fuck do you waste your time with some uptight chick that never even lets you kiss her?" Brandon seemed to love digging into Nick's sensitive areas. It was as if he saw his purpose in their friendship as chipping away at the inner convictions that kept Nick from entering deeper into his own seedy world. Brandon had little use for morals.

"That drives you nuts, doesn't it, Brandon? A girl who doesn't fall all over you and let you treat her like crap. You can't tell me you don't think Jenny is totally hot — you've told me so before. She won't give you the time of day and you can't stand it. Why can't you just admit that?" Nick was defensively incensed.

"Hey. she's a babe, no doubt. I'd do anything to get into Jenny's pants. Anything. But she isn't for me *or* you Nicky, in any way. That's all I'm saying, man. You're wasting your fucking time if you think otherwise, ya know? You gotta start living sometime." Nick kept quiet. The basic truth within

Brandon's words had stung him to the core. Jenny really wasn't any more than a friend to him and he'd spent a long time wishing it were otherwise. He feared at some point that she'd find someone else and his hopes would be dashed to pieces, but he refused to let Brandon be the one to pull him out of the dream for now.

"So where *were* you last night? You ain't been around much at all in the last few weeks." Brandon wasn't dropping the subject of Nick's absence at the party. It was obviously a sore spot for him.

"I've been jamming with a guy that moved in across the street from me. He's a solo musician. He's been traveling around the country a lot of years and he's really good. I'm learning great stuff."

"An old rocker, eh? How does he do a solo gig?"

"His stuff is pretty much acoustic. He can do rock, but he and this old guy who lives on the next street over play a lot of folk, blues and bluegrass tunes."

"You gotta be shitting me! What good is that crap? It seems like all you do anymore is waste your time being a fool, Nicky. You need to be here with us, dude!"

Nick could see that Brandon wasn't going to appreciate the kind of music that Nick was beginning to like. He wasn't sure if the bigger issue was the style of music itself or the fact that it pulled Nick away from the group that brought Brandon's fan club out to fall at his feet, with the bonus of easy money. It struck him that Jenny's assessment of Brandon might be truer to the mark than he'd been willing to see. At least with Jack's music, his mom and Jenny both approved.

"The whole world doesn't revolve around what we do here, Brandon. Just your world, that's all." Nick's comeback seemed to cause Brandon to drop his offensive tactic. He stopped his cutting remarks to turn on the charm.

"Nick, what you do is freaking amazing, man. You put a lot of time into it. People come here to hear you play and they're really bummed when you don't show. So am I and so are Benny and Diggs. What we do is *way* cool — you know that, man. We've got plans for it, remember?"

"Yeah, I know. I just don't want to get stuck in a rut."

"I understand that, man. I really do." Brandon's words seemed to come from a genuine place. *Is it real, or just the way he has to make things turn for him?*

Nick pulled his guitar from its case. "So are you getting in tune there? Let's get going." Brandon smiled his most affable smile and offered a thumb-clinch handshake.

Nothing brought Nick back into balance like playing music. They moved from song to song with a sense of timing and connection that only comes with the familiarity of musical companionship, anticipating where the next measures are going. Like a dance, it was the grace of shared movement made perfect with practice.

The time passed all too quickly. When Nick looked at the clock he was shocked to see that it was well past the hour when his mother was supposed to come home. The long summer daylight had masked the evening hour. Nick unshouldered his guitar strap and hastily unplugged from the amplifier. "I gotta jet. I didn't see what time it was getting to be," he exclaimed nervously.

"This was good stuff, Nicky. You're gonna be here Friday, right? We've got another party going on, and you can't miss two in a row. We're charging a cover for this one, so there's bucks in it for you." Brandon was in earnest, probing for a commitment.

"It'll pay for your strings for awhile, eh?"

A gig that paid money was a big incentive for Nick. It was what they'd been working toward.

"Count me in." Nick said, enthusiastically.

"That's my man. Word, dude. See you then."

* * *

Kate was sitting at the kitchen table when Nick arrived home that evening. He could tell by the look on her face that he was in trouble.

"Come in and sit down, Nicholas." He put his guitar down and walked slowly to the table to sit down. It wasn't a good sign when she called him 'Nicholas'.

"Sorry I'm late, mom. I lost track of the time."

"Where exactly were you when you did this?" Her voice was tense and she stared straight into his eyes.

"Practicing. You know, with the guys."

"No, I didn't know. When you weren't home by eight and I didn't see you on Jack's porch, I called Brandon's home to find you. When did you plan on telling me that he'd dropped out of school and moved out of his mother's house over six months ago?" He saw the anger in her face and said nothing.

"I take it you didn't plan on telling me at all."

"I thought you'd be worried…"

"You're *damn right* I'm worried! All this time you've been hanging out at a house where older boys live completely unsupervised. You *knew* that would not be okay with me, Nick. I don't much like Brandon, and I don't trust him at all." She looked down at the table to gather her thoughts, then she looked back at Nick. "Now I find that I can't trust you either. How long ago did you start deceiving me?"

Tears welled up in Nick's eyes. "I didn't, mom. I didn't do it to deceive you. I just wanted to practice. That's all I ever do over there is play music. Honest. But I knew you wouldn't let me go, so I just didn't mention where he'd moved to." Nick felt himself turn red. While it was true that his own activities at The Hanger were mostly in line, he knew that what went on there with the others went way beyond what was acceptable to her.

"It seems you've redefined what deception means in your own mind to justify this, haven't you?" She stared once again at him and he averted his eyes, knowing it was true.

"I'm sorry, mom. I didn't mean to hurt you."

"Look at me, son." Nick raised his eyes again to look at hers. It stabbed him to the heart to see the pain that was there. "You hurt yourself just as much, Nick. I've always been proud of the way I could trust you. Now I don't know if I can. That hurts us both." Tears ran down his face as he realized the serious nature of what she was saying.

"Can I still trust you, Nick?"

"Yeah, mom." He wiped his face on his sleeve.

"You know I can't be here all the time. I have to work. If I ask you to stay away from their house, can I believe that you'll do that?"

Nick hesitated. He'd already promised to play at the party on Friday, in his first paid performance. He'd given his word. The turmoil inside him turned his stomach as he answered.

"Yes, mom. You can trust me." Kate rose from her seat and leaned over Nick's chair. The long hug she gave him was nearly unbearable.

If buttercups buzz'd after the bee,

If boats were on land, churches on sea,

If ponies rode men and if grass ate the cows,

And cats should be chased into holes by the mouse,

If the mamas sold their babies

To the gypsies for half a crown;

If summer were spring and the other way round,

Then all the world would be upside down.

— The World Turned Upside Down (a traditional song)

81

ಬಿ *19* ಲ

On Thursday at noon, Jack buzzed around the house making preparations for a late afternoon cookout. Earlier in the week he'd resurrected the outdoor grill from its dusty storage in the basement and set it out on the side porch. That morning he'd placed five small, thick-cut steaks and five large chicken breasts into separate marinade sauces in the refrigerator, before heading out to shop for the rest of the side dishes.

He'd invited Sam, Kate and Nick to dinner and had asked Nick to invite Jenny as well. The idea of having a small porch party was exciting to him — it was his first attempt to bring some life back to his good memories in the old house. He was a bit nervous, never having hosted such a meal before. Sam had offered to come early and lend a hand, and Jack had gratefully accepted the help.

Sam showed up with a sack full of barbecue essentials that included a large white chef's apron, grill tongs and hickory chips. He'd also brought his dobro, one of the main ingredients for success, and he appeared to be just as excited as Jack about the party — the first one held in many years. Together they made quick work of the final preparations.

Kate had gone with Nick to pick up Jenny at her house, meeting her parents briefly and promising to have her home by eleven-thirty. They arrived at Jack's house to find the outdoor table set and kerosene lanterns hung along the entire porch. A folding table held several covered dishes, and Sam stood at the barbecue checking the coals.

"My, my, it sho' is good t' meet ya, Miss Kate." Sam's wide smile lit up as they stepped onto the porch. "We been hopin' fo' ya t' come 'round."

"Thanks, Sam. It's nice to meet you at last." She handed him a large plate covered with foil. "Jack said not to bring anything, but I just couldn't arrive empty-handed."

Sam peeked under the foil with an exaggerated gesture of curiosity, then his eyes closed as he inhaled deeply and grinned with delight. "Homemade cornbread! That be the perfect thing t' bring, Miss Kate."

"It's made from a special recipe, with sour cream, minced carrots and peppers."

"It looks like sliced heaven." Sam placed the dish on the folding table. "Good t' see you, too, Nick and Jenny. Jack is inside worryin' over the salad. He been runnin' 'round like Martha Stewart all day."

Nick groaned, "I hope he's not wearing a skirt."

They all burst into laughter when, as if on cue, Jack stepped onto the porch with a salad, wearing Sam's long white apron. "Hello folks. I bring you a gourmet salad — and it looks like I'm the entertainment as well." He looked himself over to see what they might be laughing about.

"It's so nice to see you, Martha." Nick said in a falsetto voice, adding the punch line to bring Jack in on the joke.

"Hey, there. I'll have you know that barbecuing is a *manly* thing! And I made a *manly* salad here. I used my hunting knife to cut the veggies." Jack emphasized this with a clenched fist and his jaw thrust forward. "Now that we have that settled, can I bring you all out some fresh squeezed homemade lemonade?"

Jenny quipped, "Squeezed over a rock, no doubt."

They laughed again as Jack made a false, haughty batting of his eyes and swaggered back inside for the drinks, with his hands on his hips. Sam brought out the steaks and the partially pre-baked chicken and set them on the grill. He took orders for how they each preferred their steaks cooked.

The weather that evening was perfect. The talk over their meal was light and lively and the food was delicious. Jenny and Sam both asked for Kate's cornbread recipe. Sam was full of stories that evening about his days with the railroad and the funny things Jack had done as a young boy. They'd all swapped special tales from their experiences, and many good memories.

When they circled-in at last for a time of music there was a deep sense of sharing that had already begun. It made the music all the richer. Jack's voice was strong and low as he sang the ballads and poems of bygone eras, joined in harmony by Sam and Nick. Nick played and sang a song he'd written, sharing it for the first time in front of them.

Kate's eyes shown with tears as she witnessed the talent of her son and the depth of his new-found friendship with Jack and Sam. There was no longer any doubt in her mind that these men were good companions for him at an age when he most needed them. She glanced at Jenny's pretty, smiling face, feeling a twinge of melancholy mixed with approval, that Nick's heart was so obviously turned toward a lovely and virtuous girl, whom Kate knew he was worthy of winning.

When did it happen? When did my little boy grow up to be such a beautiful young soul?

They ended the special evening with promises that there would be more of them to follow. As it turned out, that wouldn't happen anytime soon.

ℵ 20 ℭ

The night of the party Nick found himself fighting an inner battle between his promise to Brandon and the trust that his mother had placed in him. He'd given his word to both, and was now forced to make a decision. Kate was working a twelve hour overnight shift at the hospital that Friday. It started at five o'clock in the afternoon and provided the perfect opportunity for Nick to get away with an appearance at The Hanger. No matter how many lofty ideals he might have told himself about his desire to keep his word to Brandon, he knew deep down that the idea of doing a paid performance for people who wanted to hear it had driven the decision he'd finally made. It was a time of testing, like Sam often talked about, and he knew he was failing it miserably.

He opted to wait until after nine o'clock to arrive at the party. In the late afternoon he'd joined Jack on the porch for an hour of music, but when Kate called at the beginning of her dinner break, Nick made sure he was home to answer the phone. He'd never before plotted in such a deliberate manner to go against his mother's trust. His stomach was twisted into a nauseous mass and it felt to him as if a line was being crossed — one from which he might never be able to step back.

"Hi, honey." Kate had said, "How are you doing? Not playing music with Jack and Sam tonight?"

"I did for an hour or so. I got some song ideas I wanted to work out on my own, so I came home. I'm pretty tired now so I think I'll just read awhile then go to bed." Nick's gut had clenched ever tighter as he lied.

What are you doing?

He knew that lying to parents was a natural thing for most of his friends, but it wasn't so for him. His mother was also his friend who shared life with him. She'd never ruled over him without cause, and had always given good reason for the things she required from him. Most of all, he knew she loved him very much and trusted him — even when he no longer deserved that trust. When he hung up the phone after talking with her, the guilt of his scheming nearly overwhelmed him.

* * *

Nick arrived at The Hanger to find the party in full swing. A muscle-bound friend of Benny's named James was manning the door, making sure everyone paid a five dollar cover charge to get in. The place was packed and the money jar was brimming. A cheer went up as James waved Nick through the entryway with his guitar. He saw the rest of the group tuning up in the back of the room. Nick's deep misgivings began to dull and fade as he watched the focus of the party swing toward a makeshift stage that had been created, with colored lights and strobes strung across the ceiling. Brandon raised a fist high into the air as he spotted him.

"Nick—*y!* Get your ass up here," he screamed over the crowd, already showing the effects of his early start at partying. "It's out-*rageous*, man. Everyone in the fuckin' neighborhood is here, man, so we can *crank* it up." Brandon seemed unusually wired and Nick felt fairly certain he was tweaking from doing some heavy cranking of his own. His pupils were too dilated to hide it.

Nick stepped into the space set aside for the him on the short

86

stage riser and brought out his guitar, plugging it into the amplifier. Looking out at the crowd of people he saw that he was probably the only one who was not drunk, high, or both. He reflected that Benny and Brandon were likely making a tidy sum above the door and beer proceeds that night.

The rule of the event was that all illegal substances and flagrantly sexual activities were only allowed upstairs, keeping the evidence to a minimum in the event that the cops should show up. As the music started and couples moved seductively to the sounds, what constituted "flagrant sexual activity" began to get fuzzy. It didn't take long for a building intensity of rhythm to dominate the pulse of the party.

Nick was in top form, fingers flying across the frets, taking solo breaks that got wild responses from the crowd, which now filled the downstairs to capacity. Diggs was sweating and had stripped off his shirt as he pounded out rhythms, drumsticks flying. Brandon, always the showman, projected his lyrics toward every adoring female in the place, while Benny stood in a swayback stance, sporting dark sunglasses and an unlit cigarette hanging from his mouth, dipping his blond, curly haired head to his pounding bass attack.

The party increased in tension as the night progressed. Nick observed a steady stream of guys and girls making their way up and down the stairs. People were in various stages of intoxication and excitement, and their dancing became more and more erotic. A smoky haze of cigarettes and marijuana hung heavily in the air.

Around eleven o'clock Brandon called for a band break. He'd focused his singing of the last two songs, with an open-shirted, undulating seductiveness, toward a girl whose own dance motions had sent him back an undeniable invitation. He now felt compelled to take advantage of it. Nick recognized her as a girl from school named Alison Bennington, who was barely fifteen years old but dressed to be a hot twenty. She looked to be fairly out of it by that point in the evening.

Nick grabbed a glass of beer from the keg in the kitchen and returned to the room in time to see Brandon heading up the stairs with Alison, hands all over her and practically pushing her along. It was a part of Brandon that Nick hated — his complete lack of concern for age or vulnerability in his quest to score. A pang of guilt hit Nick strongly as his conscience again needled him about his own ability to participate in what was happening at the Hanger that night.

As if in response to his sudden angst, a scantily clothed girl whom he'd never before seen made her way through the crowded party toward him. Her pale, white skin contrasted with her cropped dark hair and heavy eye makeup. She stood enticingly close as she circled his neck with her arms.

"I just *love* what you do. You make me want to dance. Do I make *you* want to dance?" She slurred her words slightly as she moved in to sway her body against him, urging him to move with her. Their motion caused him to spill some of his beer onto his arm. He switched the glass into his other hand behind her back and as he did she pulled him into a hard, deep kiss. Her mouth tasted faintly of beer and cigarettes and the kiss was sloppy and demanding. Her hands moved down his sides and then behind him to grasp his buttocks. She began to grind her pelvis against his as the kiss quickly became urgent with lust. He returned it with unreserved passion, his desire beginning to surge.

Had he not been clumsy, the outcome of the night might have been quite different. As it was, the entire cold glass of beer he was holding spilled down the back of her very short shorts, dripping down her legs and into her shoes. She broke off the kiss and shrieked, *"You asshole!* Why don't you watch what the hell you're doing?" before stomping away to clean up in the bathroom. In one swift motion he had gone from being a god to being a jerk.

Nick looked toward the stage, where Benny stood laughing hysterically. He'd obviously been watching the whole episode take place. Suddenly, the seediness of the party and the reality of the lies he'd told to be there began to hit Nick hard. He felt a deep sense of shame for wanting to be a part of it. Walking back to the stage, he picked up his guitar and unplugged it from the sound set.

Benny jumped in, "Hey, Nick. Don't be so sensitive, man. You gotta admit what happened was pretty fuckin' funny. C'mon. Sorry I laughed, man."

Nick began to stow his guitar away in silence.

"Nicky, hey. That chick wasn't worth doing this. You shouldn't get so pissed about it." Benny had taken the reasons for Nick's reaction completely wrong. "Tell you what, I can get you hooked up with any girl here, man. I got a line on a few script roofies last week. You interested? No charge. I can set you up right now — you can have any chick at the party."

Nick glared back at him, stunned at the measure Benny was willing to take to turn things around, and seeing for the first time the very real differences in their ways. "Benny, you can keep this little scene you've got going for yourself. I don't want any part of it." He headed toward the door. As he did people tried to coax him to stay. Ignoring them all, he left the party and walked home. He didn't care that nobody understood why.

* * *

The next morning Jack called to invite Nick to breakfast with him and Sam at Tony's Place. Kate was sleeping late after her long work shift. Nick seemed far quieter than usual as the three friends walked the five blocks to the cafe. When they arrived they sat at a table by the window. Ruby came over to take their orders.

"Today I have special crepes with fresh Oregon strawberries. My granddaughter, she picked them herself yesterday." She poured coffee for all three without asking if they wanted it. Jack and Sam decided to try the crepes. When Nick ordered only toast, Ruby raised her finger in her most motherly manner and said, "Young men don't grow strong on toast. You let Aunt Ruby bring you my special cheesy eggs with that toast, no?"

Nick grinned weakly, "Okay, I guess."

"You gonna see — you'll enjoy." As she moved back toward the kitchen, Harvey and his fishing buddy, Marvin, entered the cafe and sat down at a nearby table. When spoken of together, they were known as Harv 'n Marv to the cafe regulars. Ruby turned around to greet them with her coffee pot in hand and to fill the mugs that were already in place on the table. "You boys are a little late today, no?"

Harvey rubbed his eyes and forehead in one movement. "I didn't get much sleep last night between the racket and the cops." He whipped the statement out into the room with the verbal poise of the seasoned fly fisherman, knowing he would likely get a bite here. He waited patiently for the fish to come.

It was Sam who finally jumped for the bait. "You had the police at yo' place, Harvey?"

"Nope. There was some big party at the house down the street last night. Bunch of unruly kids, all drinking and hopped up, playing that noise they call music." Harvey took a sip of his coffee, enjoying his role in keeping the folks at Tony's informed.

Jack looked at Nick and saw his eyes open wide, the dull look on his face turning to rapt attention.

"Well, it being summer and all, kids just get t' doin' things."

Sam played the game like a clever fish spitting the hook out, dropping the topic knowing that Harvey was dying to tell more. The room went silent for a moment. Ruby took breakfast orders from the two men, then retreated to the kitchen.

"You said there were cops?" Nick asked, looking intently at Harvey. Sam and Jack glanced at each other, then at their coffee cups.

"A little after midnight they showed up to shut off the hubbub." Harvey happily continued the story, delighted to reel in a catch on the second bite. "They were there a long time, three or four cars with lights blinking. Kept me up half the night."

Marvin chimed in with a jab toward his friend, "The lights from the cop cars kept you from sleeping, Harv?"

"No, dang it Marv, the lights weren't doing it," Harvey batted back at his buddy, "It was the police radios and all the other things. They arrested some of the kids and questioned a whole lot more on the front lawn. It must have taken three hours for them to finally all leave. I tell, you, these kids today are just itching to be in trouble."

Ruby brought the fruit crepes, along with Nick's eggs and toast, to their table. As usual, Sam paused over his food to give silent thanks. Jack waited politely to begin and looked at Nick, who sat still, staring at his plate. Sam and Jack ate hungrily and chatted while Nick nibbled at his meal, saying nothing. No one asked what had curbed his normally voracious appetite that morning, not even Ruby.

* * *

They arrived back at Jack's house after breakfast. Standing at the front walkway, Sam stated that he had chores and errands to do and would perhaps meet up with them later, then left for home. Before Nick could retreat, Jack asked him if he had time to help move a couple of bookcases out of the living room. Nick stayed to help. They went wordlessly to work and carried the shelves down the back steps and out to the garage, where Jack had planned to strip the paint off and refinish them.

When they were through with the task, Jack turned to look directly at Nick. "You want to tell me why you're being so quiet today? You don't have to, but I think maybe you ought to."

Nick said nothing and stared at his shoes.

"It's just between you and me, you know." Jack added.

"I feel like crap. I was at that party last night and I wasn't supposed to be." Nick looked up at Jack.

"I already figured something like that."

"I left before the cops got there."

"I'm glad to hear that." Jack didn't ask questions. Nick was silent for a few minutes as they stood there.

"That place belongs to some friends of mine. We play music there all the time. There's kids I know that go there a lot to hang out. My mom didn't know I was going there until the other day."

"And when she found out…?"

"She made me promise I wouldn't ever go again."

"You didn't keep your word, then."

"I'd already promised my friend, Brandon, that I'd play music at the party. I was gonna make money — they charged admission. I was just there for the music, honest."

"Very noble. In my day I would have been there for the glory, the money and the adoring girls." Jack seemed to say this knowingly, with an added wink.

"Yeah. I guess it wasn't just the music."

"So, I'm curious. Why did you leave early?"

"I didn't like what was going on. I didn't like how it was making me feel." He looked back at his shoes for a long moment. "I didn't like lying to my mom."

"Those are big lessons at your age. It took me a whole lot longer to come to those same conclusions. Except, I never had to lie to my mom. She didn't care."

"Wow." Nick paused a moment, as the small insight into Jack's past sunk in. "For me that's the hardest part of all. I looked right at my mom and told her she could trust me. Then last night I told her lies so I could get away with going there. She trusted me and I dumped all over her trust."

"Hey, Nick, don't beat yourself up too bad about this. Every guy screws up before he gets it right. Going downhill is a slippery slope that happens slowly, with each and every decision you make to go ahead and do what you know deep down you ought not to. Eventually your conscience wears down and nothing stops you. Would you make the same decision today, knowing what you know now?"

"No way. I can't stand this." Jack could see that Nick's answer was emphatic and sincere.

"Then you've learned the best thing you could have gotten from it. Even your mom might see it that way if she knew, but I don't think you should tell her. Just keep your trust with her from now on and forgive yourself the mistake it took to learn the bigger truth. You did well, Nick, overall. You really did. We'll keep this between us."

"Can I ask you something else? Something kind of personal?" Nick still seemed troubled.

"Sure."

"Did girls ever want to go to bed with you because you're a musician?" Jack was a bit hesitant to answer, but knew it was an important moment for Nick. He was concerned about what had prompted the question.

"Yep. Groupies are a pretty common thing and a lot of 'em will do anything just to say they've been with you. Some girls seem to get their identity from being with men they see as known artists, no matter how small their circle of popularity. Some guys become stage performers for that reason alone. Women performers likely deal with that, too, but they seem to handle it better. That's just a guess, though. I've never asked."

"Did you sleep with groupies?"

"Can I ask you first why you want to know?"

Nick blushed. "There was a girl last night who threw herself at me. I didn't even know her."

"Did you throw yourself back?"

"Well, yeah — but it didn't go very far. I spilled a beer down her back accidentally and she got really pissed off." Jack smiled and held back a laugh.

"I never tried that approach to cool things down."

Nick chuckled. Jack was glad to see the tension in his face fading as he did. "So — did you ever get laid?" Nick asked.

"I'm not gonna lie and say I never did. Being on the road all the time a guy never gets a chance to have a real relationship with anyone. But I've gotta say that it didn't happen a lot and I never felt good about having done it. Not ever. Most men seem to be completely okay with it, but I never could. Something inside me has always held me back from the kind of things that so many performers get into with no qualms — promiscuous sex, heavy drugs — you know, the whole thing that goes with the territory. I have a feeling that you and I think more alike about that than most would be. We're into music for the love of the song."

"Yeah." Nick grinned. "I can relate."

"You stick with fans like Jenny, son, and you'll do just fine. You've got a lot more going for you than I ever did."

Jack saw in Nick the promise of a life full of music and caring. It was something that seemed to dwell deep in the root of all Nick had become in his few short years, something elusive that Jack had seen before in others but had never grasped in his own life. There was a loving quality in this boy that he didn't see in himself, something that wasn't consciously acquired but that merely existed. The thought that he never would, or could, know it plagued his everyday life.

Run, Jack, run. You have no business being here.

* * *

A few days after the police had raided The Hanger, Nick heard that Benny and James were among the ten people who had been arrested that night. Benny had since been released from jail on a bail bond, and the charges had then been reduced to minor misdeameanors that carried some stiff fines, which he'd paid. Brandon had managed to escape arrest altogether by climbing out his second story bedroom window and hiding in the backyard — an action which was no surprise to Nick.

Once again, Brandon had avoided all consequences.

༺ *21* ༻

Kate was pleased that Nick's summer days were now focused on activities at Jack's house. It put her more at ease for the time she spent away from him. Nick had added his help to Jack's restoration projects, which were moving along quickly. She was also delighted to find that Nick's taste in radio stations was broadening beyond the hard rock which had previously encompassed his life. When she'd awakened late one Saturday morning to the gentle strains of a bluegrass band playing *Just A Closer Walk With Thee,* the degree of change had amazed her.

She walked into the dining room in her bathrobe to find Nick sitting at the table reading a guitar magazine and drinking coffee. He looked up and smiled as she said, "Good morning, babe. Thanks for letting me sleep late."

"You didn't make it home until after one so I figured you were tired. I have coffee made — sit down and I'll pour you some." Nick jumped up and ran into the kitchen as she took a seat at the table.

"Bless your heart, son," Kate exclaimed as he set the cup down in front of her.

"Do you want some toast with that?" he asked.

"Why do I get the feeling I'm being buttered up?" Kate smiled across at him, raising her eyebrows playfully.

"C'mon, mom, I just want to do something nice. So, do you want toast?"

"Not right now. It's good to just sit here with you and wake up a bit." Kate took in the comfort of the moment.

"Do you have any plans for today?" Nick asked.

"Beyond showering and getting dressed, I suppose the only other thing is grocery shopping."

"How about a trip downtown with me and Jack?" Nick looked a bit sheepish.

"Is this why you're being so sweet this morning?"

"Nope. I'm sweet to you anyway, mom." He batted his eyelashes back at her jokingly. "But I'm hoping you'll say okay to something."

"Shoot, then. Don't drag it out."

"Jack says he wants to buy me a guitar because I've been helping a lot with the house and all. We could go today and you could come with us, maybe?" Kate looked at him. It was moments like these when she still saw her little boy shine through the eyes of the young man that was replacing him all too quickly.

"I don't know, Nick. You shouldn't have to be rewarded for helping a friend."

"It's not a reward or anything. He's the one who brought it up. Please, mom? I want to practice at home and I haven't ever borrowed one of Jack's guitars even though he said I could."

Kate knew that Nick's electric guitar wasn't right for the style of music he and Jack played. She also realized that a guitar was an expensive gift that she couldn't afford to give him at this time. "Hand me the phone, son. Let me talk to Jack about this." Nick jumped up to comply as she looked up Jack's number on the phone list. He answered on the second ring.

"Hi, Jack. It's Kate. I have a very antsy young man over here saying something about a guitar you want to shop for?"

"I'd really like to buy him his first acoustic guitar. It's got a bit to do with carrying on a tradition. It's also because I appreciate all the work he's done for me."

Jack's response seemed reasonable, but Kate still felt it was too generous an offer to accept. "It's awfully nice of you, Jack, but Nick is helping you as a friend."

"It's not really payment, just appreciation. I know how it felt the day my uncle bought me my first acoustic guitar. I'd like to be able to pass that feeling on to Nick. Trust me, Kate, I can easily afford to do this, and I really want to. Nick has a lot of talent and I'd like to support that."

"Well…" she said hesitantly.

"Why don't we make a day of this, since you're off work? We'll shop for a guitar and I'll take you both to lunch. Don't say no, Kate. It means so much to Nick — and to me."

Kate sighed. "Okay, Jack. Give me an hour to wake up and get ready."

"*Yes!*" Nick cried and jumped in the air, raising his fist in triumph as he heard his mother's side of the conversation. He ran to her chair and enfolded her from behind in a bear hug.

* * *

The selection and purchase of the guitar had been challenging. Kate hadn't been prepared for the range in price of acoustic guitars, and she'd balked at the models that Jack was steering Nick toward selecting. When she'd attempted to point out lesser priced instruments, Jack dismissed them as unacceptable to consider. Finally, Kate took him aside.

"It's a lot of money, Jack. I appreciate it, but I wasn't prepared for the expense when I'd agreed to let you do this." She was agitated and inclined to call the whole thing off, but she knew that the disappointment for Nick would be profound.

"I knew exactly what to expect when we came in here, Kate. For a player as advanced as Nick the performance level of the instrument is really important, and it doesn't come with less expensive guitars that might be perfectly fine for a casual player. I know this is hard for you to feel good about. Don't worry — there's also a point where the quality levels out and the fancy fluff adds to the price. I promise to keep it at the essential level only, okay?"

"I don't know, Jack. I'm in a bad position to say no here, but you're looking at spending at least $2,000. That's way more than I feel I can allow."

"Trust me, Kate. That amount of money is a lot different to you than it is to me. This isn't causing me any hardship. In fact, it comes from my uncle's estate, not my own earnings. I want to see Nick grow to love the music he's learning, and so do you. Just let that happen."

"Well — will you at least let me buy the lunch?"

Jack smiled wide. "Okay. It's such a nice day that I'd honestly been thinking of suggesting a simple sack lunch at the waterfront. If you want to cover that, I won't object."

"You won't even permit a place where they don't put lids on the drinks?"

"Some other time. This is Nick's day."

She agreed.

* * *

The grassy area beside the esplanade bordering the Willamette River was the perfect place for their lunch. They stopped at a popular kosher deli to buy sandwiches and drinks, then found a beautiful sunny spot on a small, grassy knoll. Nick wolfed his sandwich in a few bites and uncased his new guitar. Kate wondered if she'd ever seen her son quite as glowing and proud as he was that afternoon, playing his beautiful new guitar in the middle of the open parkway while she and Jack enjoyed the impromptu concert. She admitted to him that it had an incredibly rich sound and thanked Jack again for his generosity.

A young couple had made their way across the open area to stand and listen for several minutes. Nick was stunned when the man reached into his pocket and threw two dollars into the open case lying on the ground as they turned to leave. Jack smiled as Nick thanked them. "That's how it starts, Nick." he said. "An unsolicited tip jar contribution is the sincerest form of flattery to a musician."

"Jack, this is so cool. I'm gonna get a whole new style going — I can feel it already."

"I can, too. You've sure got a good start." Jack knew it was true, and felt great about saying it. The money he'd spent had meant nothing compared to the look on Nick's face at that moment. A thought suddenly occurred to him. He turned to Kate. "The best way to really learn about new styles is to experience them in a big way. There's a bluegrass festival happening next weekend on the Washington side of the Columbia River Gorge. There're a couple of stages and a camp area where local pickers jam day and night. If you have some time off we could all go and listen."

Nick's eyes lit up. "Can we go, mom?"

"I don't see why not, if you can help get the housework done during the week, that is."

"No problem!" Nick exclaimed. Kate grinned. She knew the house would be spotless by Tuesday afternoon.

"We can do just a day trip on Saturday or opt for an overnight camp-out on Saturday night, if you can take the time off. Between tents and my camper van, we can make it work." Jack was right at home with the idea of mobile music.

Kate could see how much the trip meant to Nick. "Let me see what I can arrange at the hospital. If I can swing the time, we'll do the campout." She looked at her son who seemed about to burst at the seams from excitement. She was ready for some adventure herself. Jack had scored big points with both of them that day.

* * *

On Sunday morning, after hastily gulping down his breakfast, Nick headed over to Jack's house with guitar in hand. He was happy to find Sam having coffee with Jack on the porch, and was very excited to show off his beautiful new instrument.

"Did you hear about my guitar, Sam?"

"Heard 'bout it and was hopin' t' see it. I heard 'bout you goin' t' the music festival, too. Ain't no doubt, you'll enjoy that!" Sam's eyes shown bright with joy for Nick.

"Aren't you coming with us, Sam?"

"I done a fair num'er o' festivals in my time, but — well — this body is plum getting' too ol' t' be campin' out, truth is. I'll leave sleepin' on the ground and eatin' food from a stick t' you young folk. You jus' bring back some new tunes ya learn. That'll do fine by me." Sam bent forward to get a closer look as Nick unlatched and opened the guitar's protective case. "My, my, that do look pretty, now!"

Taking the guitar from the case, Nick handed it to Sam. "It's a beauty, ain't it? It was a blast picking it out; there were so many good ones to choose from. But the tone and feel of this one stood out. I knew as soon as I started to play it."

Sam admired the guitar, handling it with reverence and giving it back to Nick. "It's a fine lookin' thing, son. Mighty fine. Lemme hear it hum with a soulful tune."

Nick obliged, picking a lively rendition of *Baby, Please Don't Go*. Sam and Jack set in rapt attention as the deep bass line and dodging melody weaved together into a fabric of sound. Sam's foot stomped a strong, steady background beat on the old wood floor. Even in the simplicity of the moment, the effect was powerful.

"When did you learn to play that so well, Nick?" Jack asked, once the last strains of the song had faded. "It was just a day or so ago when you first tried it."

"I dunno. I practice a lot at home during the day." There was a quiet, humble grace underlying Nick's talent that Jack liked. He was confident and bold in his playing, with no hint of the cockiness that could very well rear its head in a young person with incredible ability such as his.

"I ain't never heard that song done such-a-way, Nick." Sam was obviously quite impressed. "You done found the sweet spot o' that tune."

Nick looked up with a gentle smile. "Well, it's a sweet tune. It could sure use a nice dobro part to kick it up — that is, if I could talk someone into that."

Sam scratched his stubbly face as if in deep thought. "Well, I s'pose I might could find a body willin' t' tackle that." With a wink he added, "The soul o' a good shared song is when folks all find the best part t' play in it. Ain't nothin' like it. That goes fo' music, and it goes fo' life, too. Like we done found here 'tween us three. Jack plays his way. You feel his part and come in yo' way.

When I listen, I hear that and 'fore ya know it, we's findin' harmony. That ain't no easy thing. Most folks know harmony when they hear it, but *finding* it takes practice and listenin'. Lotsa practice and lotsa listenin' — t' the music, t' the words an' the soul. Ain't many that got that gift nowadays 'cuz ain't many that know how t' listen, and a durn sight fewer have 'nough patience to practice it."

"Are we talking about the song, Sam?" Nick's head was cocked to one side and his expression was nearly comical.

Jack laughed. "Haven't you noticed? Sam is *never* just talking about one simple thing. He turns everything that happens into a life lesson."

"That's 'cuz ever'thing *is*, Jack. Don't tell me you ain't figured that out in all yo' travels?"

"I'm with you there, Sam. Being on the road, I've seen a whole lot more dissonance than harmony being practiced. And you're right — most of it comes from not listening."

"An' a whole lot o' it comes from listenin' t' the wrong tune alt'gether. If a body plays a tune ya ain't kin to, ain't no harmony can be found t' make it hum in yo' soul. They just ain't no peace when that happens."

Nick frowned. "Are you saying there are songs that are bad to play, Sam?"

"In a manner o' speakin', yes, son. As musicians, we got us a sacred job. We work hard and practice so's we can say things in song. Yo' music should say somethin' *you* wanna say — somethin' other people gonna hear with they hearts. Things folks *need* t' hear t' find peace. Music reaches deep. It changes people. That's why we remember the words t' songs we heard years ago, but can't hardly remember somethin' a body said yesterday. So, we all need t' choose careful-like which songs we let in."

Sam stopped to take a sip of his coffee. Neither Nick nor Jack spoke during the deep silence of his pause.

"In a way, it's like pickin' out that there guitar. They's a lot t' choose from, but yo' gut tells you which one is fo' you. When ya listen t' somethin' that don't ring true fo' y'own heart an' soul, then that ain't somethin' that's good fo' you t' be playin'. It ain't good fo' you t' be lettin' it in. It ain't good fo' ya t' be givin' it out. That goes the same fo' songs, an' guitars, an' people, too. But most folks don't think thataway. They jus' take in anythin' at all, not knowin' how t' separate they own voice from ever'body's noise, and not knowin' how t' find harmony w'others, down deep in they soul. And they wonder why they can't find no peace."

"Well, Sam, not every song has a harmony part." Jack's comment was openly defensive in nature.

Sam's reply was swift. "The most nat'ral harmony o' all is a chord, Jack. It's perfect harmony. Jus' a few single notes that all work t'gether t' make a strong sound. You played many songs lately that ain't got no chords, Jack?"

"Okay, Sam, you win that one."

"We ain't in no contest, Jack. We, all o' us, be makin' out a harmony, here. You, me and Nick. Kate and Jenny — they listen. They be findin' they parts, too. We' all tryin' t' find our own true part in the songs we wanna be playin'." Sam stopped talking and, for a very long moment, no one said anything.

"Wow." Nick finally broke the silence. "What did you put in his coffee, Jack?" The laughter that followed brought them all back into a lighter frame of mind, but Sam's words had hit home.

* * *

"Katy, honey, what's the scoop on your sudden need to go camping this weekend?" Kate's hasty request for time off on Saturday and Sunday had caught the interest of her friend, Sue. She'd cornered Kate in the break room on Wednesday. "Is he handsome?"

"Yes, my son is very handsome." She loved to keep the mystery going for Sue, who couldn't resist the faint aroma of romance in the air, especially where Kate was concerned.

"So you're telling me that you had the sudden urge to go camping with your son, and no one else is going along? No way. I know you too well."

"It's a music camp, Sue."

"And you and Nick are the only ones going?" Sue was in her best form, forcing a definitive answer.

"Is it so hard to believe that I would go alone with my son to a music camp?" Kate prolonged the inevitable.

"And decide it on the spur of the moment? Yes, Kate. So — is Nick the only one you're going with?"

"Well, no, as a matter of fact."

Sue's devilish grin matched the twinkle of her eye as she grabbed Kate's arm. "Who is he? Details, Kate, I want details. Don't you dare hold out on me."

"He's a neighbor who's been helping Nick with his music this summer."

"And...?"

"And what?"

"C'mon, Kate, you're going *camping* with him?"

"Him —and Nick —and a couple hundred other people. We won't be sleeping in the same tent, if that's what you're thinking."

"How old is he? What does he look like? Kate, you know I live vicariously through other people's romances."

"I hate to burst your bubble, but there's no romance here. The festival is mostly just to get Nick more involved in the styles of music he plays."

"He's a musician? Oh, this is getting juicy!"

Kate sighed. "Sue, you're hopeless."

"So he can't be a ninety four year old who plays Frank Sinatra — Nick wouldn't be too hot on that stuff. And he can't be married or he wouldn't be camping with you and Nick. Even if you don't see potential here, I sure do. How did this spontaneous invitation come about?"

"Last weekend the three of us went to buy Nick a new guitar. The idea came up during lunch."

"*Kate !?!* You've been holding out on me. You went out to lunch and to shop together for a guitar? Hey, I thought Nick already had a guitar."

"He does, but it's electric and Jack plays a more acoustic style of music, so…"

"Jack. Nice name. Tall, dark and handsome?"

Kate rolled her eyes and laughed, giving in to the relentless inquiries. "Okay, okay. He's probably forty-ish, lean, has light brown hair and a neat beard, stands a head taller than me, owns the house down the street, and plays music on his porch with my son. Contrary to your fiendish little thoughts, however, we have absolutely nothing going on between us."

"Any reason you shouldn't?"

Kate was taken aback for a few seconds and said, "Well — uh — no. Not really." She wasn't about to admit that the exact same thoughts had fleetingly danced through her own mind recently. Jack was a good man who cared about her son and was kind, responsible and *very* attractive. The festival might be an interesting way to get to know him better. She gave Sue a sheepish little grin. "C'mon. We have to get back to the unit."

"I want a full report after the weekend. And pictures, so be sure to bring your digital camera. You owe me that, since I'm taking four hours of your Sunday shift for you."

Kate laughed. "Sue, you've *gotta* get a life."

"So do you, Katy. So do you."

I couldn't agree more.

♌ *22* ♋

The three-day festival started on Friday. Since Kate had to work that day, she'd agreed to let Nick go early with Jack, to stake out a good campsite. They would stay there Friday night and she would drive over and meet up with them as soon as she could on Saturday morning.

When they arrived at the site early Friday morning, Nick was very excited. The camp ground was a large, flat, open area where a variety of automobiles and RVs were already parked. He'd never seen so many musicians gathered in one place, and was surprised to find that some of those carrying instruments around were much younger than he. Jack paid the entrance and camping fees and found a nice spot that was as close as possible to the portable restrooms and water spigots. In a short time they had staked their claim, raised two medium sized tents, and created a fire pit.

It seemed that many of the campers had arrived the day prior to establish their own camps, and were now busy cooking breakfast or jamming. The festival's attractions were beginning to come alive, and the stage groups were already playing what would be a continuous flow of music from mid-morning until late at night. Families and singles alike were everywhere and many of the people were greeting each other as old friends. Nick loved what he saw.

"All these are local people?" Nick asked.

"Most are." Jack answered. "Some people travel from pretty

far to attend, though, following their favorite annual festivals throughout the summer. A lot of well-known names play on these stages — well-known in bluegrass and folk circles, that is. These aren't necessarily the folks you'll see on prime time TV shows."

"Have you played here before?"

"Many years back I sat in with a few bands at these festivals. This isn't a style I tend to play professionally, but just for fun. You'll meet a lot of good folks this weekend, Nick, and play a lot of great music. Be prepared to watch the guys and gals that know the tunes and the moves — you'll learn a lot."

"So, what'll we do first?"

"Eat!" Jack said emphatically. Nick agreed wholeheartedly and followed him to the food stands.

* * *

In the mid-afternoon, Nick was amazed to see a group of five younger kids, a girl and four boys, take their place on the main stage. The oldest looked to be no more than fifteen, and they each played a different instrument — guitar, banjo, mandolin, fiddle and upright bass. As they strode to the microphones with the confidence of seasoned performers, the oldest boy introduced their group and began the first song with a few notes from his mandolin, after which they all came into the tune one by one. Nick was astonished to hear them play with gusto, matching the skills of many of the adult players with ease. The young girl on the fiddle was especially gifted, her bow flying across the strings and her fingers moving fast and furious to the tempo that her foot and the background bass were setting. In between musical breaks she belted out the lyrics of the songs in harmony with the boy playing mandolin, their voices clear and old-timey in nature. Their band's set lasted about half an hour, during which Nick sat

109

in rapt attention.

"How long do you think they've been playing?" Nick asked, as the band walked off the stage.

"A lot of kids start as young as four and five. Usually they have parents or siblings that play an instrument, so it spurs them to learn."

"Were you that good when you were their age?"

"Yes and no. I think kids today have far more access to music and lessons, not to mention much better equipment. It all works together with talent to produce a whole new level of young prodigies."

"I never knew anything like this existed." Nick was obviously quite deeply impressed. "Jack — thanks for this. For bringing me here, and buying the guitar, and everything."

"You're welcome Nick. You know, a lot of people in Portland aren't aware of its extended bluegrass community, since the powers that promote music don't seem to sell it here in a huge way. Jazz seems to be the favored child in Portland. Bluegrass is more widely sought in places like Tennessee and the Carolinas. It's a very grassroots genre, but then that's what keeps it rather pure. For that reason, I hope it stays in the backdrop here, promoted by people who love the life of it all." Jack smoothed his beard. "Fact is, this may also be the only kind of music venue around where folks can sing a whole lot of old gospel songs and people don't seem to mind at all. But, maybe that's just another reason it never gets overly promoted." They laughed at the thought and turned their attention back to the stage, where the act was winding to a close.

"Do you think maybe we could go back to the camp and jam a little? Listening to all this is making my fingers itchy to play."

"Sure thing." Jack replied. "Maybe we can slap together a

sandwich, too. It's also making me hungry, for some reason."

They stood and gathered up the blanket they were sitting on, then headed for the van. Making their way through the growing crowd of people, they heard someone with a heavy southern drawl yell from behind them, "Brewster, you old son of a gun!"

Nick watched as Jack turned and greeted a man with a bushy gray mustache and an oversized Stetson hat. He carried a padded guitar case on his back. "Hey there, Chuck. You're looking as ornery as ever." He stuck out his hand for a hearty handshake.

"It's been too many years since I've seen you around these parts, Jack. Did the wind blow you in for the festival?"

"Nah. It blew me in a few months ago. My uncle died back in February and I'm living in his house now."

"Hell, you say! You've stayed that long in one place?"

"Yeah, I keep waking up in the same room every day and wondering why." Jack stepped back to turn and introduce Nick. "I brought my friend, Nick, here to take in the tunes. It's his first festival. He's one helluva picker, this one. Nick Weber, meet my old buddy, Chuck Sloam."

Chuck extended his right hand and tipped his hat with the other. "Nick, always glad to meet a fellow musician. How you liking things so far?"

Nick smiled. "There's great music everywhere you turn. I like it a lot, thanks."

"You guys camping here?" Chuck asked.

Jack pointed in the direction of their camp site. "I'm still driving that same old green van. We're camped out just north of the porta-johns over there, one row back. Nick's mom is joining up with us tomorrow, so we have a double site staked out."

"I'll mosey over to your camp tonight after the main events end, if you're up for some picking."

111

"That's what we're hoping for." Jack answered.

"Nick, I hope you weren't planning for more than two hours of sleep a night." Chuck joked. "This guy is an energizer bunny — you can't shut him down once he gets to picking 'cause there's no off switch."

"You mean we have to sleep?" Nick quipped.

"Oh, *man*. He's a clone." Chuck laughed. "I pity the people who camped near you guys. See you later on, then."

* * *

When Kate arrived on Saturday morning, it took forty minutes for her to find the van amidst a sea of campers. She'd parked in the non-camp lot in front of the gate, then had made her way on foot through the many rows of vehicles, tents and campfires dotting a fenced-in field designated for the paid campsites. In all her years living in the Northwest, she'd never known that these kinds of bluegrass festivals even existed. It amazed her to see hundreds of musicians and bluegrass enthusiasts sharing food, campfires and songs in a grassy open area, surrounded by the incredible beauty of the Columbia River gorge.

It didn't surprise her, however, to find her son bouncing with excitement and stories, when she finally spotted him and Jack participating in a music circle at their campsite. A dozen people surrounded the camp, listening to the seven musicians who were playing. Jack, Nick and a man in a Stetson cowboy hat swapped breaks on guitars along with four others playing fiddle, banjo, mandolin and dobro. Together they sounded like a band that had been together a long time. Nick wore a grin of happiness that warmed her heart to see. He also wore a leather, wide-band hat and a black festival T-shirt that marked his full indoctrination into the love of the bluegrass lifestyle.

When the song they were playing ended, Nick turned his attention to the surrounding listeners and spotted her standing next to him. "Mom! I was hoping you'd get here soon! This place is cool — we've been up most of the night playing. Last night I saw a lot of great bands in the stage arena and, guess what? There were kids almost *half* my age that are up on the stage! Everyone is so great!" Nick set his guitar down and surprised her with a big hug. "Thanks for letting me come here last night. I wish you could'a seen it, but there'll be more tonight, too."

Kate glanced over at Jack, who smiled back at her and winked. "We can't settle him down long enough to take a break," he joked, "and I'll warn you, he's wired on coffee and bluegrass mania." He looked over as the man in the Stetson stepped forward and tipped his hat to her.

"Nice to meet you, ma'am. Name's Chuck. You got a great kid here and a heckuva picker. He's won his way right into some of the prime song circles happening here, and that ain't real easy to do. He sure is a natural, seeing as he ain't been doing bluegrass for more than a couple of months." Chuck extended his hand to Kate.

"Kate. Pleased to meet you, Chuck." She returned the hand shake. "I don't think I've seen Nick this enthusiastic about music since he got his first guitar. Thanks for the encouragement — it's good to see him so happy." She dipped her shoulder to drop her backpack to the ground.

"Let me help you with that!" Jack offered. "Nick and I are bunking in the tents and we have you set up all nice and cozy in the van. The mattress is pretty decent and the privacy shades make it easier to change clothes. We managed to get a spot fairly close to the portable bathrooms." Grabbing Kate's backpack, he opened the rear door of the van and placed the pack inside.

Chuck returned to the song circle and played the opening measures to a lively tune. As Jack closed and locked the van door, he turned toward Nick. *"Jerusalem Ridge.* Here's a pretty tough crooked tune for you to chew on."

Nick moved back into the circle, guitar in hand, as Kate inquired, "Crooked tune? What in the world is that?"

"When the beat of the song is interrupted briefly with an unusual rhythm change, some people call it a crooked song. If you listen, you'll hear the part where the beat goes sideways." He moved to the circle to join in. Kate was fascinated with the impromptu gathering of musicians. Each was given an opportunity to play an individual solo that featured their instrument as the song continued, and Nick seemed to know when to take his solo break, playing it with gusto. She was able to pick out the part of the song that went "crooked".

Kate was proud of the way Nick's natural ability blended with the group, and was happy to see the acceptance he'd gained from everyone. Jack was right about the importance of this kind of event. The fact that entire families were attending, and all ages of players took part, made it a good opportunity in more ways than just the practice of music. It was also a place to experience and develop a love for a traditional style of music that brought people together in a special way. She liked it.

* * *

Jack, Nick and Kate were halfway through their lunch, around the noon hour, when two men came into their campsite. The shorter, stockier man with dark hair and a goatee said, "Excuse us walkin' in on you like this."

Jack started to rise to greet them when the tall, lanky man with a tan leather cowboy hat gestured for him to remain seated.

"Been a long time, Jack," he said. We heard you were at the festival. We hate like hell to interrupt your meal, and all, but it's kinda urgent. Howdy ma'am — son." He tipped his hat toward Kate and Nick.

Ignoring the polite gesture, Jack set aside his plate and rose to shake hands with the men. "Jake. Larry. Good to see you again. These are my friends, Kate and Nick." He turned briefly to them as he spoke their names. "Jake and Larry are old band partners of mine from years back." As Kate and Nick each said a friendly hello, Jack turned back toward the men. "What's up?"

The short, stocky man named Larry spoke up. "Well, Jack, we got us a problem. Our backup, Doug, took him a spill this morning and sprained his left hand pretty good. He ain't in any shape to play and we're due on stage at eight o'clock tonight. We hate like hell to cancel and heard that you were here — wondered if maybe you could sit in. We're on for ninety minutes. We'd be glad to pay."

"And I'd be glad to help you out, but it's been awhile since I've done a bluegrass gig. I'm not sure if I can follow your set."

Jake handed a piece of paper to Jack. "Here's our set list. We can talk over any tune you might doubt and come up with alternates if needed. Anything you can do will be fine. We trust you." The three men looked over the list for a few minutes and, after some minor adjustments, settled on the final set. Once an arrangement for time and place to meet was made, they said their goodbyes and left.

"That is *so cool*, Jack!" Nick's eyes shown with excitement as he jumped up from his seat. "Those guys are playing on the main stage as a big event. That means they're a pretty well known group, doesn't it?"

"Yeah, they run the bluegrass circuit so they're very well known in those circles. You might not find their CDs at department store music sections, but stores that carry a wider selection would have them."

"So why didn't you guys stay together as a band back then?" Nick asked. The sense of adventure for the musician's life had returned to his thinking in a big way.

"It's harder than you might think to be on the road with a group." Jack answered as he sat down to finish his lunch. "Living together on a bus, egos, uneven workloads, differences of opinion in songs or locations — they all worked together with abuse of alcohol and several missed gigs to convince me that it was more work than I cared to deal with to stay in a band. I'm better off as a solo artist."

"But isn't it exciting that you get to be on a big stage?"

"Yeah, Nick, I gotta admit that it is. I haven't done it often in recent years. Frankly, it'll feel good to be on any stage at all right now. I've sure been missing it."

* * *

Jack left their campsite around five o'clock to meet up with the band and prepare for the show. Afterward, Kate and Nick managed to stake out a second-row space in front of the main stage. They laid out a large blanket with pillows and a cooler and sat down to eagerly await the opening of the evening's two top events, which started at eight o'clock. As the time grew close, the arena filled to capacity with people. Most of the smaller children were back at their family campsites by then, and the audience consisted primarily of adults and older teens who were all in a very festive mood. Stage hands were busy making last-minute adjustments.

Promptly at eight, the show started. After the announcer's introduction, Larry walked onto the stage alone, to the raucous cheers of a crowd that was obviously filled with avid fans and mildly intoxicated campers. Taking his place at a microphone, he asked the audience for a moment of silence regarding the news of their fallen band member, Doug. The crowd was instantly hushed in the wake of what appeared to be some very bad news. Larry began to give a somber account of the "tragedy" of the accident. Gradually, a wave of snickers and cat calls arose as Doug (obviously not in critical condition), slinked onto the stage with his left hand heavily bandaged and his right hand holding a gigantic mug of beer. He slowly ambled to a microphone on the opposite side of the stage from Larry, tapping it to ensure it was working then clearing his throat. Larry stopped speaking and looked over at Doug.

"Folks," Doug implored. "Please don't pay Larry no mind, and don't weep none for me. It ain't no tragedy a'tall. Yep, I did take a spill...," he said, holding up his bandaged left hand, "... but the *good* news is — *that my beer drinkin' hand is unharmed*!" As he raised the beer mug above his head, the audience went wild. It took a minute or two for them to settle down, during which Larry gave Doug a long, sideways glance, crossed his arms and tapped his foot in exaggerated annoyance.

"But the bad news is..." Doug at last continued, "...we had to find us a temporary replacement — by drawing straws. Unfortunately — the fella that won — or lost, that is — well, fact is — we just don't know whether or not he can play the *gui*-tar." Loud snickers followed.

Larry leaned into his microphone just then and blurted out, "Well, Doug, how the hell're they gonna tell the difference from you?" Once again, the crowd's rowdy laughter and cheers took over.

Before the noise began to abate, Jack walked onto the stage with his guitar, looking very handsome. Kate noted that he'd donned a black western vest and boots. Somehow, the outfit made him look taller, and quite different from his usual self. It also seemed to have transformed his personality. The more-or-less reserved and low-key man she had come to know over the last several weeks had suddenly stepped into the role of a stage performer.

Nick jabbed her lightly in the ribs and pointed at Jack. "It's backwards. He's holding his guitar backwards."

With the crowd still reacting loudly, Jack adopted a clueless and dumbfounded look on his face as he attempted to the play his guitar, which Kate now plainly saw was hanging backwards from its normal position around his neck. As his hands tried to take on opposite roles, the result was a horrible mix of disjointed sounds.

"Hold it, hold it, *hold it!*" Doug screamed into the microphone. Jack stopped dead in his tracks, stood absolutely still and, with a wide-eyed stare, surveyed the audience with a sweeping look. Everyone was laughing hysterically while Jack remained straight-faced and deadpan, which only served to heighten the comedy. Doug carefully put down his beer, shuffled over to Jack, and pointed at the guitar. Jack looked down as if trying to figure out what was wrong, then looked at Doug and exaggerated a shrug of his shoulders. In answer, Doug shook his head vigorously back and forth while pointing again at the guitar and making a sweeping arc in the air with his finger.

As if the nature of the problem had finally dawned on him, Jack gave a broad grin to the audience and nodded. He lifted the guitar strap above his head, while people hooted and clapped. He then reversed the guitar into the correct position and brought the strap back over his head, standing poised and ready to play. Doug nodded his head vigorously up and down while pretending to brush dust off of Jack's shoulders with his good hand. Scattered chuckles continued throughout the crowd. Giving Jack a final thumbs-up sign, Doug walked back to the microphone and said, "Ladies and gents, we'd like to thank our good friend, Jack Brewster, for sittin' in tonight. Jack — *hit it!*"

What followed was a blindingly fast and clean introduction of the tune *Salty Dog Rag,* by Jack. The audience stood and wildly clapped as Larry shouldered his own guitar to swap breaks back and forth. One by one, the rest of the band members took their place on stage, each taking their own song break as they entered: a man named Paul on upright bass, Jake with his dobro, another man named Brian on fiddle, and Jake's wife, Theresa, on mandolin. The applause turned to rhythmic clapping as each musician joined the group on stage with their own musical intro. Nick was on his feet, enthusiastically clapping with obvious admiration, sparked by seeing this new and unexpected side of his friend's life.

For Kate, the stage act had, in one moment, profoundly changed her own regard for Jack. She'd been surprised. She'd laughed. She'd been amazed. She'd fallen in love.

* * *

About halfway through the show, Chuck Sloam had wandered through the maze of people to find where Nick and Kate were sitting. He still wore the Stetson but had left his guitar back at his camp. When Nick caught sight of him, he waved him over and invited him to share their spot.

"Thanks, Nick." Chuck touched the rim of his hat as he looked toward Kate, smiling. "Ma'am. You mind?"

"Not at all." Kate returned the smile. "We've got a great view from here. Have you watched the show so far?"

"Sure have. Our boy, Jack, is in top form tonight. He sure can be a ham when he wants to make folks laugh. And, *man,* can that

119

bugger play."

"Yes, he can. I'm overwhelmed." Kate spoke without looking away from the stage.

"You never heard him play before?" Chuck asked.

"Well, yes. A few times on the porch of his home. But I had no idea he was this kind of performer."

"I see. Pardon me, ma'am, but I thought maybe y'all were — uh — involved?"

Kate blushed and looked at Chuck. "No, we're just neighbors. He's a wonderful friend to Nick. He's teaching him a whole new love for acoustic style music."

"Well, Nick's got himself a powerful teacher. The way your boy picks, it won't be long before we see him up on that stage, too."

Nick turned to Chuck. "I've got a long ways to go, but I sure would love it!"

"You'll get there soon enough, boy." Another song had ended and loud applause interrupted the conversation for a moment.

"How long have you known Jack?" Nick asked once things had quieted down again. He was curious. Other than Sam, Jack hadn't talked much about his friends.

"Gosh, 'bout twenty years now. We met up at different festivals like this one. Played together in jam circles and small stage acts. Did some hard partying in our younger days, too, back when we were a couple of young stallions lookin' for trouble. Later years he didn't swing through the Portland area much. But he's a good buddy, Jack is."

The next song started with gusto. Chuck turned to Kate. "Would you care to cut a rug in that there dance area yonder?" He pointed to a nearby grassy clearing that had been roped off, where several couples were dancing. "This music just makes my feet wanna move."

Kate smiled and nodded her head. Grabbing her hand, Chuck turned to Nick and said, "I'm gonna steal your mama for a bit, if you don't mind?" Without waiting for an answer he took off through the crowd, leading Kate by the hand.

Nick's attention was averted from the stage as he watched his mother move with Chuck into the dance area, to take up a lively Texas two-step. From one song to the next, they looked quite natural and fluid as they danced together, laughing and enjoying their fast-paced motions. Chuck was a good friend of Jack's and a really nice guy, so Nick wasn't sure why he felt uncomfortable watching them. He only knew that he did.

* * *

Sunday, in the mid-afternoon, Sam was surprised to see Jack at his door. He hadn't expected them to be back from the festival until quite late. Inviting him in, he went to the kitchen to pour two cups of coffee, then brought them into the living room where the two men sat down to talk. It troubled him that Jack seemed unusually somber.

They sat silently for a few minutes as Sam waited for Jack to start the conversation. When things remained quietly awkward, he asked, "Did Nick get a good taste o' music campin'?

"Yeah. Big time. He fit right in and earned his way into some serious jams. The kid is really good, ya know?"

"Yes, indeed. We both know that. Reminds me o' you at his age." Sam spoke with a sense of pride for them both.

"Better. He's got a helluva lot more class and no chip on his shoulder. He knows who he is. Hell, I still don't know who I am at forty-two."

"Now, why 'you talkin' thataway, Jack? You was a great kid and a fine musician at Nick's age, and you ain't changed none but t' get even better." Changing the subject, he asked, "So, didja get much playin' in at the festival y'self?"

"Tons. Ended up playing in one of the evening events, too. Couple of guys I used to run with asked me to stand in for their band's backup. The guy had injured his hand." Jack paused to sip his coffee. "It sure felt real good to be performing again. I've been missing that. Been missing it a whole lot."

"You miss the audience?"

"I miss the life. I dunno, Sam. Maybe I'm just not cut out for staying in one place."

Sam's heart sank. He knew Jack had struggled with settling in, but he'd seemed to have been handling it until now. He wondered what had happened over the weekend to bring on this obvious change. "What brung ya home so early today, Jack? What brung ya here?"

Jack stared at Sam for a moment before answering. "I'm thinking about hitting the road."

"I knew that, Jack, 'fore ya even said it. You ain't needin' no one's permission t' do that. What I asked is what brung ya here." He'd decided that being direct was going to be the best approach. "Are ya thinkin' o' leavin', or are ya thinkin' o runnin'? Ya done made up yo' mind right fast 'bout this. What I can't figure is how campin' and enjoyin' a whole lotta music is suddenly makin' you wanna leave. If ya ask me, it don't make no sense."

"No, Sam, I don't need anyone's permission. But all of a sudden I feel like a caged animal, the way they pace."

"Who's got ya caged, Jack?"

"No one's trying to. I dunno. The house. Memories. The more I stay, the harder it will be on people when I leave."

"Yo' sayin' it like ya ain't got the choice t' stay. Didja tell Nick and Kate you was thinkin' o' leavin'?"

"No, not yet. I couldn't. Nick — this weekend changed him. Changed his music. Those kids he's been running with are the same ones who got in trouble at that house party awhile back. He got a taste of better things at the festival. You should've seen his face. If I leave — I dunno."

Sam felt that something was still not being spoken. "And Kate? How was the weekend fo' her?"

"She was happy. She loved seeing the changes in Nick and told me so. I wasn't fair to her this weekend."

"How you mean?"

"She had a good time. When our band was on stage I saw her dancing for quite awhile with an old friend of mine. They were having a lot of fun. Chuck's a good man. Been through a couple of divorces, but a real good man. The kind of man that asks his buddy before stepping in."

"Steppin' in on you and Kate?"

"There is no 'me and Kate'. But I told him no, anyway. He took me aside and asked if I had any objections to him calling on her, and I told him I did. Like a good friend, he backed off. I had no right to do that, and I'm not even sure why I did. After all, he could help keep Nick going with the music. He likes Kate a lot. They seemed to have a good time when they were dancing. And here I am thinking of leaving. What right did I have to screw with that?"

"Ya don't know if ya screwed with nothin'. Ain't no tellin' if Kate would o' wanted that. Ya don't know her heart, ya only saw her enjoy a dance. And you ain't no old doormat t' be replaced with a new one. You and Nick is friends. You and me is friends." Sam hesitated before he continued. "Now don't ya go takin' me bad here, but I need t' say it. You had y'self a mama that could replace a man easy, like one was good as 'nother. Fo' the men she picked, that was pretty much true, 'cuz none o'em was any good. This here's different, Jack. Ain't no man can step in and be the same t' any o' us as you. No man."

Jack thought long and hard about Sam's remarks before replying. "Well you're right about one thing, Sam. You're definitely my friend. The best kind of friend. You aren't afraid to tell me the truth, and I trust you."

"So — you gonna stay?"

Jack grinned. "For now, Sam. I won't leave while the song is still playing. It just wouldn't be right."

❧ 23 ❧

"He's a doll!" Sue was shuffling through a small stack of photos from the festival, which Kate had brought out during their lunch break at the hospital. She spent a lot of time examining the pictures of Jack. "Definitely infatuation material. So, were there any romantic interludes?"

"There wasn't any time for that." Kate said this casually, but she'd been very disappointed that the trip hadn't allowed for more of a relationship to develop. "The whole point was to play music, and that's what they did. My only contribution was to cook breakfast on Sunday morning."

"Is this Jack on the stage? I didn't know he was going to perform there."

"Neither did he. He was a last minute fill-in on Saturday night. Was that ever fun to watch!" She proceeded to describe the show and Jack's part in it.

"Oh, honey, this just keeps getting better all the time!" Sue was determined to stir up the romance. "You had two whole days to get things going, dearie. Have you forgotten how to woo a man? No matter what they say, it *ain't* through his stomach!"

"Cool down, Sue. Don't forget, my son was there and the whole reason for going was to introduce him to a local bluegrass festival. Jack's been so good for Nick. I like the changes I'm seeing in the music he listens to and plays these days. He isn't spending time any longer with his delinquent friends. Watching Nick make new friends and develop a love for family-oriented music was enough."

"I agree that's important, Kate, but that can all still be happening if you strike up a relationship with Jack. The fact that he's good for your son is excellent, and it's certainly not a trade-off. You had all day Sunday and didn't get any chances to charm the man, even one a little bit?"

"Well, we didn't exactly have all day Sunday. We didn't stay until the close of the festival. For some reason, Jack was pretty quiet the day after the show. For that matter, so was Nick. I think maybe they were both burned out after two solid days of activities and music. After all, they'd both arrived on Friday and had gotten very little sleep. So we picked up camp and headed home around noon Sunday, and Nick rode home with me. He slept in the car."

"Do you think maybe something had happened?"

"No. Nothing happened." But Kate wasn't so sure about that. She'd had a fun time dancing with Chuck at the show and had been glad it remained just a friendly moment for both of them. Chuck had joined them all for breakfast the next morning but he'd left shortly afterward. Still, there'd been an undercurrent of tension in both Jack and Nick. Perhaps there'd been a deeper reason for their trip to be cut a bit short, but nothing was said.

Kate wasn't about to go there with Sue, however. It seemed best to let the whole thing drop.

ℬ *24* ℭ

Sunday was Kate's day off and she called Jack that morning to invite him and over for breakfast. The summer weather was perfect so she set a table for three out on the back deck. Nick went to work slicing onions and potatoes while Kate prepared homemade biscuits. Jack arrived about the time that the coffeemaker was groaning out the last sounds of its process. He grabbed three mugs from the cupboard and poured them each a cup of coffee. He then offered to scramble the ham and eggs, and in a short while the meal was ready. They ate their breakfast while talking lightly about the progress Jack was making on his house.

"What a beautiful day." Kate said when at last she'd finished her breakfast, leaning back her head and lifting her face to bask in the morning sun. "This is what we wait for all winter long under our gray northwest blanket." About that time the phone rang and Nick jumped up to answer it. Kate smiled at Jack and said, "One of the perks of having a teenager is that you never have to get up to answer the phone."

"The way Nick eats, you spend a lot of money for that service." Jack said, giving them both a good chuckle.

Nick returned to the deck with a smile on his face. "That was Jenny. She just got home from church and wants me to help her with her computer. Mind if I split without helping with the dishes?"

"You didn't finish your breakfast." Kate hated to waste food, and Nick's third helping was barely touched.

"I'll eat it later, I promise."

"Okay, son. Just finish your orange juice."

Nick drained his glass in one gulp, wiped his chin with his arm and ran back into the house to get ready. Kate shook her head resolutely and said, "The other side of the Nick coin is that anything to do with Jenny Dunn takes priority in life. If she sneezes, Nick will run eight blocks to her house to hand her a tissue."

"Don't be too hard on him." Jack said, grinning, "Jenny's got the looks that'll make any teenage boy she calls on become her instant slave. To her credit, she doesn't seem to know that or do it on purpose. She really is a good kid."

"Yeah, I agree. It's just hard on a mother when she's no longer the favorite woman of her son's life."

"Not always." Jack said with a somber look as he stood up and began to gather the plates from the table. Kate winced as she realized that her remark had hit a tender spot. She managed to balance the remainder of the dishes in her hands and followed him into the kitchen.

"Jack, I'm sorry if I said something that upset you."

"No, Kate. Don't think that. I don't ever want you to walk on eggshells trying not to say something that it's perfectly natural to say. You're a good mother and Nick adores you." Jack set the dishes he was carrying on the counter and turned to her to add, with a wink, "Right up until the minute Jenny calls, anyway."

"That remark will cost you exactly one sink full of dirty pans to wash. I need a new slave since my regular one just left the house."

"Fair enough." Jack said, and began the task by rolling up the sleeves of his work shirt before rinsing off the dishes and handing them to Kate, who loaded the dishwasher. Kate felt a special closeness with Jack in the sharing of such a simple chore. She wondered if he'd felt it, too. In a short time they'd finished the work and moved to the back deck once again, to finish the last of the morning's coffee. Jack leaned back with his eyes closed, deep in thought. "Where are you?" Kate eventually asked.

Jack turned to her. "I was thinking about a place my uncle used to take me to in the summer. Down southeast of Portland there's a trail loop that winds through some old growth trees toward a small lake. The lake is a little off the beaten path, but it's a fly fisherman's haven. There are trees along that trail that have been growing there since way before the Civil War. I used to love going there with Uncle Dan."

"It sounds beautiful." Kate said, then added, "Your uncle really meant a lot to you, didn't he? I wish I'd met him and your aunt before they died. We lived here, but I never had the chance."

"Yeah. They'd have liked you." He set down his coffee mug and turned to her. "It's not too far to get there. To the lake, that is. Are you interested in a nice hike? We could be back by the time Nick is through gawking at Jenny over her computer screen."

Kate smiled and nodded. She was definitely interested. She rarely got the chance to be alone with Jack and this was the first time he'd suggested that they do something together. A hike to work off breakfast on a nice day was a great place to start. "Why don't I meet you at your house in ten minutes?" she said.

"You're on."

* * *

Jack pulled his van onto a wide gravel shoulder beside the trail head, which was barely visible in the undergrowth. Two other vehicles were parked at the spot, but there was no one in sight. Kate got out and swung her small day pack onto her back. Her hair was tied back loosely to get it off her neck. Jack had opted not to fish that day and carried only a small pack of his own. He handed her his bottle of bug repellent. "The bugs are one of the reasons for the great fishing here. They eat us, then the trout eat them, then we eat the trout. It's all a very neat arrangement."

They both doused themselves with repellent and sunscreen before starting out on the trail. From the road it hadn't seemed like much of a path, but it was fairly well worn and easy to follow. Since it was not one of the more popular groomed trails, they had to step over fallen limbs and skirt around muddy and stony areas. Jack's hand was soft and warm as he helped Kate keep her balance over obstacles. She was very aware of him each time he touched her.

The trip was deeply nostalgic for Jack, evoking unspoken memories of his uncle and the special companionship they'd shared so many times on the trail. It felt good to be experiencing it once again, in a new way. He pointed out some of the old growth cedars and Douglas firs that graced the path, many of them with trunks so large that three or four people abreast could hide on one side of them. It felt as though they were in a quiet, private sanctuary with birds sounding out a choir of praise.

"How often did you come here?" Kate asked.

"April through July are the best months," Jack answered, "and we hit this spot several times during those months every year."

"So you stayed with them a lot."

"Uh-huh. Until I was seventeen I probably stayed with them half as much as I did at home, for a day or two at a time." Jack pointed out two trees that had grown together forming an

130

archway beneath. "There's a story in these trees from long ago, and we'll never know it. I love the way these deep forests keep a record of events that happened over all their years. Every windstorm, every drought, every fire — they're all recorded here." Kate had the feeling he had purposely changed the subject. She waited awhile before bringing it up again.

"What happened at seventeen?" she asked.

"Seventeen?"

"You said you stayed with your aunt and uncle a lot until you were seventeen."

Jack kept walking. She saw she'd trespassed into an area of his emotions that he kept carefully fenced in.

"I left home." Jack said after awhile. "Took my guitar and about two hundred bucks I'd saved and hit the road with my thumb out."

"Why at seventeen?" Kate asked. She knew she was pushing him to answer things he was reluctant to share. At that point they came across a smaller secondary path that led into dense underbrush. Jack took the path, pulling gloves and pruning snips from his pack to cut away some of the more thorny limbs as they walked along.

"Watch yourself," he said as he held back a large branch to allow her to pass through. She looked down through the cleared pathway as she did.

Is he merely talking about the terrain?

It was a few minutes later that they entered a sunny clearing. In the center was a beautiful lake, small but clear and pristine. A narrow trail wound around it and three fly fishermen dotted its perimeter in waders, hip deep in the water and located a good distance from where Kate and Jack stood. The men were spread apart from each other as well. Their continuous casting with brightly colored fishing lines was amazing to watch, like a dance of linear motion. The lake was calm, with bird and insect songs filling the earthy, fragrant air. The glory of the evergreens and sky reflected their portrait onto the watery canvas that stretched in front of them in Pacific Northwest splendor.

"It's incredible," Kate whispered. "I can see why you love this place."

Jack grinned and also spoke softly. "I didn't even have to tell you not to speak too loud. It's like walking into church, isn't it?"

"You can do what they're doing?" she asked.

"It's fantastic once you get the hang of it. The idea is to allow the fly hook at the end of the line to barely touch the water in spots, acting like a bug would when it skims across the surface. The motion and arc of the line comes from whipping it back and forth from a ten o'clock position to a two o'clock position, over and over. Of course, that's all easier said than done. The true art of fly-fishing is in getting the tip of the line to hit in the exact spot you're aiming at."

"It's amazing to watch." Kate marveled at how easy the men in the distance were making their fly casting look.

They found a flat, shady place to rest and Jack pulled a thin cloth tarp from his pack for them to sit on. The view was incredible. Kate had brought peanut butter and jelly sandwiches and apples, and they were both surprised to find themselves hungry again so shortly after breakfast. They ate quietly.

"I had a disagreement with my mother's boyfriend," Jack said at last, as if Kate had just asked her question. "It wasn't the first time or even the same boyfriend each time, but it was the last time I let one of them beat me up. That's why I split at seventeen, once I'd finished high school. Hit the road, found some bands to play in and that was pretty much the way it was from that time onward."

Kate was silent. In a few short words he'd revealed so much.

"I thought about going to Uncle Dan's and Aunt Eva's, but I'd gotten some idea in my head by then that life on the road playing music would be an adventure."

"Was it?"

"It had its moments. Not as many as I thought there would be, but they were there. I bought a van. After awhile I just got used to it. My trips to see Uncle Dan got further and further apart. My time in any one place got shorter and shorter. I made the weather circuit around the country. Places like Miami or California in the winter, Boston or Chicago in the summer. It becomes a life."

"What about your mother? Was she okay with you leaving like that?"

"It took her a week or so to even realize that I was gone. She thought I had split to stay at Uncle Dan's and he thought I was with her. I'd sent her a postcard to let her know."

"She wasn't worried that you might have been injured by her boyfriend?" Kate asked, incredulous that a mother would not worry about her teenage son's whereabouts for a week.

Jack took a drink from his water bottle then screwed the cap back on. "Not all mothers are like you, Kate."

Jack had been Nick's age at the time he'd left home. Kate couldn't imagine what that had been like for him. She said nothing more as she gazed at Jack in a different light. With his chestnut brown layered locks touched by silver strands and trimmed beard showing flecks of gray, he looked from his outer appearance to be a strong, capable man. But Kate now saw, for the first time, a young, frightened boy who had run for his life so hard that he'd never known when to stop. He was still running, unaware that the demons that once pursued him had ended their chase long ago. Now he was running from himself.

ᏚᎧ *25* ᏣᎦ

Jack sat on his porch with Nick in the mid afternoon of a cloudy summer day. Earlier Nick had helped him tear out the fixtures and linoleum in his downstairs bathroom. Jack had started a restoration of the room back to the original 1920's era when the house had been built, with plans that included a clawfoot tub and an elevated water tank above the toilet. Their work that day had been exhausting but rewarding, and they'd gutted the room within a few hours.

Nick sat on the wide porch railing, playing his guitar. He was working on the fingerstyle exercises that Jack had showed him the day before and was trying to control the rhythm of the alternating bass notes using his thumb, while playing the melody notes using his three fingers. As was his habit during moments of deep concentration, the tip of his tongue had crept to the corner of his mouth.

"Does the tongue help?" Jack liked to tease him about it.

"It must not." Nick said, "I can't get the hang of doing this."

"Be patient. It takes time to get the muscle memory happening, just like it did when you learned your first chords. You're doing fine. Before long you won't have to think about it at all. Then you can keep your tongue in your mouth." Jack winked.

"I give up. I'll never get to where your playing is at." Nick bemoaned, dropping his hands from the strings.

"Okay, let's see." Jack crossed his arms into an exaggerated thinking pose. "You've been learning this since last week and I've been playing fingerstyle for thirty-some-odd years. I'm not sure giving up based on comparisons at this point is in your best interest." He broke his pose to lean intently toward Nick. "Keep playing, son. You're doing just fine. You're just used to things coming easier to you on the guitar."

"Okay, you're right." Nick sighed and placed his hands on the strings again, then paused in his thought. "Thirty years? You've played for thirty years?"

"Makes me sound old, doesn't it? I was nine when my uncle bought me my own guitar, once he saw that I was serious about it and determined to learn. Before that he'd let me plunk on his."

"Did you want to be in a band?" Nick asked.

"Not really. Back then there were folks playing music on this porch nearly every weekend in the spring, summer and fall. I guess in a way that was a band in itself. People from the neighborhood liked to listen. I just loved the music and wanted to be a part of it. After awhile the music began to own me, and I couldn't stop. Best addiction in the world."

Nick laughed. "Folks actually wanted to hear the music. Nowadays they call the cops to get you to stop."

"I think that still depends on the style of music. The stuff you play with your friends tends to be a bit louder and heavier. Old ballads don't rankle people as much, ya know?"

"I suppose not. So — you started out by playing in bands. Was it easy to quit and go solo?" Nick asked.

"A long ways back, when I first started doing gigs in clubs, a band was the best way to make money. Over time I developed my own solo style and more people wanted to hear the mellower stuff. It was easier not to be tied to a group of people, too.

Musicians can be fickle. It's a part of the artist mentality that can be hard to deal with. That and the fact that people's lives change when relationships and families happen." Jack had certainly learned that reality in his years.

As they spoke, Nick looked down the street and noticed a tan Ford truck come to a stop in front of his house. Jack saw his face change to a deep frown. "Oh, hell," he said sourly, immediately handing his guitar off to Jack. "I gotta go home. Sorry."

Jack watched as Nick sped quickly toward his house. A tall man with dark, curly hair, wearing a lumberjack's red shirt and blue jeans, stepped out of the truck just as Nick reached the front yard. Nick stood in front of him as if to block his way to the house.

Jack went to his front door and opened it in order to prop the guitar securely against an inside cabinet, then he closed the door again. He stood on the porch watching Nick's encounter with the man. They seemed to be arguing. After a minute or two, the curly-haired man pushed Nick aside to stride with cocky steps up to the front door. He entered without knocking and Nick followed him in. Not liking the scenario he was seeing or Nick's response to the man, Jack headed for the house.

As he got to the door he heard their voices. "Get the hell out of our house. You aren't supposed to be here and no one wants you here. When are you gonna get that through your fat head, you jerk!"

"I'm just waiting here friendly as can be. I need to see your mom." His words seemed to be slurred.

"I already told you she won't be home for a long time and I don't want you here. If you want to talk to her, you can call." Nick's voice was angry and frustrated.

"You seem to have a new unlisted number now. So I had to

come in person."

Jack didn't like the arrogant tone in the man's voice. He knocked on the door, which was partly ajar, then swung it open and asked, "Mind if I come in?" A look of fear came over Nick's face. "Why don't you introduce me to your unwanted guest?" Jack continued.

"Who the hell are you?" The intruder asked, jumping up from the seat he'd taken on the sofa.

"I'm Jack. And you are...?"

"I'm Kate's old man and you'd best walk your ass right back out the door." The threat was matched by a stance with clenched fists. He swayed slightly on his feet.

"I've been living in the neighborhood a couple of months now and I haven't seen you around here. I haven't heard Kate or Nick mention you at all. That kinda makes your story about being her old man pretty weak." Jack wasn't taking his eyes off the man's movements. "Nick has asked you to leave and I'm going to make sure you do just that."

"Who the fuck do you think you are? You been hanging around with my woman?" A dark rage flashed across the man's face.

Nick jumped in between them and said, "No, Tom. He's my friend. He's just protecting me, that's all. Leave him out of this."

"He's in it." The man took a step forward and flung Nick to the sofa with the sweep of his arm. As his body was turned in that motion, Jack jumped in with all his weight to land a hard jab to the man's stomach.

Jack's punch had no effect whatsoever, other than to further enrage the man named Tom, who sent a flying left hook to Jack's jaw as he turned back to face him. Jack flew backward three feet in a circle and landed on his hands and knees, dazed by the blow.

Before he could recover he felt a hard kick to his ribs that sprawled him onto his back, a sharp pain stabbing instantly through him. He knew at that point that he would be no match for this man's strength and anger. He had roused an angry lion.

Tom reached down to grab the front of Jack's collar, lifting up his head to deliver another punch to his face. As Jack fell, he saw Nick dart from the room into the hallway. Several more blows landed powerfully on his body and face as Tom jumped on top of him to pummel him with his fists, before rising up to kick his arms, thighs and torso. Jack rolled over and curled into a ball for protection. He was immersed in pain and could only try to cover himself.

The sound of a shotgun's sliding pump action broke the air as Nick returned and yelled, "You piece of shit! You get out of here *now* or I swear to God I'll blow your fucking head off! I'll do it!" Nick was in a shooting stance in the hallway opening, finger on the trigger of a twelve-gauge shotgun aimed at Tom's heart.

Tom backed away slowly, hands in the air, looking wary and surprised. "Now, son, there's no need for that here. I'm just protecting myself."

"I'm not your son and Jack is no threat to you. You're just doing what you love — thrashing people." Nick was slowly moving forward as Tom was backing uneasily toward the door. The shotgun seemed to sober and scare him quite a bit. "There's a restraining order on you, and you know it. I have every legal right to shoot you dead right now. I'll put you in the ground if you ever try to show your face here again. That's not a threat — it's a promise. Now get outta here, and don't you *ever* come back!"

Without saying another word Tom strode quickly out the door, down the steps to his pickup and climbed in. The truck started with a load roar and he took off.

Jack groaned as he lay on the floor. Nick put down the shotgun and knelt beside him. "Jack, how bad are you hurt?"

Jack turned his head toward Nick. "I don't know yet. It hurts everywhere except my little toe." Nick was relieved to hear him try to joke, but saw that he was bleeding from a nasty looking gash on his head.

"I'll call an ambulance," Nick said and started to get up.

"No, don't do that. I've had my ass kicked worse than this. I'll be okay." Jack tried to get up into a sitting position but the pain in his ribs brought him back down to the ground. "Help me up," he said.

Nick rose up and grasped Jack's hand in a thumb clench to pull him to a sitting position. Jack winced and said, "There now, that was worse than I thought it would be." He started to chuckle, then groaned in pain. They managed to get him over to the couch and Nick ran to get wet washcloths and a first-aid kit. By the time he got back, Jack was wiping the blood from his head wound with his shirt to keep it from dripping on the furniture.

"If you won't let me call an ambulance, at least let me call my mom, okay?" Nick asked in a shaky voice. Jack knew this was a lot for him to deal with, so he agreed. He put pressure on his head wound with the washcloth Nick had handed him.

Nick glanced out the window to make sure that Tom hadn't stuck around nearby, then grabbed the phone to dial the hospital where his mother worked. After asking for a connection to the floor she worked on, he requested that Kate Weber come to the phone, then waited nervously for her to pick up the line.

"Hi mom, it's Nick." He twisted the phone cord around his finger mindlessly as he spoke. "Tom was here a few minutes ago." He paused to listen. "No he's gone now. Jack came by to help me and Tom beat him up pretty good." Nick paused again.

"I think he's okay but Tom worked him over a lot. He's on the sofa here." Another pause. "Nah, he says he's okay and doesn't want an ambulance." After listening to Kate's response he said, "Okay. See you," and hung up.

"Mom's coming home," Nick said as he walked back over to Jack, whose eye was beginning to swell shut. "Man, your face looks real bad. I'll get some ice."

Jack hurt all over. Tom had been a powerhouse with knuckles of steel. Jack had only landed one punch that hadn't even made the guy flinch. He looked at Nick when he returned from the kitchen. "I didn't know your mom had a shotgun."

"She bought it because of Tom." Nick was laying ice cubes wrapped in a towel over Jack's eye. "I got really scared when I saw you at the door. He can get pretty ugly."

"Has he hit you or your mom before?" Jack asked.

"No, but he's got this jealousy thing. He used to wail on guys that looked at her, even when she didn't know them. They broke up a long time ago but he keeps coming back. Every time his latest woman dumps him he starts thinking he can get back with mom."

"Your mom used to date this guy?" Jack asked in disbelief.

"He used to not be that way when they first met. He seemed okay at the beginning. He was a sober alcoholic but she didn't know that until he started drinking again."

"I see — but right now only from one eye."

Nick chuckled and Jack started to join in when a pain spasm hit and made him wince. "Stop trying to make jokes, Jack. It isn't worth it."

"If I don't laugh I'm afraid I'll cry," he answered.

* * *

141

It took about half an hour for Kate to show up at the house. She went immediately into the living room and took Nick's place beside the sofa. Jack's face was quite swollen by then and his shirt was covered with dried blood. "Oh, my God, Jack." she said, "I'm so sorry about this." She asked Nick to bring her several of the thin gelatin ice packs she kept in the freezer along with more washcloths and iodine from the bathroom cupboard. "Where does it hurt?" she asked.

"Where doesn't it hurt might be a better question," Jack responded. "Some defender I turned out to be. That guy is a tough character."

"He was a middleweight kickboxing contender until he was thirty," Kate said, examining Jack's eye which was now swollen completely shut.

"That would have been nice to know before I threatened to heave him bodily out the door." Jack tried for a smile but it ended with a look of pain as his facial muscles protested the movement.

"Don't joke around, Jack. He could have done a lot worse damage. He has before. I probably should have warned you about him but I never thought it would come up again. This time he'd stayed away for a few years. Until now." Kate looked worried as she cleaned a jagged gash on his forearm and dabbed iodine onto it. He grimaced but made no sound. She had Nick hold one of the ice packs on the side of Jack's face.

Kate unbuttoned Jack's bloodied shirt and they lifted him up gently to slide the sleeves down and pull it off. Jack's arms and torso were discolored in numerous places that she knew would soon become large bruises. She pressed into his ribs as gently as possible and determined that, while one or two might have hairline fractures, none appeared to be dangerously broken.

"We really should get you in for X-rays, Jack," she said. As she leaned over him to examine the opposite side of his chest,

Jack noticed a faint scent of lavender. "I can't tell if your ribs are cracked."

"I'm okay. It hurts but nothing feels too serious."

Kate continued gently cleaning the scrapes on Jack's chest and arms that the kicks had caused, then taped his ribs. She saw that the bruising went down beneath the belt line and asked Nick to remove Jack's shoes and socks. "Sorry, Jack. We'll need to get you down to your skivvies to make sure your kidneys and legs are okay." She had Nick remove his trousers.

Despite the pain in nearly every part of his body, Jack was embarrassed to see that Kate's nearness and touch had caused an unexpected side effect for him. There was no mistaking the evidence in his briefs when Nick pulled off his jeans. Kate said nothing and continued with her clinical examination. Nick was less subtle.

"Dude!" he said, a rather natural reaction from a seventeen year old boy. Kate shot him a warning look.

Jack turned even redder than his swollen face had already become. "Sorry about that."

"Well, at least we know you aren't made of stone." Kate quipped, trying to bring some levity to the moment.

"Some parts sure do look like it," Nick chuckled.

"Enough!" Kate snapped with a glare that stopped Nick short. "Go get a blanket from the closet." She turned back to Jack. "Don't worry about it, Jack. At the hospital that happens more often than you'd think."

Jack smiled faintly and said, "Around you I'm quite certain it would." She ignored the comment but took note.

Nick brought a blanket back to the sofa. Kate said, "Tonight you'll sleep on our couch. There's no sense in you trying to move, and we can monitor how you do. I'll send Nick over to lock up your house." She fluffed out the blanket and slid it upward from his legs toward his neck. In the movement her forearm slid lightly over his partial erection, shooting a new wave of awareness through him.

Jack wondered. *Did she mean to do that?*

* * *

Kate knocked on Sam's door early the next morning, while Jack was still asleep on their living room sofa. He'd seemed to do well through the night but Kate was concerned about leaving him there attended only by Nick while she went to work, since complications still could arise.

She was glad to see that Sam was an early riser. When he answered his door he was fully dressed and listening to a gospel music station. His expression wore a mix of surprise and concern.

"I hate to bother you this morning, Sam."

"No bother a'tall, Miss Kate. Come in."

She stepped in through the door. Sam's living room was simple and filled with old furniture. The room suffered from infrequent dusting, but was otherwise tidy.

Kate explained, "Last night there was a bad situation at my home, with a man that had no business being there. Jack was roughed up when he tried to intervene and help Nick. He seems to be okay today, but I need to ask if you can help Nick keep an eye on him." Kate hoped this wasn't too much for Sam to handle at his age.

"Lord, lord. What happened?"

She described the situation as briefly as she could, then said, "Jack stayed the night on the sofa so we could make sure he was going to be alright. I feel terrible about the whole thing. It's my fault that he was hurt."

"I'm sure Jack don't see things thataway, so why should you? Ya can't help what that guy done t' him and I know Jack 'nough to know he'd a jumped in no matter what. It ain't the first fight Jack's knowed, that's fo' sho'. I seen him get busted up pretty good b'fore."

"He fought a lot when he was younger?"

"Not ever once when he wanted t' fight. I hate t' talk ill o' his mama, God rest her, but she weren't much good at pickin' out the men she took company with. They was a heap many o'em and ain't none o'em ever treated her o' her boy much good. Some was downright evil t' him, usin' they fists to make a point."

"They beat him? Why?"

"Sometimes cuz he defended his mama. Sometimes cuz he defended hisself. Sometimes jus' cuz." Sam shook his head. A deep frown furrowed his face.

"She didn't try to stop them?"

"No, ma'am, it don't seem so. I think maybe she didn't know how. She didn't keep on with 'em afterward, so maybe that be how she stopped 'em. I never did fig're what set her t' those ways. She weren't always thataway. It ain't easy t' tell you how bad things was fo' that boy at home, but it's good fo' you t' know 'bout it. His Uncle Dan was a good friend t' me and like a daddy t' Jack. That's how he come t' spend so much time here. When he was growed, Jack took t' runnin' 'round the country. He ain't never settled and, tell ya the truth, I ain't sure he knows how. But he's tryin'."

"What happened to his mother?"

"Long about a dozen years ago she took herself a handful o' pills. Jack didn't even find out 'till all was said an' done an' she was buried. I ain't never asked how that was fo' him an' he ain't never said. They's things that Jack jus' don't talk 'bout. But he's a good man, and ya have no account to worry 'bout yo' son with him. No, siree."

"Well, he certainly stepped into trouble to defend Nick last night, although if he hadn't no one would have been hurt. Nick was in no danger, but Jack certainly was."

"Jack jus' did what Jack does. He be okay."

"Perhaps, but if something is wrong, Nick may need help. It'll be very important to make sure there's no blood in Jack's urine this morning, and no extreme pain anywhere."

"Yes, ma'am. Now, don't you go worryin' over things today. They'll be jus' fine, Miss Kate. I 'spect Jack'll think it's a bit too much fuss, but we'll watch o'er him."

Thanks, Sam. I won't tell Jack we spoke about things in his past, but you're right — it's good that I know them." Kate left to get ready for work, relieved that Sam was able to help and disturbed by the deep undercurrent of Jack's life that never showed on the surface.

* * *

Kate arrived home that evening to an empty house. Nick had left a note saying that Jack had returned home and he and Sam were there with him. Sam answered the phone when she called.

"Well, hello, Miss Kate. We done moved o'er here 'cuz Jack wouldn't stay put there. He sho' is an ornery cuss, but he seems t' be feelin' a heap better this evenin'. Nick is in the kitchen stirrin' up a pot o' chili I got goin' earlier. I even made some o' yo' cornbread. Maybe you'd like t' join us fo' supper?"

Sam's cheerful invitation was welcome after a long day at work, and she gladly accepted. She washed up, changed into jeans and a cotton shirt, then grabbed her first aid kit before heading over to the house. She knocked and heard Jack invite her in from the living room.

Jack was sitting upright on the sofa across the coffee table from Nick, who sat cross-legged on the floor holding a handful of cards. They were playing cribbage.

"Hi, mom." Nick didn't look up as he spoke. "Jack taught me how to play cribbage today." He pegged his points on the board as he counted them, "Fifteen two, fifteen four, and a double run for twelve."

"He picked it up way too quick." Jack added. "I'm being beaten up all over again today."

"Well, don't worry about the damage; I brought a first aid kit. How do you feel otherwise?" Kate saw that the facial swelling had subsided.

"Not bad, considering. Pretty stiff and sore. I managed to walk back home and these two have tagged along beside me all day, like worried puppies."

"They were just following my orders." Kate replied as she moved closer to examine Jack's purple eye. "I don't want to hear any arguments about it."

"Mom, can you please let me and Jack finish the game before you do that?" Nick was immersed in his new challenge.

"Okay, son, I'll go help Sam." She walked into the kitchen where Sam was taking the cornbread out of the oven. "Can I help set the table?" As she asked, she washed her hands at the sink.

"That be real nice. Things went jus' fine today, Miss Kate — jus' fine indeed. I told ya our boy was a tough one. He been givin' us a bad time 'bout doin' things fo' him but we went ahead an' did 'em anyway."

"I knew I could count on you, Sam." Kate piled the

silverware onto the plates she'd taken from the cupboard. "The cornbread and chili smell delicious."

"Nick's been keepin' Jack restin' by playin' cards and I been busy with the rest o' it." He followed her into the dining room with a serving bowl full of chili.

The meal was simple and satisfying. Jack insisted on sitting at the table with the rest of them. He seemed to be recovering quickly after just one day of rest. Their conversation was light, and they all steered away from any discussion about Jack's injuries or the events of the prior day. Kate was glad to have Sam's gentle support making the evening easier.

When the supper had ended, Sam stood to clear the dishes from the table. Kate stopped him. "No, Sam. You did a lot today. Let me finish this up. I insist."

"Truth is, I am a might tired, Miss Kate. I sho' do thank you for doin' that." He'd been through a long day.

Jack spoke up. "I'm not used to sitting around while people do things for me. Why don't I…"

"No!" The others all answered in unison.

"Alrighty, then." Jack backed down.

Sam turned toward the door. "Long as you two got things covered here, I best get m'self home."

Kate stood up. "Thank you for everything, Sam. The chili was wonderful and you've done so much. Before you go, I want to make sure you have our phone number. You know you can call on us anytime at all, and I'm glad we can do the same."

"Yes, ma'am."

After they exchanged contact numbers and Sam left, Kate cleaned up the dining room and kitchen, placing the leftover chili in a container and the cornbread in a bread bag. She walked back into the living room to find Nick dozing in a chair and Jack reclining on the sofa.

"Poor kid wore himself out worrying over me today." Jack said. "It was nice having him and Sam here. Thanks for that."

"You're the one that deserves the thanks, Jack. I hated to see you hurting so bad over something you had nothing to do with. I wasn't about to leave you alone like that."

She walked over to Nick and shook his shoulder gently. "Honey, why don't you go home and get to bed early tonight. You put in a good long day." Nick looked up drowsily and pushed himself up from the chair.

"The chili put me to sleep," he answered. She squeezed his shoulder. "Are you leaving , too?" he asked.

"In a little while. I want to stay a bit to make sure Jack will be okay." She brushed the hair from Nick's forehead then kissed it. "Thanks, son."

Nick said goodnight to Jack and left, taking his guitar with him. Kate walked over and sat on the coffee table across from where Jack reclined, bringing along the first aid kit. "How are your ribs feeling? They were pretty badly bruised."

"Still sore but they seem to be fine. I can take a deep breath now without it hurting too much."

"That's a good sign. I see the swelling is also down in your face, but the gauze on that gash needs changing." She worked silently, removing the old dressing and cleaning the wound, then applying a clean butterfly bandage.

When she finished Jack spoke up. "How long have you been dealing with this kind of stuff from Tom?"

Kate sighed. "Some mistakes you make just keep coming back to bite you. I first met him about ten years ago. He was a nice man and treated us well — until the day he started drinking.

I hadn't known about his problem and he'd been sober a couple of years, evidently."

"Did you live with him, back then?"

"No. When Nick's father died I was a mess for a few years, trying to keep it together. Nick and I lived with my mother until I got a job at the hospital and could afford day care and a place of my own. Back then we lived in an apartment. We moved here seven years ago."

"Why didn't you stay with your mother?" Jack asked.

"Because of my stepfather. He was egomaniacal and verbally abusive, and I hated to see Nick growing up in that environment. We were forced to be there for awhile, but I worked like hell to change it."

"It must have been hard for you."

"I'd wanted a different way of life than my mother's. Believe it or not, I was a Woodstock baby — born in May exactly nine months after her wild weekend at the biggest party of the century. She married when I was seven and we both spent the years afterward paying for that decision. He moved us out here from Boston, where I was born. After I got my associates degree I married Nate — Nick's father. Who knew that the Gulf War would take him from me fifteen months later? Being widowed at twenty-one wasn't what I expected to happen. I poured myself into being a mother and felt pretty alone, but I was wary of bringing a stepfather into the picture. My own experience with that made me determined to avoid it. That's what makes this whole thing with Tom so hard to deal with — I was so wrong about him, and now he won't stay away. I hate that Nick had to go through what happened yesterday. Even worse, look how it turned out for you."

"Don't feel bad about it, Kate. Anyone can misjudge a

person. You saw the ugly side of Tom and you got out right away. That says a lot about the difference between you and your mother. This time, Tom may not be back. I think Nick put a good scare into him yesterday. You should have seen how your son handled himself — you'd have been proud. If he hadn't stepped in when he did, it sure might have gone a lot worse for me. He's a tough kid and pretty resourceful." Jack shifted his weight and slowly sat up on the sofa.

Kate's eyes became watery as she thought about her son. "He's the best thing in my life and always has been. I see him growing up so fast and I'm trying hard to give him the space to do it. The day he goes off to college will be harder than anything else I've been through."

"He's not the kind to just drift away, Kate. He has no reason to and he loves you very much. I don't think you have to worry at all about any abrupt changes from Nick. He'll ease into adult life quite nicely, and you'll stay a part of his life no matter what."

Kate looked intensely at Jack. "It wasn't at all that easy for you, was it?"

Jack got silent for a moment. "Well, I can certainly understand the problems that a mother choosing the wrong man can cause, especially when she keeps on doing it over and over." The pain behind the words showed in his eyes. "For me the answer was to leave, but I didn't have any plans beyond that. I just kept living and that was about it."

"You had your aunt and uncle. They must have been a comfort to you?" Kate was trying to understand why Jack had chosen to cope with things on his own.

"They were wonderful. Aunt Eva was so very different than my mother — like night and day. She was a saint. We never talked much about things when I stayed here, but I saw what life was like for her and Uncle Dan. They loved each other so much.

My mother relied on my uncle a lot more than Aunt Eva would have liked, but they both endured it for me, more than anything. When I got older I was determined to move on, so things could change for them. I think they did."

"What happened to your mother?" Kate asked. When she saw Jack flinch she realized that her questions were stirring up very hard memories.

"She died a long time ago." He said nothing else and she didn't press for more information. There was no hint from him that her death was a suicide.

"Now here you are, all at once living your life in a completely different way than you ever have before." Kate watched his eyes register a deep inner tension.

"It doesn't feel like my life. It feels like I'm starting to live someone else's life. I'm becoming someone I don't know anymore. Not better or worse — just not me."

"I only know the Jack I've seen over the last few months. He's a very good man. I suspect he's you." Jack looked troubled as he turned away.

"And I also suspect he's tired and needs rest. I'll leave now and let you get some sleep." Jack sat wordlessly on the sofa as Kate got up and slipped out the door, locking it behind her.

ಚಿ *26* ಆ

"How are things with that gorgeous hunk of man?" Sue couldn't be counted on to be subtle. Ever since she'd seen the pictures from the music camp, her conversations with Kate had been focused on hearing about Jack. Kate hadn't told Sue of Jack's incident with Tom the week before, wanting to avoid any new lines of questioning. Fortunately they were the only ones in the hospital break room.

"Nick and I always get along, Sue." Kate flashed her a wide, exaggerated smile.

"The *other* gorgeous hunk, dearie. Don't keep putting Nick out there as your standard defense. You know I meant Jack."

"I've told you time and again, Sue, we're just friends."

"So he hasn't made a move yet. Do you think he's secretly gay?" There was no avoiding Sue's line of interrogation.

"No. He's just a nice guy adjusting slowly to living in a neighborhood lifestyle after years of traveling around."

"In all the time you've spent with him, he hasn't given you any sign of interest?" Kate had thought a lot about that herself, but talking it over with Sue was like throwing a lit match on gasoline. She didn't like exposing the troubled life that Jack had come from. It was his business.

"I haven't exactly encouraged him, either. Things are better when they go their natural course over time."

"Honey, just take a short look in the mirror. That's all the encouragement any healthy guy should need. You must be doing something to *dis*-courage him, like you've done with the guys around here." Sue meant well, but often did it quite offensively.

"What do you mean by that, exactly?"

"Every guy that's asked you out around here you've turned down flat."

"I don't date the men I work with, Sue."

"Honey, you don't date anybody. Sooner or later they give up asking. I understand wanting to protect your son, but not every guy is a jerk. Jack sounds like such a nice man and he's great with Nick. So what's the problem? It's way past that natural course of time you talk about — things should be happening."

"Sue, give it a rest. Jack's made a big impact on Nick. I like the changes I see in him. He's not spending time with the friends that I've long suspected of being hoodlums and criminals. He's doing great."

"So what has all that got to do with you and Jack? That should be making things easier for you, not harder. Answer me one simple question. Are you interested in a romance with Jack or aren't you?"

Kate paused, then answered softly, "I am."

"Well it sounds like he never learned how to make the first move. So you need to look for the next opportunity and make it happen yourself."

"Maybe."

That's what good friends are for, Kate. Listen to her.

෨ *27* ෬

It was a hot summer day and Nick had ridden his bike to Tony's Place to buy an ice cream cone at the market. He was standing near the door reading the billboard while eating the cone when Alison Bennington walked into the store.

"Hi, Nick." She greeted him with a brief wave of her hand.

"Hey there, Alison. How're you doing?"

"Okay I guess. I came in to buy a soda."

"I came in for ice cream. It sure is hot today."

"Yeah, it totally is. Hey, how come you haven't been around The Hanger lately? Brandon is really pissed that you aren't coming around anymore."

"Yeah, I know. He even called me once or twice, but I didn't have a lot to say. I'm not allowed to go over there."

"I'm not supposed to either. The cops called my mom to come pick me up when the party got busted. I was grounded for a week after that. Did they bust you, too?"

"No. I got pissed off and left the party early. Lucky thing, as it turned out." Nick finished his ice cream and tossed the napkin into the nearby trash can.

"Then how come you aren't allowed to go there? You weren't busted."

"I wasn't, but my mom doesn't like the place."

"Mine either, but I still go so I can see Brandon."

"You have something special going on with him?" Nick was

upset to think that Brandon had a steady thing happening with a fifteen year old.

"I dunno. Maybe. He's nice to me." Alison said this with an unsteady conviction.

"The stuff that goes on there doesn't bother you?" Nick was dismayed to think that this young girl was getting deeply involved in things that could just bring her more trouble.

"Well — sometimes, yeah. But Brandon's such a doll. I just love him."

Another one bites the dust.

"How do you get away with going there when you aren't supposed to?"

"My mom and her boyfriend are never home, so they don't know about it."

Nick felt sorry for Alison. She needed attention and was hoping to get it from Brandon, but the kind of attention he was giving her wasn't doing her any good. "Look, Alison, this isn't my business, but I know Brandon pretty well. He's just using you, and he's way too old for you. Maybe you need to think about finding someone else."

"But he says I'm special." Alison began to get defensive.

"I'm sure he does. With Brandon, those are just words he uses to get what he wants." Nick felt a little sick being so abrupt with her, unsure that he should comment at all.

"I thought he was your friend."

"He is. He's a friend I have fun playing music with, but most of the other stuff he does rubs me the wrong way. I hate to see him hurt people, Alison, and I think he's hurting you."

"You play music with him but you hate the other things he does, so you're willing to ignore them to have a good time. How is that different from what I'm doing?"

Nick was taken aback. *It really isn't, Nick. It isn't.*

* * *

Nick went to Jack's house later that same afternoon. It took Jack a few minutes to answer the door. "Hey, Nick, come on in. I'm staying down in the basement where it's cooler."

The house temperature was only slightly different than the outside air. Nick followed him down to the basement, where it was far more comfortable. Jack was using a plane on some shelves that were laying across sawhorses.

"Whatcha been up to?" Jack asked.

"Just bumming around. I went swimming awhile ago and it cooled me down a lot. Hey, this is a big room." Nick hadn't noticed it before when it had been cluttered.

"Yeah. I'm thinking I could section off part of it to build a small recording studio." Jack pointed to an area in the corner that had been completely cleared out.

"Sweet! Let me know how I can help." The thought of a place to record music was exciting to Nick.

"Oh, don't you worry about that. You'll be in on making it happen if I decide to do it."

"Why wouldn't you?" Nick asked.

"It mostly depends on whether or not I stay here."

Nick stared at Jack. "What do you mean? You own the house, don't you?"

"Of course. It's not a matter of the house. I'm just not sure if I'm cut out for a neighborhood lifestyle. I haven't played a solo gig for months now and the festival was the closest thing to traveling that I've done in long while."

It had never occurred to Nick that Jack would consider

leaving. He was shocked. "But Jack, what about the music we do? I mean, doesn't that feel good? We play some great music together."

"I love jamming with you and Sam, Nick. That's one of the things that keeps me here. I know it's difficult for you to understand, but twenty five years of never settling down anywhere is hard to just shake off."

"But you're doing all the work on the house. Doesn't that make you want to stay?" Nick was beginning to feel frightened and he wasn't exactly sure why.

"The projects keep me busy. Either way, whether I decide to stay or leave, doing this work will have been worthwhile." Jack seemed to sense Nick's agitation. "Hey, don't look so worried. I'll be around for awhile. We have plenty more porch jams in our future."

"When you first got here you told me it wasn't so great not getting to know people. So what is it that you miss now about being on the road?" What had initially seemed to be such an adventurous type of life to Nick was now threatening to take away his friend.

"Nothing is ever exactly the same. The day you pull out for the next place, there's a sense of starting fresh — starting over again. You get to see people that you know again, whenever you arrive in their town, and enjoy going back to venues where folks have been looking forward to having you return. There's a lot of me out there in a hundred places — and not enough of me here in one place. Does that make any sense?" Jack's question was more to himself than Nick, born from his introspection in recent weeks.

"How can there ever be enough of you in one place if you don't stay around to make that happen?"

Jack looked at him intently. "That's exactly the battle I'm in,

Nick. It seems it can't be won overnight."

Nick was lost in his thoughts for the next few minutes. The revelation of Jack's struggle to change the course of his life mirrored his own turmoil over the choices he'd been making. For both of them, their passion for music had brought them into situations that fed their need, but not their souls. He wondered if that reality applied to everyone at some level, where their deepest desires led them to ignore the penalties they paid to sustain them.

"Jack, if you couldn't play music for some reason, would you still feel the need to keep traveling?"

Jack stopped his work and thought for a moment. "That's a hard question, Nick. I suppose it's the music that's made my travels possible. I can't imagine not playing."

"Neither can I. Until I met you, my whole focus was hard rock and heavy metal. That's all I knew and all I played. In a way, it defined my friends and ruled my life. Music can do that, you know. None of my Hanger friends understand how I can stay away lately, but I'm seeing that the only music I've played and loved is part of a way of life that isn't good for me. I've hated the life and loved the music that causes me to be there. I'm not even sure you can separate the two, at least not in this neighborhood. So it's like living in two places at once — who I am at home and who I am when the music calls me. But it isn't the music causing that; it's me. Sam was right about music needing to reflect what your soul wants to say. 'Play what you feel, and feel what you play', right? Isn't that what you told me awhile back? I just wasn't seeing it that way."

Jack had been looking at the ground as Nick spoke, and he raised his head to stare at him, "So, you're willing to change the focus of your music life to be in a better place. Is that what you're trying to tell me, Nick?"

"I think I am. What about you?"

159

"I get to keep the same music. It's the life around it that I need to be willing to change. But I hear you, Nick. Loud and clear; I hear you. You have a wisdom way beyond your years. It takes a lot of courage to see it and change it. You've proven you have it in you."

"I think you do too, Jack."

* * *

The recent days of record-breaking temperatures had made swimming at the local community center a daily habit for Nick, helping him to cope with the heat. One afternoon, as he climbed out of the pool, he saw Jenny walking to the poolside from the locker rooms. She wore a one-piece flowered suit and her long hair was swept back into a French braid. Spotting him, she waved and walked over to where he stood.

"Great to see you here, Jenny. These days have sure been crazy hot!"

"Uh-huh. Fortunately, we have air conditioning at our house, but it still seems like a good time to get in some swimming." Finding a place to lay her towel, flip flops and lotion, she walked to the pool, bent one knee, then trailed her other foot in the water. "It feels just right."

"It's perfect. Why don't you dive in?"

"You first!" She gave Nick a surprise shove, and he faked an awkward, arm-waving back flop into the pool. Laughing, she dove in beside him.

They spent the next half hour splashing, diving and racing in the pool. Nick was delighted to make Jenny giggle, doing floating duck imitations and demanding to know why she'd forgotten to bring crumbs to feed him.

When they finally got out of the water, he managed to grab two side-by-side deck chairs. As they relaxed in the sun, Jenny re-applied her sunblock, offering some to Nick, who politely refused. With his tawny olive complexion he never burned, and he'd developed a deep tan over the last few weeks.

"I burn so easily." Jenny capped the bottle and set it aside. "I spend the whole summer slopping on lotion. That's why I wear a one-piece. Less exposed skin."

"Keeps the wolves at bay, too." Nick winced inwardly after he said it. He didn't want to sound crude.

Jenny didn't seem to take it badly. "If only it was that easy. Being pretty can be a curse if you want people to see who you really are. Too many guys gawk at the outside and couldn't care less about the rest."

"Too few girls bother to care about the rest."

"I suppose so." Jenny laid back and closed her eyes. "It's so nice that you're my friend, Nick. I never have to worry about your intentions. We just have fun."

Nick was dismayed at the remark. In his heart he wasn't just a friend, but if he told her that he felt more for her, he might lose her friendship altogether. His inclinations were somewhere between friend and wolf, but if he had to choose one, he was resigned to being her friend.

"You're fun to be with, Jenny." He decided that was safe enough to say. "My mom thinks you're terrific. We need to think about having another cookout."

Jenny looked over at Nick. "That'd be so nice! It's weird how easy it felt to be around your mom and Jack and Sam. We all got along great. It's like our ages didn't matter. Jack is such a nice guy and he's so cool. How does your mom feel about him?"

"I'm not sure. They seem to just be friends, but I wonder if maybe she'd like more." The irony of this statement, in light of his own feelings about Jenny, hit him hard. He'd never before thought that his mother might be experiencing a similar situation to his own.

"Would you like it if they got together?"

Nick had to think before answering. He was amazed that the idea had never consciously crossed his mind, but he pondered whether some part of him hadn't already put them together. His thoughts flashed back briefly to the evening that his mom had nursed Jack after Tom had beat him up. "I guess so. Jack seems like a friend, and it's strange to think of him being anything else."

"I think they'd be good together. Don't you?"

"Yeah. I guess I do." *And us? What about us Jenny?*

Jenny got up from her chair. "So, how about it, Nick. You ready for more?"

Oh, yeah!

He got up and followed her back to the pool.

* * *

When the heat wave had finally broken, a series of soft summer rains had soaked the parched ground and the temperatures had dropped significantly. Jack was able to work in the upstairs areas of the house once again. The steady progress was slowly transforming it back to being the showplace it had once been.

Jack and Nick sat on the porch early one afternoon, taking a break from a morning spent laying tile in the bathroom. They were working out vocal harmonies for an alternative folk song that Nick had recently written — a genre of music he was beginning to appreciate for its acoustic depth and expression. The

162

melody was captivating and powerful, weaving through unusual chord changes that were almost haunting in their beauty. Jack had been impressed with the song, and Nick had asked him to help fill out the chord structure with fingerstyle patterns. Nick's ability to develop intricate melodic arrangements was still somewhat limited, but growing steadily stronger from practice. His prolonged experience with loud electronic effects had produced a vastly different set of skills than those required for acoustic styles, but his unique abilities were making both come together in original ways.

"It's an amazing song, Nick. Do you think Sam's dobro could add some depth to the breaks?"

"I had that in mind, too. Maybe we could ask him?"

"I need to get something to drink. I'll go give him a call while I'm at it. You want some lemonade?" Jack got up and started for the front door.

"Sure, thanks." Nick said, then turned his focus back to the song as Jack went inside.

Nick's concentration was interrupted when a four-door low rider pulled up to the front of the house, the forceful blare of its stereo's subwoofer taking over the quiet of the neighborhood. The sound ceased as the car's engine was cut and four guys got out and stepped onto the sidewalk. Despite the warm weather, they wore leather jackets.

As they started up the walkway, Nick set aside his guitar and stood up. He'd seen them before at The Hanger and knew they were some of Benny's crew. He didn't like the look on their faces as they approached the steps.

"Dude — need to talk with your little poser ass." The leader of the group moved up onto the porch and took an aggressive stance.

163

"Do I know you?" Nick asked.

"You're sure as shit *gonna* know me. I ain't letting no punk like you take my action."

"Your action? I don't know what you're talking about." Nick began to get nervous.

"I'm talkin' the three bills you clipped from your pal, Brandon. It was mine. I'm collectin' my green."

"I don't know what Brandon told you, but I don't have anything that's yours." As Nick spoke, Jack opened the front door and halted on the doorstep.

"Can I ask what you're doing on my porch?" Jack had heard Nick's words. He turned and set the glasses of lemonade on the porch table.

"Back off, dude. This is for me and this little fuck to drill out."

"Are you insulting my friend on my porch? I'm asking you again why you're here."

"He took what ain't his, bitch. And don't you *even* think of messin' in on this." As he spoke he pulled back his jacket to reveal a pistol stuck into the waistband of his baggie jeans."

Nick turned to Jack with a nervous look. "Brandon told them I stole their money from him."

"How much money are we talking about?" Jack asked. He seemed to remain calm.

"Three hundred," the accuser answered.

"Lucky break for you. You just happened to catch me at a good time for that." Jack pulled his wallet out from his back pocket and counted out two hundred ninety dollars. "It's all I have. Will you take it and call it even?"

"Jack..." Nick started to say as Jack held up his hand to silence him.

"I ain't runnin' no fuckin' charity, man. It's three bills."

Jack turned to Nick. "Do you have ten?"

Nick took out his wallet and produced eight dollars. "It's all I've got."

"Cool enough. We're square," the young man said, grabbing the money from Jack and Nick.

"You're square with us," Jack retorted as they turned to leave, "but Brandon is your bigger problem. Sooner or later he'll run out of other people to blame."

Ignoring him, the four young men headed back to the car. As they got in, the driver started the engine. The deep bass boom of their music assaulted the air once again as they drove away.

Nick stood in silence for a moment. "What just happened here? Why did you do that, Jack?"

"Street hoods mainly defend their pride and whatever they own. We took care of them and they went away."

"But I didn't owe them anything — and neither did you." Nick was beginning to feel angry.

"You weren't about to get a fair trial on this porch, and I didn't want it going any further once I saw the gun. The money is nothing."

"I can't believe Brandon would send them here looking for me! I haven't even seen him for weeks now. There must have been some mistake. I'm sorry, Jack. You keep getting involved in my problems."

"Be careful about where you think the mistakes lie, Nick. I was glad to help keep you safe this time, but you need to do your part and decide who your friends really are."

❧ 28 ☙

Kate loved the cozy breakfast nook in Jack's kitchen, where she sat one morning drinking a glass of iced tea. The nook's bay window looked out onto the small backyard garden that Jack had planted in late spring. The plants were healthy but running over the tops of each other, having been planted too close together. She smiled, remembering her first few gardens and the trial and error that was a natural part of learning how plants grow. To his credit, there were few weeds and the soil was well tended. For a man who had spent his entire life living in small, ever-changing spaces with all his worldly possessions in a duffel bag, the garden was quite an accomplishment. In a way it symbolized his fledgling attempt to take root in his own garden.

Jack returned to sit at the table across from her, his attempts to find his telephone directory having failed. "There are a lot of hiding places in this house. I know I saw the thing somewhere. I've thrown a hundred of them in the recycle bin and only kept one. Now I can't find it!" His eyes moved to the side as he thought hard about where it might be.

"Never mind," Kate said, "Just have Nick look it up online when he gets home later. He loves to do that for me." Nick had opted to ride the lightrail downtown and spend the day at the waterfront with his guitar, hoping to make some tips. Kate and Jack had been discussing the need for a plumber to install the bathroom fixtures, now that the tiling and flooring in that room had been finished.

Jack agreed, then remarked "There's so much work left to do. I've never had to organize so much junk in my life. They must have kept everything they ever bought. I don't even want to think about starting work in the pantry. There's stuff in there that may date back to World War II."

"It can't be that bad," Kate said.

Jack rose from the table once again. "Come on in here and look." She followed him to a narrow door that opened off the side of the kitchen. As the door swung out Jack snapped on a wall switch to light up a small, six foot square room. Its three inside walls were covered with deep shelves that lined them floor to ceiling. Wire storage bins were attached to the entire back of the door and hooks lined the walls on either side of it, laden with cleaning tools. There was not a single inch of unused space in the entire room, with canned goods and packages stuffed far back into the dark corners. There was very little room in which to stand.

"I think you may have been too optimistic," Kate remarked as she shuffled some of the bottles and cans aside to peer into the back recesses of the pantry. "I'd say World War I is a better guess." The contents of the shelves were a mixture of food, kitchenware, appliances and household items.

"Scary, isn't it?"

"I don't scare that easily." She turned to look at him. "You go get the napalm and I'll find the camouflage suits. We can do this." The organizer in her was not daunted.

"Are you nuts? You aren't seriously thinking of tackling this mess? It's not a great way to spend your day off."

"Take the offer, Jack. Who knows, we may find an entirely extinct species in here that you can donate to the Museum of Science." She nudged him out the door. "We'll need a bucket of

167

soapy water, some rags, garbage sacks and a small stepladder. You have these things?"

In a few minutes they had prepared themselves for the task. Jack brought in a bright light on an extension cord and they set to work clearing out the small, enclosed space,. They worked their way downward from the top shelf. Kate handed items down to Jack, designating what should be done with them. "*Garbage*", "*Wipe off and save*" and "*Donate*" were the primary commands. Jack stood at the door managing the flow of stuff being given to him. The top two shelves were cleared and she was halfway through with digging out items on one of the middle shelves.

"Why would anyone need fifteen large bottles of dishwasher spot reducer?" Kate was amazed at the strange assortment of goods that had filled the room to excess.

"Aunt Eva was a sucker for a bargain. What can I say?"

"She couldn't possibly use it all in ten years." Kate forged on with the process until the shelf was cleared.

"What's this for?" she asked, reaching far back into the shelf space to bring out a glass jelly jar that contained a brass key.

"I don't know," Jack said with a puzzled look. The key was small and ornate, and didn't appear to be for a modern lock. "It must be important for Aunt Eva to have kept it in a jar. I don't recognize it. I have the keys for all the locks around the house, including her jewelry case. She kept them all in one location."

Kate opened the jar to examine the key in her hand. "This was stashed way to the back of the shelf behind one of the supports, as if it had been hidden there on purpose. It wouldn't have been easy to find unless the shelves had been cleared or you knew exactly where it was." The dust on the jar was evidence that it hadn't been touched for many years.

"I can't imagine my aunt or uncle wanting to hide something

that way. I wonder what lock it belongs to." Jack took the key from Kate and placed it back in the jar. "Maybe I'll find out as I sift through other stuff." He placed the jar on the window sill in the breakfast nook.

Another hour of work allowed them to clear away the remainder of the pantry contents, which now lined the baseboards and counters of the kitchen. They'd managed to eliminate about two thirds of the inventory. Jack placed all the garbage and donation bags outside the back door while Kate began scrubbing down the top shelves.

When Jack came back to the pantry he grabbed a rag to clean the bottom shelves. The space was tight with both of them in there at the same time, but with the pantry now empty it took little time to prepare the shelves for storage once again. Jack finished wiping down the lower shelves and stood up just as Kate turned to face him and jump off the stepladder. As she did she lost her footing and caught herself with her hands, using Jack's shoulders for balance. He put his hands on her waist and gently lifted her down to the floor in front of him.

They stood inches apart, still touching. Neither of them moved. As Jack gazed down at her, Kate was aware of the closeness of his body from the tip of her toes all the way up to her lips and everywhere in between. Jack remained motionless with his eyes fixed on hers. Her feelings raced as she waited for some clue as to what she should be doing and what he was thinking.

She finally went with her instincts. Sliding her hands from his shoulders to the back of his head, she pulled him down toward her to tenderly kiss his lips for a long moment, then slid her cheek against his. She heard his breath quicken, but still he made no move or response toward her.

C'mon Jack, why is this so difficult? You can't be that shy.

169

Kate kissed the soft nape of Jack's neck behind his beard, flicking her tongue lightly against it, then moved her face across his cheek, slowly and deliberately seeking his mouth once again. Their lips met in a series of deliciously small kisses, each lasting a little longer and becoming a little more fervent until, at last, Jack's hands moved from her waist to encircle her and pull her against him in a deep, passionate kiss. As his tongue sought hers, a sigh of pleasure rose in her throat. She slid her arm down to the small of his back and they began to slowly move with each other, wrapped in a long, ardent embrace. Kate groaned with the desire that was overtaking her, having waited so long for this moment.

The sound of Kate's passion seemed to rouse Jack from the spell of their sensuous interlude. He broke off the kiss and stood back. She looked at him foggily as her senses tried to register what was happening.

"What's wrong?" she asked.

His words came in a hoarse whisper. "Oh, Kate, I can't. I'm so sorry."

"Sorry for what?" Kate was now confused.

"I didn't mean for this — I wasn't — I can't do this."

"Do what? Kiss me? Jack, you're not making any sense." Kate was embarrassed.

Did I read things all wrong?

"I just don't know if I'll be here, that's all. It isn't fair to Nick if I can't. If I don't." Jack's reasoning was sketchy and unclear.

"What isn't fair? What has Nick got to do with this?"

"I just don't want to make his mother a whore."

Kate was stunned. "A *what?!?*"

Her slap landed hard across his face and her hand stung as she turned and bolted out of the pantry. Jack shot out after her and raced her toward the front entryway, bracing his hand against the door as she started to open it.

"Stop, please, Kate." Jack's voice was wavering and desperate. "I said that all wrong. That isn't at all what I meant. Don't leave like this. I want you to understand."

"I understand perfectly, Jack." Kate turned and answered. "In your world there are only two kinds of women — the untouchable saints like your Aunt Eva and the promiscuous whores like your mother. There isn't anything in between. And I stepped down from my sainthood when I kissed you. That's all it was, Jack — just a kiss. A kiss that somehow made me a whore."

Jack stared at Kate, blinking, and said nothing for a very long moment. Her pain, humiliation and embarrassment was overwhelming as she waited during the awkward pause for him to say something. His inability to do so finally prevailed.

"I can't handle this, Jack. Whatever your problem is, you need to deal with it on your own. Leave or stay — it's up to you to decide. You won't need to worry about hurting me or Nick because we aren't going to be hanging around here anymore."

Kate shoved Jack's arm aside then ran out the door and across the street toward her home. Once inside, she closed her front door, leaned back against it and began to sob.

* * *

Nick arrived home that evening as the sun was setting. When he opened the door the room was nearly dark. He turned on the living room light and was surprised to see that his mother had been sitting in the gloom on the sofa, staring blankly at the coffee table.

"Why are you sitting in the dark, mom?" Kate's expression seemed odd to him. She blinked but didn't look up. He laid his guitar down cautiously, sensing something was very wrong. As he walked toward her he could see that she looked upset and had been crying. "What's the matter?"

Kate looked at Nick and patted the seat next to her. "Hi, baby. Come sit down a minute." He moved slowly to sit beside her and braced himself to hear something serious. "How was your day?" she asked.

"Mom, don't do this. Don't ask me how my day was when something is obviously wrong. You're sitting in the dark crying and you called me *baby*? C'mon."

"I'm sorry, son. My day wasn't so hot. I was with Jack and we had a fight."

"What *kind* of a fight?" Nick's heart leaped for fear that Jack had struck his mother.

"Just words, honey. Don't worry, just words."

"Sometimes words are the hardest way to fight."

Kate reached out and smoothed his hair. "You're so right about that, son. We said some hard words. No — I said some hard words."

"What did he do to make you say them?" Nick was having trouble imagining that Jack would be a jerk or that his mother would be cruel to him.

"That has to stay between Jack and me, okay son? He didn't do anything bad — we just — disagreed."

"Yeah. But you're cool with him now, aren't you mom? I mean, you got it all straightened out?"

"No, baby, it's not something that's easy to fix. It's complicated."

"Was he a creep?"

"No, he wasn't. Jack is a good man but he's going through a tough part of his life. It may not seem like it because he keeps it all bottled up. Today I saw that it may not be good for us to be in his life right now."

"Both of us?"

"Yes, son. Both of us." Kate saw the sting of her words in Nick's eyes. Jack had become a special part of his life.

Am I being fair here?

"For a little while, anyway."

"Does he know that?"

"Yes, he does. I told him as I left his house."

"Were you mad when you said it?"

"Very mad — and hurt. For now we just have to leave it this way, okay? I don't want to see him and I don't want you to see him. He knows that. It's hard to explain, but our being in his life is confusing for him and he needs to sort things out in his mind. I know that hurts, Nick, but please don't go against this, okay?"

Nick hesitated. His mother hadn't told him much but he knew she wouldn't ask that without a good reason. He suspected it had something to do with Jack's indecision about staying around in the future. The thought frightened him, but he kept it to himself as he processed a new understanding that the evening of music he'd planned was now canceled — as were all the porch jams for an unknown duration.

"Okay, mom. I promise."

She kissed his forehead. "I love you so much, son. I'm sorry that this hurts and I can't tell you when or if things will change. It's a hard thing to ask you to do. It's just for now, okay?"

Nick got up from the sofa. "If it's okay with you, I think I'll go to my room. I'm not hungry for dinner."

Kate sighed. "Neither am I, son — neither am I. Sleep well." He picked up his guitar and went to his room.

173

What are you doing, Kate? Is this just your pride or humiliation talking? Is this even right? Is it really necessary to keep Nick from seeing Jack?

But the answers didn't come to her. She wept silently.

* * *

Kate found it impossible to sleep that night. She laid awake thinking about what had happened and the things she'd said to Jack. The turn of events had made her feel very foolish. She'd been so certain that Jack's feelings toward her were deeper than just friendship, but now she wasn't so sure. As for her own feelings, Kate was much clearer. She had fallen deeply in love. Where to take that from here was the question that was breaking her heart.

From down the street, the distinctive sound of the van engine starting interrupted her thoughts. Kate jumped up and looked out her bedroom window just in time to see Jack's van pull away from the curb outside his house. Glancing at the clock on her nightstand she saw that it was a little after three o'clock in the morning. Her heart sank. She knew instinctively that his leaving at that hour could only mean one thing. He would not be coming back anytime soon, if at all.

❧ *29* ☙

Sam was heartsick as he began his morning prayers. Jack had been gone for nearly a week. He hadn't said goodbye, nor had he phoned to explain. When Nick had come to visit the day before, he'd confirmed what Sam's heart already knew.

Jack was on the run.

There wasn't much said about the cause of the departure, but it was obvious that Nick was sad and confused. Sam didn't know how to convey to such a young soul the depth of the struggles that had caused Jack a lifetime of unresolved pain. He and Nick had played a few songs together, without much gusto, then ended the session rather quickly. The desire to be sitting on the porch with their good friend had been too overwhelming for them both.

He didn't know what to ask in his prayers, but Sam held to his unswerving faith that the human heart doesn't need to know what to ask in words. In fact, the times when God had most powerfully answered him were almost always the times that Sam felt powerless to say or do anything. He simply asked for help. That seemed to be the very nature of faith itself — relying on an unseen God for things that are beyond human ability to speak or understand or control. And God seemed delighted to prove himself faithful in unexpected ways, no matter how faithless Sam's own heart got. There was no use trying to ask for a specific thing to happen, but just to live on and let things unfold as they would. Knowing that had always been a comfort to him, as it was that morning.

In the midst of his thoughts, a profound awareness of Jack's inner war had emerged. Perhaps this was a transition time for Jack. He was fighting against habits and actions that had enabled him to cope for so long with the unrest and brokenness that plagued his soul. But in all his years, Jack had never allowed himself to be needed. Things were different now. The people who had recently entered his life had nothing to do with his past. They were offering him a future in which he'd had no prior experience. A future of belonging. A future that frightened him because his ability to live it had never before been tested.

Sam smiled. He somehow knew that the seeds of love that had taken root in Jack's heart were strong enough and deep enough to prevail. He took great comfort in one simple, enduring truth. Love never fails.

* * *

Sam looked up from his breakfast to see Kate enter the cafe and walk toward him. She was dressed in her nurse's uniform and had her dark brown hair pulled up into a French roll. He wasn't entirely surprised to see her there.

"Hello Sam. Do you mind if I sit down with you?" Her voice was soft as she glanced around to see the three other customers at Tony's Place pretending not to notice her entrance.

"Not at all." he answered "Are you coming from work or are ya goin' t' it?"

"Going to, but not for a little while yet. I've been putting off coming to see you long enough. I made up my mind this morning to talk with you, and if I don't follow through I may get cold feet again. When you weren't at home I thought I might find you here."

"Yes, indeed. I get tired o' oatmeal and come here fo'

176

somethin' t' give a body a good case o' heartburn."

"I heard the food was actually quite good." Ruby came out from the kitchen as she said this.

"You like home cooking?" The mother in Ruby was shining hard that morning. "Let Ruby make you a nice breakfast, no?"

"Just coffee, please."

"Don't you listen to Sam. He no gonna get heartburn from *my* cooking. He's all talk."

Kate smiled. She liked Ruby instantly. "I'm sure it's delicious, but I don't have much time. Perhaps another day?"

"You don't stay away too long or you'll make me think you don't mean it." Ruby poured a cup of coffee for her and refilled Sam's cup, then went back behind the counter but stayed in the room and busily checked the salt and pepper shakers, which already looked full.

Sam chuckled at Ruby, then turned his attention to Kate with a more sober look. "I s'pose I know what ya come here t' talk 'bout. I ain't seen Jack around fo' a couple weeks now. You got any ideas what might o' set him on the run?"

"Yes." Kate's eyes became misty.

"I thought maybe so. Don't you worry yo' pretty head that ya maybe done somethin' t' set him off. He done it hisself, and don't have no doubt there."

"I guess I just don't understand. I want to."

"No one does, child. That boy has done wandered all his life. It's hard t' watch a heart be so afraid o' itself."

"Afraid of itself?" Despite her confusion Kate felt comforted talking with someone who seemed to know Jack so well.

"Truth is, I ain't never knowed Jack t' take a such a shine t' anyone. It's kind o' a new feelin' fo' him, I think."

Kate blinked. "You mean me?"

"Yes, m'am. I surely do."

"He told you that?"

"He don't have t' say it. With Jack you jus' gotta read it."

"Well, I think I read it all wrong." Kate sighed.

"No, m'am. Like I said, he jus' done what's always been nat'ral t' him. He run hisself away. This time it ain't gonna work, though." Sam chuckled lightly to himself at his remark.

"I don't know. He's been away a long while."

"And he hates it, be sure o' that. What worked b'fore ain't gonna work no mo'. He'll be back by and by."

"Even if he does come back, I'm not sure what that means."

Sam looked intensely into Kate's green eyes. They were deep and filled with sadness and quite striking. He saw instantly why Jack was drawn to her. Sitting across from him, with no makeup, she was attractive in the most natural and unpretentious way a woman can be.

"Give him time, Kate. He's a man comin' out o' a hard lot in life. Got a whole heap o' things he's sortin' through but he'll come 'round. He ain't never had t' wake that up b'fore."

"How can you be so sure?" she asked.

"I seen the change in him and I know he wants t' keep it thataway. I seen the way he looks at you. Ya didn't read nothing wrong, girl. You and yo' son are an itch under his skin, and sooner o' later he'll be back t' scratch it. Just you wait and see."

Kate looked at Sam and smiled. "I want to believe you. You sound so certain."

"Never more. I know that boy deep down. And I know the good Lord's got his hand in it all. Ain't no doubts here."

Ruby returned with the coffee pot to refill their cups "You

listen to Sam about our Jack. That's a good one, he is." She raised a finger in the air and shook it. "But don't go listening to him about my cooking. Heartburn? *Madonna mia!*" She walked away to pour coffee for the other customers.

Kate shrugged. "I guess the conversations here don't go unnoticed?"

"Nothin' does here. This be the place t' get things goin' 'round the neighborhood. But when it comes t' Jack, ya got friends here."

Kate reached out to place her hand over Sam's. "Thank you, Sam. Jack is lucky to have you for a friend." She thought for a moment and added, "So am I."

You may esteem him a child for his might,

Or you may deem him a coward from his flight.

But if she, whom Love doth honor,

Be concealed from the day

Set a thousand guards upon her,

Love will find out the way.

Some think to lose him by having him confined

Some do suppose him, poor thing, to be blind;

But if ne'er so close ye wall him,

Do the best that you may,

Blind Love, if so ye call him,

Will find out his way.

You may train the eagle to stoop to your fist.

You may train inveigle the Phoenix of the east.

The lioness, you may move her

To give o'er her prey;

But you'll ne'er stop a lover;

He will find out his way.

— Love Will Find Out the Way (a traditional song)

❧ *30* ☙

In the midst of a hot summer day in Los Angeles, Jack walked into a plush, dimly lit dinner lounge that had long been his favorite music venue in that town. Black leather seating, deep mahogany woodwork and elegant touches of subtle lighting created a low-key mood that featured the small corner stage — a very pleasant venue for solo musicians.

He sat at the other end of the bar from the only other patron, a man with a laptop computer who appeared to be drinking a late business lunch. A pretty woman came out from a room behind the bar wearing a very curvy and short-skirted version of a bartender's suit. Her auburn hair was cropped short and sassy, with lighter streaked tips. Jack winked at her.

"Jack! Oh, honey, it's *so* good to see you!" She hurried out from behind the bar as he swiveled in his stool to stand for a warm welcome. She planted a brief, hard kiss on his mouth.

"Lindy, my sweet, how are you?" He sat down on the stool again as they remained in a loose embrace, with her arms dangled across his neck.

"Fine as ever. What in the world are you doing here this time of year? I never expect to see you until at least November, and you usually call first."

"My travel schedule was a bit interrupted this year. Hey, can a thirsty guy get a drink around here?" Jack said, changing the subject.

"On the house, love. A Rum Rickey?" Lindy moved around the bar to serve his drink.

"That's my poison. You remembered." He thanked her as she slid his drink across the bar then went over to the other man to take his next order. Jack had always loved the open, no-nonsense way that Lindy had with people. It had made her a highly successful bar owner.

She returned to talk with him. "So, Jack, I wish I had an opening in the schedule for evening music, but I'm booked solid through October."

"I'm not here to book a gig, Lindy. Just visiting."

"Well, in that case, my personal calendar can be *very* easily rearranged." A grin spread across her face and she placed her hand over his.

"I was hoping. You free for dinner?" Jack asked.

"I am now. The evening crew comes in at four-thirty if you'd care to stick around."

A couple walked into the lounge and sat at one of the tables. Lindy walked over, took their order, placed the food order with the cook, then served their drinks. She returned behind the bar to stand across from Jack.

"How long have you been in town, hon?"

"I just pulled in from San Diego an hour ago. Caught a couple of small gigs there then decided this morning to come up here. I wanted to beat the worst of the traffic."

"Is there a way to do that anymore?" she joked. "It sounds like you're just wandering aimlessly around southern California. You sure picked some hot weather to visit — I can't remember when we last had this kind of a summer."

"I'm never around this time of year so I wouldn't know the difference." Jack took a long draw on his drink.

"So what brings you here now, doll?"

Jack stirred the ice in his glass with its lime wedge garnish. "Wanderlust, I guess. My uncle died this past winter and willed me his house up in Portland. I've been up there since early spring. Now — well, I'm taking a break from it all."

"You've never have been able to stay in one place very long, but I'm sure glad your itchy feet brought you to my door today. Let me refill that drink."

* * *

Kate arrived from work late in the afternoon to find the house quiet. The stereo was off and Nick was asleep on the sofa. She went to her room to change from her scrubs, then headed for the kitchen to start dinner, just as Nick awakened.

"You feeling alright, babe? I was surprised to see you asleep in the middle of the day." Kate poured them both a lemonade and handed a glass to Nick.

"I'm okay. Just bored, I guess. I went swimming this morning then popped in at Sam's house. There's nothing but soaps and women's shows on TV during the day, so I fell asleep reading a book."

"Did you and Sam play any music?"

"Nope. Neither of us has had much enthusiasm for music. We just talked, and he made sandwiches for lunch. I'm gonna help him do some things online."

"Good for you, son. I'm glad you're taking time to see Sam. He thinks the world of you. He's such a dear man."

Taking chicken breasts and broccoli from the refrigerator, she asked Nick to prepare brown rice in the cooker. They went silently about their tasks for a few minutes.

"Sam misses Jack." Nick turned to look at Kate. "And so do I. He never calls. Sam keeps tending the garden and making sure it's watered. He thinks Jack'll be back soon, but me — well — I just don't know. He's been gone almost a month. What if something happened? How would we know?"

Kate covered the skillet to let the chicken cook, then turned toward Nick. "I miss Jack, too, babe. Don't worry, I'm sure he's okay. He's probably miles from here in that jalopy van. In a way I feel responsible for him leaving. It never occurred to me that he would just vanish like that."

"I know you don't want to talk about what happened, mom, but why do you think he left?"

"It's hard to say, Nick. Maybe he thought that we were going to abandon him, so he abandoned us first. People do that. The things I said might have seemed that way to him. I was angry. All I really wanted to do was give him some space to work things out." Kate folded her arms and shrugged her shoulders. "This probably would have happened at some point no matter what triggered it. Sam seems so sure that Jack won't be able to stay away. We can only hope he's right."

"I sure do." Nick's reply was sprinkled with doubt.

Kate placed her hand on Nick's shoulder. "If he does return, you know that things may not go back to the way they were, don't you? Jack needs to make that happen, not us. Whatever he's wrestling with has been there for a long time and no one else can put it to rest."

"So what do we do if we see he's back?"

"Let him make the first move, son. Be kind, say hello when you see him, tell him we missed him — but let him be the one to invite us back into his life. I think that's important."

Nick nodded wordlessly as Kate drew close to hug him.

* * *

Jack awoke to early morning light filtering through the drapes across a sliding glass door. A dull throbbing in his head reminded him of the evening's indulgence in far too many Rum Rickey's. He turned over in the king-sized bed to find it empty and became vaguely aware of the sound of a shower running.

Slowly he stretched, then rose to a sitting position at the side of the bed. He was naked. The faint memory of having dinner with Lindy began to surface. When he recognized that he was in her bedroom a strange feeling of shame came over him, but he wasn't sure why. He stood up to put on his briefs and trousers and brush his teeth at the vanity sink. As the sound of the shower stopped he sat back down woozily on the edge of the bed.

A few moments later, Lindy walked out from the bathroom in a white terrycloth robe, her hair wrapped in a towel. She smiled. "I didn't expect to see you awake before I left for work. You did some pretty serious drinking last night. I've never seen you do that, Jack."

"I never do. What time is it?" Jack looked at his bare wrist, then around for a clock.

"It's only six-thirty. You can go back to sleep if you'd like. I need to get to work sometime this morning." She walked over and gave him a quick kiss.

"I thought this place looked way nicer than a motel room." Jack's head was beginning to clear, but his headache persisted. He spotted his wristwatch on the nightstand.

"It's a good thing we brought your van over here before we left for dinner. There's no way I would have let you drive anywhere."

"I'm a little fuzzy about things, unfortunately. I hope I wasn't too much of a jerk. You get enough of that at work." He was uncomfortable that he couldn't remember much beyond arriving at the restaurant in Lindy's BMW.

"You were just fine, love — though rather intoxicated." She smiled. "I heard a lot of very funny stories about being on the road. It's all you talked about over dinner."

"So I was a bore?" Jack was feeling rather foolish.

"Not at all, sweet. You were very, *very* attentive and I enjoyed every minute of it." She sat next to him to give him a more long and lingering kiss, after which she said, "I have only one question for you."

Jack smiled. "What would that be?"

"Who is Kate?"

He froze and stared at her. "Why do you ask?"

"Don't look so stricken, Jack. I'm not asking as a jealous witch. You and I have always been strictly casual and I'm okay with that. I'm just curious to know who you thought you were making love to last night."

"Oh. Lindy, I'm so sorry. You don't deserve to be treated that way."

"Don't be sorry, Jack. Whoever she is, she sure missed out on what you were doing with her."

"I feel like such a cad." Jack covered his eyes with his hand and shook his head.

Lindy laughed. "Don't be so hard on yourself. I'm not at all upset. But I really am curious about your mystery woman. Why am I getting the feeling she was at the bottom of every drink you ordered last night?"

Jack looked at her long and hard, saying nothing.

"I thought so." she said. "Do you care to talk about it?"

"Do we need to?"

"Not for me. But everyone knows a bartender is a great confessor, and I think maybe you need one."

"Don't you have to go to work now?" It was Jack's attempt to avoid the moment.

"It can wait. I own the place and other people are opening it up today." She stood up and began to fluff her hair with the towel that she unwound from her head. "I tell you what. I'll dry my hair and go make us some breakfast. You take a nice hot shower and get dressed. We'll talk over food."

When he came out of the bathroom, Jack found his duffel bag on the bed, which was freshly made. He dried his hair and put on clean clothes, then brought his bag into the dining room where Lindy was setting the table.

"I made pancakes and eggs. That always seems to sit best on my stomach after a night of drinking." Jack was grateful for Lindy's gracious way of putting him at ease.

"I seem to recall that you didn't drink at all last night. It must have been a real joy to be around me."

"You forget, I have a lot of practice being sober around people who are drinking. If it bothered me I sure wouldn't own a bar. Sit."

"Touché." Jack responded. He gingerly took a seat at the table while Lindy brought in coffee and pear juice, along with their breakfast plates. After taking several bites he began to feel his headache fading. They ate silently for a few minutes.

"Why did you come to California, Jack?" It was her way of opening up the conversation.

"I thought about that in the shower. I'm not sure I have any answers. Being in one place for so long is the hardest thing I've done in twenty five years. I guess I had to feel my normal life again."

"So how long ago did you leave Portland?"

"Almost three weeks." Jack finished the eggs and sipped his coffee.

"Does Kate live there?" Lindy's questions were softly spoken, not at all like an interrogator but with concern.

"Yes. She's a neighbor and a friend."

"She's not married?"

"No." He gave her a sideways look of admonishment. "She's a widow. She has a teenage son."

"Do you get along with her son?"

"He's a musician. We're good buddies."

"Does she know how you feel about her?"

Jack quietly said, "How could she? I'm not even sure myself."

Lindy reached across the table to grasp his hand. "Take it from me, Jack. You have a lot of feelings for her. But you already know that. You're not traveling anymore. You're running away. I sensed it at dinner, long before I knew anything else."

Jack wandered into his thoughts as he spoke them out loud. "I thought things could just go back to normal if I got on the road again. But life on the road is just as strange to me now as living in a house. I'm not sure who I am anymore. I'm hurting everyone I know trying to figure it out — Kate, Nick, Sam — even you."

"I'm not sure who all those people are, Jack, but let me assure you that you haven't hurt me. I never had illusions about being more to you than an occasional companion as you pass through town — gee, that sure makes me sound like a slut doesn't it? — but something is different about you this time, Jack."

Jack wrapped his fingers around hers as they continued holding hands. "You're not a slut, Lindy. I know better and so do you. It took a long time for us to go beyond friends. But I'm a bum in the truest sense of the word. A wandering bum. I always have been. I've tried to be otherwise lately but I keep feeling that I can't sustain it. What can I possibly offer anyone?"

"The best of you. The part that never happens on the road. You've been living a half-life, Jack. The older you get, the harder that's gonna be. Maybe you're being offered something, here. Maybe you came to me to find that out. We seek what we need, even when we aren't conscious of doing it."

"How can you be so good about this, Lindy? Here you are caring about me finding love with another woman, when last night I was in your bed."

"That's what I've been trying to tell you, Jack. You weren't in my bed last night. You were in hers."

౸ *31* ౦

Sam opened the door and smiled wide when he saw Jack standing there. "My, my. It does me good t' see ya at my door, yes indeed. You just step right in here and sit y'self down, boy. I got t' finish stirrin' up oatmeal. You eat yet?"

"You go ahead, Sam. I already ate. Maybe I should come back?" Jack remained hesitantly at the door.

"Now you just get that outta yo' head. I been hopin' t' see ya and I ain't about t' let ya go." Sam hurried into the kitchen and called out to Jack. "You comin' in here?" Jack closed the front door and strode into the kitchen as Sam poured him a cup of coffee. "Now I know ya ain't gonna turn down a cup o' coffee."

Jack smiled and took the mug from Sam. He sat at the kitchen table. "It's good to see you, Sam. I missed you."

"That's pure music t' my ears, Jack. I been itchin' t' sit on the porch with ya'll. I knowed if I waited you'd be 'round by and by. Ya musta got in here right early from wherever ya been." Sam set down a steaming bowl, poured milk and honey on his oatmeal and began to eat.

"I've been in California. Down the coast and up again. Played a few places. Saw a few old friends." Jack made the journey sound light and casual, knowing Sam understood that it was anything but that.

"Well, now, you sho' did leave a big, empty space here. I 'spect ya knowed that, though." Sam looked down at his oatmeal as he spoke.

"I not only knew it. It frightened me, Sam."

"But yo' back. You thinkin' o' stickin' around awhile, or did the road feel real good t' ya?" Sam looked Jack in the eye as he asked.

"Nothing feels good right now, Sam. I did a lot of thinking while I was away. I'm not sure that I have any answers, but last night for the first time in my life I walked into a house that felt like it was mine. I'd missed being here. It was like I'd been gone from a place that wanted me back and waited for me. I guess that's something." Jack sipped his coffee and felt the quiet of the morning come over him.

"That's somethin'. It is indeed."

After a pause, Sam said, "Ya know, Jack, I don't try t' push nothin' with you. I sure would like t' know what set ya t' runnin' though. I know it has t'do with Miss Kate."

"We had some words, Sam. She saw something about me that I never had seen before, but I realize it's true. I haven't been fair to her — never told her enough about me. I've hurt her and she doesn't want anything to do with me. I don't blame her, either."

"That jus' ain't true, Jack. Kate and Nick both been worried fo' ya'll. They miss you somethin' pow'rful."

Jack felt confused. "Kate said she and Nick were out of my life. I pretty much called her a whore, after just one innocent kiss. I didn't mean it that way, but it came out sounding like I think of her as a tramp. How do I recover from that? Should I even try? What if I do choose to leave for good, after all? I don't want to be a man who was a momentary fling in Kate's life. I won't be the one to make Nick see her like that."

"What's it take t' make a woman a whore, Jack?" Sam frowned as he asked.

"What do you mean?"

"I knowed yo' mama befo' you was born, even when she was jus' a wee girl. Now, I don't rightly know what set her t' what she done, but I sho' do know that no little girl starts her life wantin' that t' happen. Not a-one. Not even yo' mama. Most women don't take t' those ways. The twists o' life can bend a heart thataway, but it ain't the nat'ral way that God made a woman's heart t' run. But in yo' life, you maybe ain't knowed many hearts that didn't. Since ya ain't never married o' stuck 'round much, the only women ya been with are ones that don't need t' marry o' commit much t' be with a man. These days that's pow'rful many o' 'em, Lord knows. Are they all whores, Jack?"

Jack stared at Sam. "That's exactly what Kate tried to say." His time with Lindy came briefly to mind as he reasoned with the flaws in his thinking.

"Kate's a good woman, Jack. You seen the kind o' mother she is, too. She got her a good son. No matter how she grows her feelings for you, that be true. Nick won't never see his mama the way ya done seen yo's. You won't never see yo' mama the way he sees his. Try and see Kate through his eyes, Jack, not yo' eyes. He got the better picture."

Jack nodded. "You're right about that, Sam."

ℬ 32 ℭ

Kate answered the door and looked up at Jack. She'd seen his van parked at the house for a few days but had been unsure whether to approach him.

"Hello, Kate. Can I come in for a bit?" he asked.

"Of course." She stepped aside to let him enter.

"Is Nick here?"

"He went to the community center this morning."

"I was thinking he might be gone. I wanted a chance to talk with you alone."

Kate sat down in a chair and invited Jack to sit on the sofa. Her heart was racing. She'd wanted this moment to happen, yet now felt apprehensive. "I'd wondered many times if you'd be coming back."

"So did I. It turned out that it was just as difficult to stay away as it was to come back. Nothing seemed the same anymore."

"Where did you go for so long?"

"Mostly California. I spent a lot of time just driving."

"You left so suddenly. I didn't expect it."

"I figured I wasn't going to be seeing you or Nick."

"Is this how you always deal with conflict, Jack?"

He stared at the floor as he answered. "Please don't make this harder than it already is."

"Do you think it hasn't been hard on me? Or Nick? I've watched my son with anguish over the past few weeks, trying to adjust to abrupt changes that he's had no control over." She wasn't sure why her anger was beginning to rise. "You never gave things a chance to settle. You just took off."

"How were things supposed to settle? Everything you said to me was absolutely true. Where was it supposed to go from there? I don't know how to do this, don't you understand, Kate?" She saw the confusion in Jack's face and her heart melted and softened her voice.

"I'm trying to, Jack, if you'll give me the chance. Just talk to me. Maybe we can figure it out together."

"Nothing has felt familiar for a long time. I tried to go back to my old ways, and now even that isn't the same. While I'm bouncing through it all like a ping-pong ball I'm hurting everyone else. I don't have the right to do that." He combed his fingers through his hair, shaking his head.

"The only way not to ever hurt people is never to get involved with them at all. Is that what you want, Jack? Are you sorry to have stepped into our lives?"

"Honestly? Yes." It wasn't the answer Kate had expected, but she'd asked for it.

"You can't mean that, Jack."

He looked at her with tears in his eyes. "At least it would be a helluva lot easier. A half a year ago I wasn't expecting any of this to happen. I just lived. I never had to worry whether what I did made other people unhappy. I didn't ask for the house or to come here. I didn't ask for any of it to happen."

"What on earth is making things so awful that you feel this way? I don't understand. You have people that care about you and a beautiful home that you own. It makes you want to run?"

194

"I never asked for people to care about me."

"It isn't something you ask for, Jack. It's something that just happens."

"It doesn't happen to me! Don't you understand? I'm a drifter. I'm a bum who never had a home and suddenly it all changed. Now I can't leave or it hurts you. I can't stay around or it hurts me. I can't play music without thinking of Nick and Sam. I can't make love to a woman without thinking of you. I can't take to the road without feeling the need to be here. *Nothing* is the same as it used to be and I'm not sure why I can't be happy about that, but I can't!" He stopped his rant, agitated and breathing deeply.

Kate stared at him in stunned silence. Finally she asked, "Why did you come here today, Jack?"

"I don't know, Kate." He looked at the floor, then back up at her. "I'm sorry. I really don't."

"Neither do I. Maybe you'd better leave before Nick gets back. Nothing has changed, Jack. Until you have a better answer than 'I don't know', nothing ever will. You need help, and none of us seem to be able to give it to you."

Jack looked silently into Kate's eyes for a long moment, then rose from the sofa, crossed the room, and left without saying a word.

Kate began to rock back and forth in her chair, tortured in her thoughts. She'd never dealt with anything like this and had no idea what to do. She'd hoped that Jack's return was a sign that he'd found answers, but he appeared to be more unsettled than ever. Worse than that, she realized from his remarks that he'd attempted to work things out by sleeping with another woman, or perhaps more than one. Kate's heart ached — for Jack's pain, for her son's loss, for the love she was unable to share, and for the

195

situation she now found herself crying over. As the tears fell, she considered that Jack might not be the only one who wished they had never met. But in her deepest heart, she knew it wasn't true.

* * *

Kate and Sue sat at an outdoor table at their favorite restaurant, sipping drinks and waiting for their lunch. The morning's trek through the small shops along Twenty-Third Street had been less than adventurous. Kate was quiet and Sue's attempts to lighten her spirits had had little effect.

"Kate, honey, I hate to see you like this. How long is this thing going to eat at you?" Sue knew that Jack was in town but was not communicating with her or Nick.

"It's not like the flu, Sue. I can't tell you it'll be over in two days." She was sorry she'd agreed to the day's outing.

"Is this guy really worth it?"

"It isn't just about me. Nick has been devastated over the situation. When Jack first returned, I'd thought about letting Nick continue to play music with him. After talking with Jack, I changed my mind. There's been no music happening with the neighbor, Sam, either — it's just stopped. It's like he's trying to shut down whatever he thinks is hurting him. He's got these demons bottled up inside him and none of us know what to do about it."

Sue softened as she saw her friend's pain. "It sounds like whatever he's dealing with has been ignored for a very long time."

"Jack had the childhood from hell. To his credit, he didn't bury it with drugs and alcohol, like most others would. He got addicted to music and a gypsy life, and he stuffed the pain so far down that, every time it started to surface, his comfort came from running away and changing the scenery and the people. That's how it seems, anyway. But how do I explain that kind of thing to Nick when I'm not sure I understand it myself? If I wasn't in the picture, I'm not sure that Jack's problem would be so severe. I think he simply doesn't know what to do about me and Nick, since we come as a package, so to speak."

"And he lives a few houses down, so it's pretty hard to ignore." Sue remarked.

"Yep. That's what keeps me on edge. I just can't shut him off from my mind and my heart. Frankly, I'm surprised he hasn't taken off again."

"Maybe that's a good sign?" Sue said hopefully.

"That's the kind of thinking that'll drive me nuts."

"You love him, don't you?"

Kate sighed and paused for a long moment before answering. "Yes, I do. The other side of Jack is incredibly wonderful and worth the wait. It's like living in the path of a hurricane, waiting for an inevitable event and wondering how bad it'll hurt when it finally comes — or if anything will be left standing. I'm living in the path because I fell in love before the storm ever hit."

"How is Nick holding up through all this?"

"That's what has me really worried. He won't talk much about it and he doesn't really know what's behind it all. He trusts me, but it seems like I'm keeping him apart from something he loves. He's been to Sam's house to play music a few times, but I see him being drawn back to his heavy metal stuff more and more. I guess we all have ways of retreating to what feels familiar, don't we?"

"What do you retreat to, Kate?"

"Work. Nick. Books. Old movies on the late show. Having

lunch with good friends." Kate smiled at Sue and held up her glass. "Thanks for being there and putting up with all my misery, Sue."

They clinked glasses. "Anytime, my friend."

ಬಿ *33* ಲ

Early on a Friday afternoon Nick headed over to The Hanger, shouldering his electric guitar in its gig bag and ignoring his inner convictions to stay away from the place. He felt a strong need for a music jam but he knew that any attempt to visit with Jack would be in plain sight of his house and would likely get back to his mother. He didn't want to make Jack's position with her any worse than it was right now. Nick loved playing music with Jack, but that was no longer an option for him, not until his mother changed her heart about things. He hoped she could. In the meantime his need for a dose of driving, hard rock music consumed him that day.

Nick was pretty sure he could talk Brandon into jamming with him if he found him at home. He was disappointed when he didn't see Brandon's car in front of the house. After parking his bike and locking it to the side fence, he strolled to the front door and knocked. It was Diggs who opened the door and stepped back to let him enter.

"Hey, Nick! Good to see your face here, man."

The room was strewn with the remnants of paper cups and empty food bags left over from a recent party. Nick put the guitar down near the coffee table and strolled into the kitchen, tossing some coins into the food fund jar and grabbing a soda from the refrigerator. He then went back into the living room to plop himself on the sofa where Diggs was slouched, watching a movie.

"Looks like you had some fun here lately." He said this more from a need for conversation than anything else. "Don't you guys ever clean up? The place looks like shit."

"It's Brandon's turn. I did it last time." Diggs hoisted himself up to a sitting position and opened a stash box sitting on the coffee table. "Wanna smoke a doob?" Diggs grabbed a nearby lighter and proceeded to light up and take a hit, not waiting for Nick's answer.

"What are we watching here?" Nick asked.

"Some old Bogie flick about three convicts that escape from Devil's Island. It's pretty funny. Turn of the century stuff with some tight-assed family that these dudes end up helping. My bets are on Adolph the snake."

Diggs offered the joint to Nick, who shook his head to decline. Instead he got up and grabbed his guitar out of its gig bag, then settled down in the nearby chair to play some leads in the key of D. The guitar wasn't plugged in and the tinny sounds of the strings could barely be heard over the TV. It seemed that Diggs wasn't in the mood to jam, so he continued to play unplugged for quite awhile.

"When's Brandon gonna be back?" Nick finally asked.

"He's upstairs. He went up there a couple of hours ago with Jenny Dunn." Diggs spoke her name while raising his eyebrows to indicate his amazement at Brandon's ability to make such a conquest.

"*What?!?*" Nick's eyes flew wide open. It had to be a mistake.

"True story." Diggs said, "I was surprised, too. I didn't think he'd be her type. She seemed kind of drunk, though."

Nick's heart was pounding. "What do you mean, drunk? That was before noon. No way — Jenny wouldn't step foot in this place, let alone be drunk in the morning."

"I dunno, but she looked fairly wasted."

Nick rose to his feet feeling confused and heartsick. All the while that he'd been sitting down here killing time with Diggs, Brandon was upstairs doing God knows what with Jenny.

With Jenny.

It made no sense. As Nick headed for the stairs, Diggs turned and hollered back toward him.

"Hey, man, I don't think he wants to be disturbed."

"I gotta — I don't know — find out what's — I don't know." He kept thinking this was a practical joke or some mix-up. Nothing could stop him from finding out.

The door to the bump room was closed and the sign over the door was lit — [**No Clothes --- Anything Goes**]. The thought of what that probably meant made him tremble. Nick stood at the door, afraid, not knowing what to do or how to handle this bizarre situation. He heard muffled sounds from inside the room that told him his worst fears were not unfounded. Quietly turning the doorknob, he slowly and steadily opened the door to peer inside.

What he saw made him freeze on the doorstep.

They were both naked. Jenny lay face up on the bearskin rug with her hands clutching the fur of the rug. Her legs were curled at the knee and spread wide to accept the powerful thrusts of Brandon's hips. They didn't notice him at the door. Brandon's throaty gasps rose up in tempo with their urgent sex, sending a wave of nausea to Nick's stomach.

He backed away and quietly closed the door. Unable to move, he leaned his head against the door jamb.

My Jenny. Oh, god, my Jenny.

His thoughts raced, reminding him of the earnest feelings of disgust she'd expressed about Brandon. *Sure, he looks good, but I wouldn't want anything to do with a guy like that. Not ever.*

What had happened? Why was she here, doing this? From inside the room came the loud and unmistakable cry of Brandon's release. The sound sent tears to Nick's eyes. They had been in there for two hours, and he wondered what all had transpired in that time. He wanted to be numb, but the pain he was feeling was so very intense and real.

The next memories that came to his mind reversed his thoughts completely, with a shock.

Brandon: *I'd do anything to get into Jenny's pants. Anything.*

Benny: *I got a line on some script roofies last week. You interested?*

Diggs: *I dunno, but she looked fairly wasted.*

Nick came to the sickening realization that Jenny was probably not in the bump room knowingly or willingly. As the horror of that thought crystallized, it drove a flood of raw courage into his veins. This time when he opened the door, it was not slowly or quietly.

Jenny now lay alone on the rug. Her legs were still parted and her eyes were closed. She turned slowly toward the sound of Nick's noisy entry, opening her eyes slightly and staring at him as if through a fog. She smiled as she recognized him. The fact that she made no move to cover herself, and registered no surprise or embarrassment on her face, had confirmed Nick's suspicions.

He stood at the door, heart racing and frozen in a moment of dazed thought and crushing emotion, unsure of his next move. His good friend had inescapably gone far beyond the limits of behavior that Nick had imagined him capable, and had done the unthinkable. It was time to confront him, not as a friend, but as the enemy and the monster that he'd become.

He crossed the room to where Brandon knelt, attempting to light a partially smoked joint that he'd grabbed off the small table in the corner, which also held a square mirror tile with a short straw laying beside it. As he turned to face Nick their eyes locked briefly in a stare-down, and a smirk of triumph, barely perceptible, moved across Brandon's face. He grinned at Nick and said, "You want some of this, Nicky?"

Nick was unsure if he was being offered to share the joint or Jenny. It was probably both. The cavalier attitude that Brandon was taking about the scene brought Nick to a point of rage he had never before felt. In one swift move his foot slammed into Brandon's chest, sending him into the wall. "You dirty *bastard!*" he screamed, "You slipped her a roofie, didn't you? *Didn't you!?*"

With a mix of astonishment and fear on his face, Brandon unconsciously guarded his bare genitals with his hands. It provided the clear opportunity for Nick's next kick to land hard on his jaw, spinning him around and onto the ground with a whelp of pain, momentarily dazed. Before he could react, Nick grabbed his arm and wrenched it into a wrestling hold, jumping at the same time onto Brandon's back to pin him. "Is there any limit to how twisted you allow yourself to get, you sick *fuck!?*" Nick choked this out, close to tears. Brandon said nothing.

He broke his hold and stood up. Brandon rose to his hands and knees, struggling to get up, with his back to Nick and his testicles exposed. Nick's last kick sent Brandon writhing back to the floor, unable to breathe. He made chortling sounds of agony and then turned away to lay in a quivering fetal position, with no hope of recovering for a long while.

Nick turned his attention back to Jenny. She hadn't moved and appeared to be falling asleep. He gathered up her clothes which were strewn nearby, finding her bra, panties, shirt and jeans but only one of her flip-flop shoes. Kneeling beside her, it was impossible not to gaze at her nude body. Even in this awful situation she was beautiful to him. A moan from Brandon brought Nick back to the moment and he knew he had to get her out of the house as quickly as possible.

He pulled Jenny into a sitting position and she flopped against him and mumbled something incoherent in his ear. Wrestling with her bra, he determined how to put it on and then worked to slip the loops over her arms. Nick had only ever unhooked a girl's bra once, which had been tricky. He now found it almost impossible to fasten one, particularly when blindly attempting it from the front as she lay motionless against his torso. He managed to get one of the two hooks clasped and gave up on the other one. In the process of dressing her he became very aware of her nakedness pressed against him, her warm breath upon his neck.

Down, Nick. Not here. Not like this.

The shirt was easier to put on, but not much. Her dead weight and loose posture worked against it. She mumbled unintelligible words under her breath. He laid her down again to button it up, then picked up her panties from the floor. At this point his focus moved to her legs, which had still not moved. He saw for the first time that they were slick with moisture, and became suddenly cognizant of the strong smell of sex. With a deep stab of pain he also realized that the wetness on her legs was mixed with a small amount of blood.

Jenny had been a virgin.

It took every bit of his strength to keep himself from turning back to Brandon with renewed wrath. He looked instead for something to use to wipe off her legs, but the thought occurred to him that he might be destroying evidence. There was no doubt about this being a rape and, most damning for Brandon, while Jenny was a minor, he was not. Nick knew in that moment that he would gladly testify against Brandon, with no qualms, if given a chance in court.

Once her panties and jeans were on, he attempted to awaken her, hoping she could stand and negotiate the stairs. He had a growing concern that her ability to remain conscious was diminishing rapidly. Nick had no idea what the effects of a roofie were, other than the loss of memory and inhibitions. The thought crossed his mind that she could be in serious danger as well. He tried to rouse her, but Jenny could only mumble, keeping her eyes closed. Taking her pulse, he was somewhat relieved to find it quite slow, but strong and steady.

With a glance to Brandon, who still lay on the floor in the corner, Nick lifted Jenny to a vertical position, then draped her over his shoulder to carry her out of the room and down the stairs. When they reached the bottom landing, he saw Diggs look back toward them then jump up from the sofa.

"What's going on? What's wrong with Jenny?" Diggs asked.

"She isn't drunk, Diggs. I think Brandon gave her a roofie." Nick swung Jenny off his shoulder and gently sat her on the floor. Her incapacity was obvious.

"Oh, *shit.*" Diggs was visibly shaken. "I didn't know, Nick. I really didn't."

"Her parents both work and won't be at home. You gotta help me get her over to my house. She won't be able to walk it. Can you drive us over?" Nick asked.

"Yeah, sure." Diggs reached into his pocket for his keys. "Oh, man, this is fucked. This is *so* fucked." He helped Nick lift Jenny to her feet by wrapping her left arm around his neck while Nick supported her other arm. Together they managed to get her from

205

the side door of the house to the car parked in the driveway. They lowered her into the back seat. Nick climbed in beside her, laying her head on his lap and giving directions to Diggs. They drove the short trip to the house and pulled into the driveway that ran along the side yard, parking toward the back door for privacy.

Half carrying and half walking her, they brought Jenny through the kitchen and into the living room and laid her on the sofa. She was nearly unconscious by this time, and Diggs seemed more frightened than ever.

"Nick, this is bad, man. I feel like a creep for just letting it happen. God, I never thought Brandon would do such a stupid thing. I didn't know, man. I didn't even think."

Nick knew that his plea was sincere. Deep down below the tough outer shell, he saw the real Diggs at that moment and liked what he saw. Even he hadn't comprehended how low of a pit Brandon was able to drag himself down to. Nick felt sure Diggs would never have let this happen, had he known Jenny as anything other than a pretty neighborhood face and a name.

"I'll take care of Jenny." Nick said. "Go home, Diggs. Get the house clean for the cops. They're probably gonna get called at some point, so the place is hot now." They were both slowly comprehending the gravity of what was happening, playing it a moment at a time. "Diggs — don't be there when they come. As far as I'm concerned, I never saw you today, okay?"

Diggs nodded soberly and put his hand out to clasp Nick's in a handshake of brotherhood. Before leaving, he looked down at Jenny lying on the sofa and, with genuine regret and eyes filled with tears, said, "I'm sorry, Jenny. I'm so sorry."

Right after he left, Nick realized that Diggs had never asked what had happened between him and Brandon upstairs. He had a feeling that he didn't much care.

Turning once again to the sofa, Nick panicked. He'd said he would take care of Jenny but now he wasn't sure what his next move was. She moaned lightly and moved her arm. Nick took that for a good sign. Looking at his watch he saw that it was about three o'clock. His mother would be coming home within the next few minutes and he knew that, as a nurse, she would know what to do.

He knelt beside Jenny. Brushing a lock of hair away from her face, he thought for the first time about what this day would mean for her. The loss of her innocence was only a part of the shock, embarrassment, trials and consequences that would now be thwarted upon her life. She herself would probably have no memory of the events that had occurred, and Nick was unsure how much he would need to divulge to her, to her parents or to the police about the terrible scene. Placing his hand gently on her face he marveled once again at her beauty, then took one small advantage of the situation.

He leaned down to tenderly kiss her lips.

It was more than an hour beyond the normal time for his mother to arrive home from work. Nick was worried about leaving Jenny alone but felt that he shouldn't wait any longer to get help for her. A brief online search had revealed that gradual loss of consciousness was the anticipated effect of a roofie and was not life-threatening. She seemed okay for the moment, but he was still not positive whether the overall effects of the drug might be dangerous. This was not a time for concern about the issues between his mother and Jack. He knew that going to Jack for help was the right thing to do.

Jack answered the door with a paintbrush in his hand. He

smiled broadly and started to give Nick a friendly greeting, then saw his expression and grasped that something was very wrong.

"Can you come over, Jack?" Nick asked. "Mom's not home yet and I need your help."

"Sure," Jack replied, "just let me put this brush in the sink and clean my hands. Come in the kitchen and tell me what's going on."

While Jack quickly washed up, Nick gave him a brief summary of what had happened, leaving out the help that he'd gotten from Diggs. He watched Jack's face register grave concern as he described the condition Jenny now seemed to be in. Without wasting another second Jack turned off the water and dried his hands on his shirt as he ran with Nick back toward the house.

Kate's car was in the driveway. Imagining a bad scene, Nick raced toward the house and took the front steps in one leap, charging through the front door that he'd left unlocked.

Kate was in the kitchen, humming lightly and putting away groceries. She'd entered the house from the side door and had not yet stepped into the living room. The sound of Nick's overcharged entry made her turn toward the doorway with a startled look on her face. When she saw her son stop his advance midway toward the kitchen, she smiled. "Hey, captain, where's the fire? I was just about to make something to eat. You hungry?"

Jack stepped in behind Nick and Kate froze. There was an awkward silence while Nick struggled to catch his breath and find the words to explain what was going on.

Nick's voice shook as he said, "Mom, don't jump on this yet. Something's happened."

The tone of her son's voice caused her a momentary panic. She felt her knees weaken as she sensed the ominous nature of his words. "Is it Sam?"

"It's Jenny. She's unconscious and it may be serious. Someone gave her some drugs and I don't know if she's okay. You were late getting home so I went and got Jack."

Kate's face went pale. She looked briefly at Jack then back at Nick once again. "Where is she? Why on *earth* didn't you just call an ambulance?"

"She's on the couch. She's probably okay, so I didn't know if I should call. There's more to it." Nick's voice wavered. All the things he'd rehearsed saying while he'd waited for her to arrive had vanished from his mind in an instant.

Kate ran to the kitchen table to grab her knapsack then hurried back to the sofa where Jenny appeared to be sleeping peacefully. She was relieved to see that her color looked good, but knew that whatever more there was to the story would have to wait until she'd checked Jenny's vital signs. She felt her pulse. It was quite slow, but steady and strong. Pulling her stethoscope from the bag, Kate listened to her breathing and heart. They seemed to be functioning in a range that was acceptable. Satisfied for the moment that Jenny was in no critical danger, she turned her attention back to Nick.

"What did she take?" Kate asked.

"She didn't take it. It was given to her without her knowing," Nick answered.

"Okay. What was *given* to her?" Kate replied, becoming agitated with the reluctance that her son was displaying in telling her the whole situation.

"A roofie."

Kate held her breath and closed her eyes. Fearing the worst, she opened them again and stared at Nick with an intensity that made him cringe. "*Who* gave it to her?" She braced herself for his answer.

He hesitated. *There's no getting out of this one. Jack would never let it slide.* His answer was almost a whisper.

"Brandon."

Kate heaved a ragged sigh of fear and remorse that her worst fears of Brandon's behaviors were confirmed and that somehow her son had been involved. At last she turned to Jack. "How long ago did you find out?"

"About a minute before we came through the door," Jack answered.

"Mom," Nick interjected, "it isn't just the drug that's the problem. It's worse."

She didn't have to wonder much what the bigger problem was. "He raped her?" she guessed. His silence was her answer. Kate felt the blood drain from her face. "Son, did you have anything at all to do with this?"

"No. *Hell* no. I beat the crap out of him for doing it then I brought Jenny here. Her parents both work during the day and might not be home yet."

She decided to let the rest of the story slide for the present time. Kate knew that the most important thing to do right then was to call Jenny's parents. They should be making the decisions about how to handle their daughter's situation. "Do you have Jenny's home phone number, Nick?

"No," he said "I only have her cell phone number."

"We need to phone her parents. It'll be better to call than to just show up at their door with Jenny and not find them home. Where is her cell phone? It probably has a number to reach them stored in it."

When he'd gathered Jenny's things in the bump room Nick hadn't seen a purse and hadn't thought to look for it. He knew she never went anywhere without one and now wondered what might have happened to it. The thought of going back to The Hanger to find it made him ill.

"I don't know if she had her phone with her. I didn't see a purse but she usually carries one."

Jack intervened at that point. "Nick, maybe you and I should go and see about finding it right away. It'll just take a few minutes. Would that be okay with you, Kate?" Nick knew that Jack's presence there wasn't altogether comfortable, but they all understood that Kate was the best person to stay with Jenny. He was glad that his mother wasn't going to be involved in returning to face Brandon.

"Yes." Kate answered. "I'd feel much better if you went with him, Jack. Please be as quick as you can. Jenny seems to not be in danger, but I'm worried that her parents don't know what's happening or where she's at." She paused, then added, "Thank you."

They left immediately. Nick knew it wasn't going to be easy, but he no longer feared Brandon. He didn't know what a mistake that would turn out to be.

* * *

Nick and Jack had returned to Jack's house to get his van. Since Nick had left his bike at The Hanger, the van seemed the easiest and quickest way to retrieve the purse and bike and get back to the house. On the way Nick worried about bringing Jack into the situation. Considering the kind of activities that took place there, Jack's unwanted presence would not be appreciated by Brandon or Benny. If Brandon had been tweaking lately, as Nick had long suspected, he was likely to be paranoid about things. He was also worried that Diggs might still be around, and

Nick didn't want to disclose the role he'd played in what had gone on that afternoon.

Nick asked Jack to park a little way down the street from the house. Jack seemed to understand the situation enough to comply without asking for a reason. Since Nick was unsure what would transpire in the next few minutes, he decided to load his bike into the van before entering the house. He quickly ran to the side fence, unlocked the bike and wheeled it to the van's back doors.

"Jack — I have to go into the house by myself." Nick said firmly as he lifted the bike into the van.

"I don't know about that, Nick." Jack wasn't comfortable with the idea. A rape had occurred there today. He was fairly certain that this house was tied to illegal activity and that the occupants might get ugly about defending their interests. "Brandon won't be happy to see you."

"I know, but he got a pretty good scare this afternoon. He'll cooperate better if he's just dealing with me. Having you there would threaten him even more." Nick reasoned.

"Do you know where to find Jenny's phone?" Jack asked.

"No. I didn't see her purse or I would have taken it."

Jack pulled a cell phone out of a cubbyhole in the van. "Give me Jenny's cell phone number," he said "and I'll call it a few seconds after you get into the house. I'll keep dialing it. The ring will tell you where her purse is located, if it's there. When you find it, get out right away. Don't confront Brandon unless you have to."

The idea sounded good. Nick gave the phone number to Jack, who added, "I won't stay back too long, Nick. If I don't see you out here in a few minutes, I'm coming in. That's not negotiable. Understand?"

There was not time to argue the point. Besides, the last thing

Nick wanted to do was to stick around nixing it up with Brandon. He closed the van door and headed for the side entrance to the house, which he knew was usually left open. Nick hoped to find the purse without encountering Brandon at all.

As he'd thought, the door was unlocked. When he entered the house it was unusually quiet — no music, no TV. He was glad to find that Diggs had cleaned up the place, removed the stash box and now appeared to be gone. He'd completely forgotten about his guitar and saw that it had been returned to its case and was leaning against the side of the stairs. It was the first time ever that he'd left it somewhere without a thought.

A moment later he heard the distant sound of a cell phone ringing. It came from upstairs and sounded like Jenny's ring tone. He ascended the stairs and was dismayed to discover that the sound came from behind the closed door of Brandon's room. Taking a few deep breaths, he knocked on the door. As he did the sound of the ringing stopped. There was no response, but he heard movement behind the door.

He knocked again, a bit harder. "Brandon, it's Nick. Open the door." A few seconds elapsed before he heard the click of the latch. The door swung inward and Brandon stood a foot or two back from it with his right hand behind him, out of sight. The inside of the room was dark. He was bare-chested, wearing only a pair of jeans. A swollen, purple welt marked his left jaw line and his red, swollen eyes indicated that he'd been crying. Something in the look on his face sent a shiver down Nick's spine.

The phone rang again and Nick glanced for a moment behind Brandon to the bed, where the light from the hallway revealed a purse laying at the foot.

"You got a lot of balls showing up here, Nicky." The menace in Brandon's voice was thick. He glared intently at Nick, not blinking or moving.

213

"I just need Jenny's purse and I'm outta here. I didn't come for any more trouble." Nick replied steadily. He was surprised at how calmly he was able to stand there and say this, as if his resolve was tapping a deep well of strength that he hadn't known was there. He'd never before stood his ground with Brandon in this way, and would never have thought himself capable of it.

"You fucked me over, Nicky. I don't owe you shit. Get the hell out of my house, *now!*" Brandon's anger was visibly rising. Nick wasn't sure how far he could wisely take this, but he knew that failure to obtain the purse would send Jack into the house. He couldn't risk that.

"All I need is the purse, man. I know it's here. Hand it to me and I'm gone. I swear." Nick voice was smooth, and he was trying hard not to sound threatening in any way.

"You swear." Brandon jeered. "You *swear??* Like I can *trust* you? Like you're my *buddy?* Like you didn't *fuck* me over this afternoon?" He lunged toward Nick, grabbing his arm tightly with his left hand and bringing his right hand around to Nick's head, holding a 9mm pistol. "You aren't taking anything out of here, Nicky. Not even yourself."

Nick stood motionless, not saying a word, remaining amazingly calm. His perception of the moment was almost surreal, coming from somewhere outside the spot on which he was standing. He'd never seen Brandon like this and he was pretty sure that the threat he was making wasn't idle, but he also somehow knew that it was coming from fear.

"Why are you doing this, Brandon?" Nick said softly.

"I don't have to tell you a fucking thing." Brandon's voice was going deeper and was filled with malice. "I'm a dead man now, Nicky. Thanks to you, I'm gonna be a dead man. And I'm taking you with me, plain and simple."

Rather than fear, Nick's strange reaction to the situation was starting to be anger. His voice rose as he faced off with Brandon, who still held the gun to his head.

"You think I betrayed you? You think I'm the cause of your problems? You sell drugs to grade school kids, but I'm the problem. You give blow jobs in park bathrooms to pay your rent, but I'm the problem. You steal drug money and almost get me killed telling them I did it, but I'm the problem. Today you gave an innocent girl a roofie so you could finally get into her pants, and *I'm your problem?* When are *you* ever your problem, Brandon? When do the things you do ever catch up to you? Now you threaten to kill me. You might kill me right now for spite, but I don't think you have the guts to kill yourself or you'd have already done it."

The look on Brandon's face told him that the words were hitting home hard. His grip on Nick's wrist loosened.

Nick continued, "There's no death sentence for anything you've done so far, but you pull that trigger and there's no going back, Brandon. It'll be the worst mistake you've made yet and you'll have to find someone new to blame 'cause I'll be dead. My mom and Jack know I'm here. You have nowhere to go, nowhere to hide. You'll be in prison giving head for free to save your pretty little ass from beatings worse than I could ever give you. Be smart for once, Brandon. Put the gun down, hand over the purse and I'm gone. Nothing that just happened here goes any further. It's forgotten."

The expression on Brandon's face shifted from one of anger to one of confusion. It looked as if a fight was happening behind his eyes, shifting them back and forth as he struggled with his decision. Within a few moments the look of fear that had been wrestling for control vanished and became a blank expression. Brandon lowered the gun to his side and flung it backward onto the bed. Stepping back to grab the purse, he turned to hand it to Nick without saying a word.

They stood locked in a gaze for a few seconds as if an understanding were being communicated. Yet Nick knew inwardly that the only way he could ever really understand the motivations of a heart like Brandon's would be to have one himself. He resolved at that moment that he didn't need to try. Saying nothing, he turned, went back downstairs with the purse, gathered up his guitar and left The Hanger for the last time.

* * *

It was about five o'clock in the evening when Nick and Jack returned to find Kate sitting on the sofa with Jenny, who was still extremely groggy but slightly more responsive and able to support her own weight as she sat. Nick was incredibly relieved, knowing that the drug was finally wearing off. The phone call that Kate immediately made to Jenny's parents was painful and awkward. The events of the last hour had shaken her as a mother. Delivering such hard news affected her very deeply.

Jack decided that his assistance was no longer needed and his presence might complicate things. He opted to leave. Before he did he walked over to the phone, where Kate was still standing after ending the call. Her eyes were closed and she was trembling. He pulled her into a comforting embrace that lasted much longer than a few seconds, calming her. Nick rejoiced when he saw that his mother accepted it gladly, returning the gesture with genuine feeling. It was the only good thing that the entire day's events could claim.

Mr. and Mrs. Dunn arrived at the house shortly after Jack left, in great distress yet amazingly reasonable considering the circumstances. Nick was grateful that they weren't angry with the decision to wait and contact them before taking any other kind of action. Their demeanor toward Nick was gentle and understanding, seeing him as the one who had come to Jenny's rescue and kept her from further harm. Their grace in the moment of deep trauma was the evidence of the unswerving faith that Jenny herself had often displayed to Nick — the steadfast belief that good would always, ultimately, triumph over every evil.

It was obvious that they loved their daughter very much and were deeply heartbroken for the turn of events that would now bring her such pain. They asked surprisingly little about the details, much to Nick's relief. The shock of what had happened seemed to have numbed them from any urgent need to assign blame. Jenny's father carried her like a small child to their car. When they left, it was with the understanding that the police would now be involved and Nick's full testimony would be essential. He had no problem with that. The few details he'd leave out would have no bearing on the case. Leaving them out served a better purpose — keeping his word.

Later that evening when Nick sat with his mother on the sofa talking over the events that had happened, there was no longer any anger or disappointment on her part. They both knew that his foolish visit to The Hanger that morning had been his last, and that Jenny's well-being had been secured as much as possible by his act of disobedience. The weight of all that had transpired that day came upon him suddenly and heavily as they spoke. Nick's strength finally collapsed, and he laid his head upon his mother's chest and sobbed.

* * *

After breakfast the next day Nick was happy to hear Kate suggest that he pay a visit to Jack. There was no doubt for either of them that Jack's role in yesterday's events had helped to bring them through the toughest spots, and he deserved to know how things had gone once Jenny's parents had taken charge. Aside from that, Nick felt he needed to talk things out in a way that, as a young man, he was unable to do with his mother. He also needed to stick close by the house since the police would undoubtedly be calling upon them soon.

Kate smiled faintly when she saw Nick walk out the door that morning with his acoustic guitar. He noted in her eyes that there was something in the connection he had with Jack, and the way music played a part in it, that brought her comfort, and perhaps even a touch of envy.

Jack sat on his porch with a cup of coffee, sketching in a notebook. He looked up and smiled when he saw Nick coming up the walkway. "It's good to see you here, Nick," Jack said. "How are you doing today?"

"Pretty fair, I guess. Mom said I could come over. I didn't have to ask her — she brought it up herself." Nick saw that it meant a lot to Jack to hear that. They had never spoken about the things that had caused his mother's anger toward him, but Nick knew that the separation had caused them both a lot of pain. The loss of Jack's friendship to him and his mother had created a hole in all their lives that might now be mending, at last. That morning there was hope.

"Get yourself a cup of coffee and come sit down. Grab a couple of the muffins for us from the kitchen counter, too," Jack said as he laid his notebook and pen aside. Nick put down the guitar and in a few minutes he and Jack sat across from each other, drinking coffee and nibbling on fresh-baked blueberry muffins.

He told Jack about Mr. and Mrs. Dunn and their courage in handling the whole situation. It was no less amazing to him in the light of another day. The fact that they had taken Jenny immediately to the hospital was no surprise. The police were now involved, without a doubt. He spoke through a flood of emotions about what he was experiencing and his profound sorrow over what had happened.

"Why Jenny? Why someone so sweet and so good?" Tears flooded Nick's eyes. "That bastard didn't care, he just took what he wanted. He stole her innocence and changed her life for a selfish minute of sex. He knew how much she meant to me and he didn't give a damn about that either. He never used to be like that when we were kids. Somehow he changed and I didn't see it. How could I be so blind about him? What's Jenny's life gonna be like now?" In his release of emotion, what he couldn't reveal was the guilt he felt. He'd sat with Diggs for a long time before discovering that Jenny was upstairs. What if he'd asked for Brandon right away? Could he have stopped the worst of it from happening? Revealing those thoughts to Jack would break his promise to Diggs.

"Those are questions that you can beat yourself up over for a lifetime and never answer." Jack's voice was calm and soothing. "Whatever the reasons, what happened just happened. At some point, Brandon crossed a line in his heart that should never be crossed. To your credit, you hung in there as his friend and believed him to be better than he was. More importantly, you didn't let his ways become yours. Right now, the one who needs your support is Jenny. She's a strong young woman and she'll survive this, but it's gonna get tough. There'll be a trial. You ready to talk about what occurred?"

Nick took a long pause, then began to recall the events of that day to Jack. It was terribly painful to bring to light the memories that were still so fresh. When they'd left The Hanger the night before, Jack had asked no questions. Now he asked for details.

He seemed to sense that something malevolent had occurred when Nick had gone to retrieve the purse. True to his promise to Brandon, Nick revealed nothing of the gun threat but only said that strong words had been spoken between them. That part was essentially true, but he had a feeling that Jack didn't completely buy his whole story. He also didn't press the matter.

"I'm really proud of the way you handled things yesterday, Nick." Jack spoke with admiration. "You were a man. You did what any man should do when dealing with something like that. I know it hurt deeply. I know that Jenny means the world to you and Brandon has been a close friend. You may feel you had to hurt and betray your friend to rescue her. But it's Brandon that betrayed you, and he alone caused the punishment he'll face. You have to see it that way as you move forward."

Nick knew he was right. Brandon was even willing to point a gun to his head, and that was never the action of any kind of friend. It seemed that the longer Brandon indulged in the sort of activities that hardened his heart, the deeper he was willing to take his darkest actions. All the looks and charm that he possessed would not continue to shield him from consequences.

In the next few weeks or months, Nick knew he'd have to stand up for Jenny, in testimonies and in court, against Brandon. The thought frightened him a bit, but he was sure his mother and Jack would be there for him. With no memory of his own father, Nick's love and respect for Jack was a great comfort that somehow made things easier.

* * *

Later that same day a police car arrived at Nick's house. Jenny's parents had permitted them to divulge all information and the results of serology tests taken the night before, which had confirmed the presence of the drug flunitrazepam, otherwise known as "roofies", in her bloodstream. Her condition that morning was good and, as expected, she had no memory of the previous day beyond a mid-morning encounter with Brandon at Tony's Place, where she'd bought a soda. Brandon had talked with her for quite awhile about Nick's new interests in music. It was suspected that the drug had been slipped into her drink somehow at that time.

Nick was questioned at length about the events that had transpired. He was glad that his earlier talk with Jack had prepared him for their questions and taken away some of the sting from remembering. The police obtained enough information from him to issue a warrant for Brandon's arrest, which was carried out later that evening at the address Nick had provided. The room in which the police knew the rape had allegedly occurred was thoroughly examined for evidence. During the search, drugs had been found there, and also in both Benny's and Brandon's rooms. They were both taken into custody. Diggs hadn't bothered to warn either of them, and Brandon had said nothing to Benny.

Neither had he run.

ℬ 34 ℭ

Sam rose early, as usual, and turned on the radio to hear the daily gospel music hour. It was the time of morning that he devoted to talking with God, and his heart was heavy with the events of the last few days in the lives of the people he'd grown so close to. His daily prayers were never formal. He simply offered up his thoughts and the day that was about to begin, then remained silent, the way his father had taught him to do long before. On this particular day nothing had entered into his silence.

As he stood at the kitchen sink looking into the backyard, a movement in the window of his outdoor tool shed caught his eye. He wasn't much concerned — there was nothing of any value in the shed. It mostly held old lawn tools that would be of little interest to thieves. It was more out of curiosity that Sam decided to investigate. He donned his socks and shoes, pulled on his old sweater and headed out the back door.

When he reached the shed he heard faint sounds coming from behind the door. The lock had been broken for years, but the hasp that usually kept it shut was unlatched. He cautiously swung the door to peer open to peer in.

A young man with tawny complexion, shoulder length black hair and a thick horseshoe mustache stared back at him in shock. He'd been rolling up a sleeping bag when Sam's entry had interrupted him.

"Hello, boy." Sam smiled as he addressed the lad, hoping to

ease his apparent fright.

"I wasn't stealing anything, mister. I just stayed here last night, man. I was packing up to leave early."

"Don't worry yo' head. I ain't thinkin' ya did nothin' wrong. Spent a few nights in odd places m'self."

The boy looked relieved. "I was trying to be gone before anyone woke up."

"I rise up early. Thought I saw somethin' movin' in here and come t' see. You want some breakfast, boy?"

"I can pay."

"I weren't askin' fo' that. Just bein' friendly, and I know you's prob'ly hungry. I ain't eaten yet m'self if ya care t' join me."

"Sure. Thanks. That's real nice of you."

They walked back to the house and Sam offered him a seat at the kitchen table. "Eggs and toast okay with you?" Sam asked.

"Sounds great, man."

Sam began the preparations. "You drink coffee?"

"Yes, sir. Thanks."

"You can call me Sam." He offered his hand.

"Anthony. But just call me Diggs." He shook Sam's hand.

Sam poured a cup of coffee and set it in front of Diggs. "Diggs. Now that be quite a nickname. I like it." He set the table and poured orange juice for them both, then started the toaster and began to scramble eggs.

"I don't know how it started. I've been called that since I was a little tyke."

"So how you come t' be in the shed?"

"My family lives in Salem somewhere, but I've been up here awhile and lost track of where they are. I had to move from the place I was staying at. I slept in my car two nights, then it got towed. I found your shed unlocked and — well — I've stayed there a couple of nights already. Sorry, Sam."

"Nothin' t' be sorry for, boy. It ain't comfy but it kept the dew off. You plannin' t' find yo' folks in Salem?"

"Nah. I figure I'll try to find a cheap room somewhere. I looked in the paper the last few days but I need to get my car back before anything else. My computer and other tools were in the trunk."

"My, my. Troubles do pile up, don't they?"

Sam prepared two plates and set them down on the table, pausing for a moment to give thanks before beginning his meal. Diggs ate hungrily while Sam silently gave thought to the situation. He felt instant peace about his decision.

"Tell you what, son. I got me a spare room that could stand t' get some use. It might help y'out while you set y'self right again. I live simple and trust in God, and I don't want no drugs bein' here. If that abides with ya'll, the room is yo's."

Diggs set his coffee cup down. "You don't even know me, Sam. You met me a few minutes ago because I'd snuck into your shed, man. How can you offer me that?"

"I'd feel a heap worse if I didn't. We all get into bad times now an' again. Been there m'self and folks done right by me. I take you fo' an honorable man. Am I feelin' that right?"

Diggs looked bewildered. "Yeah. I try hard never to hurt people, Sam."

"Ain't much risk fo' an old man like me. I 'spect ya could use the help."

"I can, but would you let me pay you back for it?"

"Ain't gonna cost me nothin'. When folks help each other, it ain't s'posed to be with the thought o' bein' paid. It means later, when they get right on they feet again, they do the same. I'm payin' back the folks who helped me right now. Ya see?"

Diggs smiled. "I see."

* * *

Jack sat on his porch in the afternoon, drinking iced tea and playing his guitar. The peace that had eluded him in his music for several weeks was beginning to flow again, and his spirits were improving. When Sam came up the walkway with his dobro, he was surprised to see him accompanied by a young man Jack didn't recognize, who sported a bushy mustache, an unshaven look and a Maori forearm tattoo on each arm.

"It does me good to hear ya playin' with yo' soul, Jack." Sam said, walking up the steps. "It been awhile now that it ain't seemed to be so."

"It feels good, Sam." Jack set aside the guitar and stood up to greet them.

"I'd like ya t' meet my new friend, Anthony. He calls hisself Diggs, though. — Diggs, this here is my good friend, Jack."

Jack and Diggs shook hands. "Nice to meet you, Diggs. Can I offer you both some iced tea?" When they accepted the offer, he excused himself to bring it to them from the kitchen. He glanced at Diggs, who was staring across the street in the direction of Kate's house and appeared to be quite nervous. "Sugar? Lemon?" he asked.

"Both. Thanks, man."

When Jack returned with the drinks they all sat down. Sam took his dobro from its case and Diggs looked at it curiously. "Is that a resonator guitar?" he asked.

"That be exactly what it is, Diggs. Ain't many folks that know that." Sam seemed delighted.

"I like music. I've seen these played before in blues bands. They're cool. It looks like a regular guitar, but you hold it flat to play it."

"Do you play an instrument?" Jack asked.

"I play the drums."

Sam spoke up. "Well, that is *good* news, you bein' a musician." He turned to Jack. "Diggs is stayin' in my spare room for a spell. Ain't it fine that he plays music!"

Jack tried not to show his surprise. "When did you take on a boarder, Sam?"

"Early this mornin' when I found Diggs had been sleepin' in my tool shed."

Jack was alarmed. He worried that Sam had taken in a young homeless stranger who he knew so little about. "Well, Diggs, how did you come to be holed up in his tool shed? I've seen it and it isn't exactly luxurious." He smiled and tried to sound friendly as he probed for information.

"I ran into some tough times and had nowhere to stay. When I saw that the shed didn't have a lock on it, I sort of moved in. I only planned to do it quietly for a few days until I could find a place, man. I was packing up to leave early this morning when Sam found me." Diggs looked embarrassed as he spoke.

"I had t' talk him into stayin'." Sam added.

"Well, you couldn't find a nicer guy than Sam to help you out, Diggs. We go back a long way."

"I sure do appreciate it. I want you to know that I respect the offer. I won't abuse it, man." Diggs seemed to sense Jack's unrest and was attempting to put him at ease.

"I'm sure you'll be a welcome guest. Trust me, you can learn a thing or two from this man's wisdom." Jack exclaimed.

"I already have."

Jack relaxed and picked up his guitar. "Would you like to hear some tunes?" Diggs nodded. Sam started off with a soulful riff in the Piedmont blues style. Jack took up the tempo in the old ragtime rhythms of Blind Blake, and Diggs sat in full attention. None of them had seen Nick come up the walkway, toting his guitar. He waited silently for the song to end.

"Diggs?" Nick had an incredulous expression on his face.

Diggs turned toward Nick. "Uh — hi, Nick. You know these guys?"

"I was about to ask you the same question. What are you doing here?"

"Listening to some great music. I got to know Sam earlier this morning and he brought me over to meet Jack. Are they your friends?"

"Yeah. We jam together a lot."

Jack noted an undercurrent of tension between the two, putting him on alert. "Sit down, Nick. We're just getting to know our guest."

"Sure." Nick answered. Taking a seat across from Jack on the porch railing, he pulled his guitar from its case.

"I've never seen your acoustic. Never seen you play anything but the Stratocaster." Diggs looked curiously at Nick, as if a mask had just been removed.

Nick laughed. "You've never heard me play the kind of stuff we do here." Jack relaxed a bit seeing that they were obviously old friends with no animosities.

"Diggs told us he's a drummer." Jack stated. "Have you two played together before?"

They both smiled. Nick answered, "Many times. He's a great drummer."

Sam had been sitting back, watching their interaction.

"Mighta knowed you two was friends. Ain't it a kick? We should show this man what we do, ya know?" He started into another blues tune. Nick and Jack moved into the song and made it come alive. Diggs watched as each swapped breaks, adding their rich solo riffs and finally winding down to the finish with the ease of musicians who read each other's minds and hearts.

"That was amazing. How long have you been doing this, Nick?" Diggs was genuinely dumbfounded.

"Ever since Jack moved here back in April. Isn't the style great?" Nick seemed glad for his friend's approval.

"I always knew you were good, Nick, but this is killer stuff. Makes me wish I had drums." As he said this, his look became somber. Nick said nothing, but it was clear to Jack that a story lay under their silence.

"Has your playing together got anything to do with Brandon?" Jack decided to ask it straight up. The look on their faces answered Jack's question.

Nick replied. "Diggs was one of Brandon's roommates. He isn't anymore. When he realized what had happened to Jenny, he moved out. He didn't want any part of it or of Brandon." Nick carefully avoided any implication that Diggs had been around that day, but Jack was quick to note that Nick hadn't been around any places where he could have gathered that knowledge. He'd also observed that Nick would have needed help to move Jenny to his house, in the condition she'd been in that afternoon. He said nothing of these thoughts.

Jack looked at Sam, who seemed to have taken it all in before commenting. That was Sam's way. "I knowed you was an honorable man. You took t' livin' in my tool shed instead?"

"Once my car was towed." Diggs hung his head. "I wasn't trying to hide it, Sam. I didn't think there was a need to tell you."

"You lived in Sam's tool shed?" Nick was floored.

"Only at night. I didn't have anywhere else to go. I had no idea who he was or that you all knew each other."

Sam slapped his knee. "Well that done beat it all. Ya didn't know ya was runnin' t' friends. Ain't that jus' the way the good Lord works? He seen that you was okay fo' doin' what was right."

Jack turned to Nick. "Sam offered for Diggs to stay in a spare room." He waited carefully to see Nick's reaction.

"Cool!"

Jack was relieved, trusting Nick's honest endorsement.

೩ *35* ೫

"There's something about a good music store that makes your whole body want to wag a tail." Jack closed his eyes and breathed deeply as Nick smiled and chuckled. They had just entered a small music shop where the walls, shelves, and a good portion of the floor were filled with interesting instruments and quality sound equipment.

"Every time you walk in one with me we're spending your money. I guess that doesn't wag my tail quite as much." Nick wasn't sure why they were there. Jack had asked him to go along that morning, but had been vague about his purpose.

"Ah, but we're on a mission of mercy." Jack grinned. "I can't take another day of playing music while Diggs sits on the sidelines watching."

"You're buying a drum set?"

"Not exactly. A percussion set is more like it."

"What's that?"

They stood in front of a small line of conga and djembe drums. "You have an acoustic guitar. These are the more 'hands-on' version of modern drums."

"I don't know if Diggs knows much about these."

"Every percussionist should, as far as I'm concerned. Trust me, he'll be thrilled. You'll love what they'll add to the kind of songs you're writing. Let's call some help over, shall we?" Jack winked, then began a four-three rhythm on a large conga. Within moments a sales clerk appeared. Nick snickered.

They spent the next hour weighing the pros and cons of various congas, snares, cymbals and percussion devices. Nick had fun learning to stretch his natural talents into the realm of rhythmic sounds. They decided on a small collection that included a large and a medium sized conga, small snare, a cymbal, dual cowbells and chimes, completing the set with the associated hardware. He also opted for a djembe drum to give to Diggs as a portable instrument.

"This is quite a setup." Nick said when at last they loaded the equipment into Jack's van.

"It seemed like I needed to grow my collection of instruments to accommodate the needs of wayward musicians that keep showing up on my porch. Don't you think?" Jack raised his eyebrows. "Won't Diggs get a charge when he tags along with Sam this afternoon?"

"It sure fills up the back of the van. Isn't that a problem for you, Jack?" Nick asked slyly.

"Problem?"

"I mean, it's a lot to pick up and run with."

Jack closed the van doors and faced him. "Nick, I won't leave again like I did, without a word. I promise." He added as he shuffled the van key to his other hand, "I'm not even sure that I could ever leave again at all. I'm working on that. Will you trust me?" He offered him a handshake. Nick accepted it, then pulled Jack into a strong hug that settled all their unspoken feelings.

* * *

Diggs was more than just charged when he saw the percussion setup that afternoon. He was overwhelmed. Jack had

231

brought the instruments onto the porch and arranged them as best he could. When Sam and Diggs arrived shortly after lunch, Jack and Nick were already jamming. They stopped to watch the others approach. Diggs walked up the porch steps, then halted. He stared at the drums, then at Jack.

"Welcome to our music, Diggs. Care to take your place with us?" Jack's grin widened as he watched Diggs walk slowly toward the conga set, with a look of utter astonishment on his face.

"Jack, what did you do, man?" Diggs could barely get the words out.

"You ever play congas?" Jack asked. As if in reply, Diggs stood in position and began a lively Latin beat.

"Guess so, eh?" Nick chortled as he playfully slugged Jack's arm. "Hey, that sounds pretty cool, Diggs. I didn't know you played congas!" Diggs stopped to answer and admire the drums.

"It was the first kind of drums I ever played. My uncle was a cool dude and he played congas. Gave me lessons when I was just a short stack. Man, he was good! From then on, I wanted to play percussion. Took up the drums in school."

The joy on Diggs' face made Jack smile. "Well, now. There's a lot to be said for inspiring uncles. My Uncle Dan was a cool dude, too — taught me to love making music. He'd be so proud to see what's happening here now, on this porch. It's how his music lives on. It's his legacy."

"It do seem the old life o' this porch may be comin' back, don't it, Jack?" Sam was excited. He'd set his dobro case flat on the wide porch railing and was preparing to take it out to play. "Those days was special. The neighborhood had good things happenin'." He sat on the porch rail and began to warm up, playing lively, sliding blues riffs to the rhythm that Diggs had now moved into. Jack and Nick jumped in. The sound was full and bold.

As if in response to Sam's remark, a middle-aged couple walking down the street stopped in front of the house and listened to the improvisation. When the music finally ended, they clapped and gave a friendly wave, then continued on their walk.

Jack spoke loudly to them as they passed by. "All listeners are welcome here. Anytime you hear the music, just drop in and pull up a chair to listen, no matter how many people you see here. It's always open."

"Thank you!" They both turned to say this in unison. "We'll be back sometime," said the man.

"That be the way it starts!" Sam's eyes were twinkling. "You got the gift yo' uncle had, Jack."

"I only hope to have half his gift, and that'll do." Jack turned to Diggs. "That was fantastic! When I bought the congas, I wasn't sure if you knew much about them. I figured what you didn't know you could learn. A standard drum set didn't make much sense for the music we play here. Man, did you surprise me! Far more than I surprised you."

"It feels good to be on congas again. *Really* good!"

"Well, it's great to have you join us. What you do fits right in. Then again, I knew it would."

"Yeah!" Nick was tickled. "More! We need more!"

The music started up again. They all felt the tide of new beginnings, and the feeling moved deeply through the song.

ℰ𝒪 *36* 𝒞𝒮

Diggs waited, as he had each morning, for Sam to finish his prayer time before he headed downstairs to the kitchen. He felt it was important to respect the simple faith by which Sam lived — he knew he owed him at least that much. Diggs had also honored his promise to refrain from drug activity while he stayed at the house, including the making and selling of pipes, roach clips and other marijuana-related implements. That had felt like part of his promise, for some reason, even though Sam hadn't specifically required it. His inclination was to honor the gentle and kind man that had opened up his home and his life to help someone to whom he'd owed nothing. It was the first time ever that someone had believed in him.

Jack had helped Diggs retrieve his car from the towing impound. They had been relieved to find his computer and silversmith tools still safely in the trunk. Once he'd reconciled the overdue orders that had accumulated during the disruption, he'd worked diligently to expand his inventory of jewelry to compensate for the loss of sales in drug paraphernalia. Jack had also paid for the installation of fast internet access in Sam's home, asking in return that Diggs assist Sam with his online claim forms. He'd happily agreed.

Sam and Jack had both put their trust in Diggs, and he was determined to live up to it. He'd blown it in a lot of other areas in his life, but felt like he was being given a clean slate and a new direction. Thus, he used the quiet time of Sam's morning to fulfill online orders and work on new creations. The sense of peace he was feeling in his new situation was unlike any in his past experience.

That particular morning, however, Diggs was troubled. He'd visited Brandon in jail the previous afternoon and what he'd found had distressed him immensely. As soon as he heard Sam moving about in the kitchen, he went downstairs to help prepare breakfast.

"Mo'nin', Diggs. Gonna be a glorious hot day. We best done keep the drapes an' windows closed 'til the evenin' cool comes 'round." Like many houses in Portland, Sam's home was not air conditioned. It was seldom needed.

"Sure thing. How about I get the coffee going?"

"Ain't it funny how the hottest days still start best with a cup o' hot coffee?" Sam handed the coffee jar to Diggs.

They worked like a team to set out fresh fruit, yogurt, oatmeal and coffee for their morning meal. When they were seated, Diggs kept quiet while Sam took his usual moment of silence to give thanks. That morning, Diggs had even closed his eyes and bowed his heart, hoping that some residual strength of Sam's prayer might seep into his own disquiet. At the close of the prayer, he'd moved his lips to a soundless amen.

"You ain't said much since yesterday, Diggs. Ya got somethin' on yo' mind?" As usual, Sam didn't let things go unsaid. It was one of the hardest things for Diggs to get used to, but at the same time was something he admired. There was never an ill motivation for Sam's questions.

"I went and visited Brandon yesterday." He hadn't yet told anyone about it, but he felt that Sam had the best distance from it all to see things clearly.

"I know you was his housemate. Was ya close, too?"

"In a way. I talked more with him than I ever did with Benny, but none of us had a whole lot in common, other than the band and sharing the chores and rent. Brandon was always a lot friendlier to me." Diggs set his plate aside and twirled his coffee mug mindlessly in front of him. "But he wasn't too happy to see me at the jail."

"I 'spect he ain't feelin' good 'bout bein' locked up."

"It must be rough, man. He had a black eye and a swollen lip. Never said anything about it, and I didn't ask. He was pretty angry about me taking off the way I did, like I should have stuck around and been arrested."

"Don't let that get ya down, son. Ya didn't do nothin'."

"I know. That didn't bother me."

Sam sat back in his chair, frowning. "What got ya so troubled, then?"

"I dunno. It was the way he talked, not so much his words. Said I could go to hell with the rest of his family. I doubt he's getting much support from his mom. She didn't have a lot to do with him, anyway, even before this. They maybe talked three times the whole while I lived there."

"The boy done put hisself where he is. Still, family is what comes alongside, even when ya done wrong. It ain't right for him t' go this alone. You was doin' nice t' go see him there."

"He sure didn't think so. This is huge for him. He's gotten away with things he's done in the past, but this is too big to charm his way out of. I think he's scared — *real* scared. He expected to get away with it. I've never seen him the way he was yesterday. It's got me worried." Diggs took a sip of his coffee and brushed his fingers across his mustache.

"Worried? 'Bout what?"

"Something is really different in him – like – mean. Sinister.

Crazy. I dunno, man. His talk jumped all over the place. Some of it I understood and some was just rambling and weird. He mentioned Nick. He don't know about me living here or hanging with him. The way Brandon talked was spooky, man. Like Nick was a traitor and a liar. Then, like a coin flipped, he talked about going away — like he was planning a trip. There's something — not safe — going on in him. If he ever got out, I'd be scared for Nick."

Sam's brow furrowed deeply as he listened. He closed his eyes for a long moment before speaking. "It ain't likely t' happen. They's too much evidence and too much bail."

"Brandon has gotten away with so many things, it's hard to believe this one'll stick."

"Still, it ain't good for a body to be worryin' where there ain't no need." Sam paused to think. "Was Brandon doin' serious drugs?"

Diggs hesitated. He didn't want to lose Sam's respect by revealing too much about life at The Hanger, but he also felt compelled to be truthful. Sam was a kind man who seemed to be savvy beyond his simple ways. "The last few months it seems he was. He had a lot of access and connections. I just ignored it."

"You wasn't into the serious stuff?"

"No. Just pot. I saw what hard drugs did to my older brothers. One OD'ed and the other is in the pen."

"That's a hard way t' learn such a thing, but I'm right glad ya done learnt it. You become a good man." Diggs was glad Sam thought so and wished he could believe it himself.

"D'ya think the crazy way Brandon is talkin' is 'cause he ain't been getting' no drugs?" Sam asked.

"Man, I hadn't thought about it, but maybe. It does weird things to come down from crank cold turkey. And he's dealing with a lotta shi — uh — stuff. In a few weeks maybe he'll be getting past this."

"I 'spect that jail gives a body lotsa time t' think. He may start t' see things more real. Whoever caused his black eye may be takin' some o' that hate off o' Nick, too. Take the edge off for now."

"But sooner or later there'll be a trial. Nick'll have to testify. It may get ugly."

"They's things that best work themselves out in time, Diggs. We don't need t' worry. We jus' need t' pray."

"That's your department, Sam."

"Jus' the same, you kin be sayin' a little amen to it. God ain't that hard t' talk with. He ain't tucked away like the president."

Did he see me say that amen?

☙ *37* ❧

Jack and Nick walked into Tony's Place just after noon, when the lunch crowd was at its peak. Several of the cafe regulars heartily greeted them.

"Hey, when're you guys gonna join us down at the lake? The trout are so fat this year it takes a wheelbarrow to haul 'em home." Harv and Marv looked like twins that day, with red suspenders, white t-shirts and bellies overhanging their faded jeans.

"What time you heading out there these days?" Jack asked.

"Four-thirtyish, like always."

"Then you won't be seein' me anytime soon." Jack threw out his banter knowing good and well that their departure time was closer to six-thirty. It was still too early, as far as he was concerned. "I' got other fish to fry," he added, drawing loud, scattered groans.

They found a table in the corner by the window and Ruby soon came to take their orders. "The special today is a nice, lean corned beef on rye with my special cheesy potatoes. You like?"

"Hey, Ruby," Marv spoke up from his seat at the counter, "how come everything you serve is always cheesy?"

Ruby turned, her index finger waving. "I make things how you ask. You say cheesy things, so I be sure the menu has them for you."

"She gotcha there, pal!" Harv guffawed heartily, pulling the brim of Marv's hat down over his eyes. Jack and Nick also laughed. They both ordered burger platters.

"Make those burgers *cheesy*, wouldja please, Ruby?" Jack winked.

"*Madonna!*" She protested as she returned to the kitchen.

It was then that Jack caught the stares of two young men seated at a table in the opposite corner. They weren't amused. He watched as they rose and threw money on the table, leaving the cafe with their meals half finished. He recognized one of them from the group of boys who had threatened Nick on the porch.

Nick hadn't noticed them. He was in a better mood than Jack had seen for a long time, so he decided not to mention what he'd observed. Still, it had made him uneasy.

It wasn't long before they were eating their burgers and talking idly of porch jams, performance tips and how Diggs was fitting nicely into their music. Any talk of recent events was avoided altogether. Jack made a mental note to ask Nick about his interest in fly fishing, but he didn't want to bring it up at that moment. There were too many ears willing to join in on that discussion, and he wanted to keep the conversation between the two of them. They finished their meal and stayed quite awhile, just talking. Nick sipped on several refills of soda, looking relaxed. At last, Jack went to the counter to pay for their lunches while Nick drained his glass and chose to wait outside. The lunchroom was busy, and it took quite a few minutes before Ruby noticed Jack and moved to the cash register to take his money.

When he finally walked outside, Nick was nowhere in sight. He looked down both directions of the sidewalk, then thought perhaps he'd walked into the market. As he moved toward the entrance he heard distant voices coming from the parking lot around the corner of the store. One of the voices sounded like Nick's. He looked down the side of the building.

Nick was standing with his back against the wall at the far corner of the store. The small parking lot was full of cars, making it difficult to see what was happening from the street. A young man with curly blond hair was facing him in a stance that couldn't be mistaken for friendly. He stood a good head taller than Nick and looked to be several years older. The two boys Jack had seen earlier were leaning against a car a few yards from them, with their backs toward Jack, watching the encounter. The voices were barely loud enough for him to hear what they were saying.

"Don't hand me that shit, Nick!" The blond man's tone was hostile. "I never did buy your little saint act. The only reason I ever trusted you was 'cause of Brandon. Shit, you sure proved how you can screw your good buddies."

Nick was standing his ground. "I never did anything to you, Benny. Brandon either..."

"You brought the cops down on us! Twice! I've had to pay a whole shitload of money 'cause of you, ya little twerp."

"Whatya mean? I never called the cops!"

"That night when you conveniently left the party a few minutes before they arrived? You think I didn't know? We never saw you again after that. Don't tell me you didn't narc on us, you fuckin' pussy!" Benny poked his finger into Nick's shoulder for emphasis.

"I didn't! The loud music brought the cops, not me!"

"Well there sure as hell wasn't any loud music when they showed up at my door the other day."

"Brandon *raped* Jenny, dude! Her *parents* reported it."

"How the fuck did they know it happened? Who told? Why do the cops think I sold him a roofie? You think I'm *stupid?*"

Jack didn't like where this was going. He turned and went quickly back into the cafe, wishing he had the habit of carrying his cell phone with him. Not wanting to create a scene of gawkers, he quietly asked Ruby if he could use the phone in the kitchen, then called 911 and reported an altercation in the market's parking lot. When he left the cafe, he went to the opposite side of the building and around the back wall. Standing just out of sight around the corner, he listened.

Nick's voice was now filled with fear. "I swear to God, Benny, I'm not a snitch. I'm not a narc. I don't work with the cops. Please!"

Jack stepped out from behind the corner, just a few feet from where they stood. Benny and Nick both turned at the same time to look at him. Benny held a pistol to Nick's belly.

"Who the fuck are you?" Benny's initial look of surprise turned into a menacing sneer.

"Nick's friend." The answer came from the youth Jack had recognized earlier. "Sorry, man. I thought he was gone." He seemed uncomfortable. "Shit, this is outta hand." The other one turned to talk discreetly with his pal.

As Jack stared at them, Benny quickly grabbed Nick's collar, pinning him to the wall, and turned the gun toward Jack. "You walked into the wrong scene, dude. I got a score to settle with this little shit. You get to be part of it. Get over here. *Now!*"

Nick's face was white. "Run, Jack!"

"*Shut up, puke!*" Benny didn't take his eyes off Jack as he shouted.

"Easy, now. I don't have a gun." Jack lifted his open hands to shoulder height as he stepped toward them. The parking lot was hemmed in by tall hedges that blocked any side views from the street. He worried about what would happen when the police arrived, if this could even last that long. His eyes stayed focused on Benny, waiting for any opportunity to shift the control.

242

The two punks had had enough. "Hey, Benny, this is your deal, man. We're gonna jet. Ain't our score to settle. We done our part — just — keep the money, man." Their part was obviously to tell Benny where to find Nick and to get paid. They were probably even good for some idle threats, but this threat was no longer idle. They weren't about to go to prison for accessory when it wasn't even their problem. As they slunk out of the lot, Benny never said a word and never took his eyes off Jack. He kept Nick pressed to the wall with his fist. Jack didn't like what he saw, as if something irrational had taken over.

Nick seemed strengthened by Jack's presence. "You can believe me or not, Benny. I never did anything wanting to hurt you. All I wanted was the band. The music. That's all. We were making that happen, remember? That's what kept me there. We aren't great friends, Benny, but you aren't my enemy. You've never been my enemy." Even with these words, Benny's eyes never shifted from Jack. He didn't see Nick as his target at this point, but he seemed indecisive on what to do. It was one thing to be angry enough to threaten. It was another to follow through.

A car left the parking lot. None of them had noticed anyone walk up. Jack wondered if the driver had seen what was going on as they left. He doubted it, or they'd have either left in a hurry or backed away on foot. A minute or two went by and no one moved or spoke. A few times Benny shot momentary glances at Nick. One of those times he'd said, "You fuckin' turd," in a voice bitter with malice.

It was a police cruiser pulling into the lot that finally broke Benny's attention for a split second. A momentary warble of the siren sounded and the door opened. As Benny turned his head for a quick side glance, Jack sprang into action. He lunged at the gun arm and grabbed it in a two-handed grip, yanking it backward and away from him and Nick. He attempted a kick to the groin at the same time, but the kid was young and fast. Benny let go of Nick and began a struggle for the weapon with all his muscle. He was strong and Jack was barely able to keep the gun from swinging inward toward him.

Jack managed a throaty yell. "Get *outta* here, Nick!"

Nick backed away, mesmerized by the fight for the gun. The patrolman's weapon was now drawn and aimed. He yelled, "This is the police! Drop the gun *now* and put your hands on your heads." Without looking at Nick, he yelled, "Take cover, kid!"

Nick shouted, "It's the blond guy! Don't shoot Jack!"

In one swift move, Benny found control and wrestled Jack into a headlock with the gun pointed at his temple. He backed against the wall holding Jack in front of him. Benny was scared and breathing fast and hard.

The patrolman stood behind the cruiser's open door in a shooting stance. He was no longer yelling. "Stay calm and put the gun down. Nobody has to get hurt here."

"I'm going to my car!" Benny's voice was shaking. "Don't try to stop me! I'll kill this asshole, I swear I will." He started to slide along the wall toward the front of the building, dragging Jack with him. A small pipe sticking out from the wall caught his pant leg. He stumbled.

Jack felt the headlock grip loosen and in one sweeping motion he jammed his elbow into Benny's stomach and jerked himself free, lunging to the ground. Instinctively, Benny swung the gun toward Jack.

Two shots rang out, and the fight was over.

Nick watched with horror as Benny's eyes flew open wide, then slowly went dead as his life ebbed away and he slumped to the asphalt.

❧ *38* ☙

When the doorbell rang at eight in the morning Jack was tempted not to answer. The last two days he'd had a lot of official visitors asking him to recount the incident at Tony's Place and the events which he'd just as soon start putting to rest. Added to his last few restless nights, the result was a weariness he was unable to shake. Resignedly, he plodded to answer the door.

His heart quickened when he saw Kate. She was dressed in jeans and a white shirt tied at the waist, and her hair was braided loosely back. She looked about as tired as he felt, but she looked good all the same. He smiled and invited her in.

They made their way to the breakfast nook. To Jack, that was somehow a special spot — the place where their turning points always seemed to happen. There was an undercurrent today that made him hope for another, but this one a good one, not like the last.

When Kate sat down, Jack noticed her red, swollen eyes. She'd been crying. It wrenched him deep in his gut. He reached across the table to grab her hand, and she let him. It was a good sign.

"Everything okay with Nick?" The boy had been through a lot more than Jack. Being threatened at gunpoint was bad enough, but watching a friend die in front of his eyes was as tough as it gets.

"He's still asleep. He's handling things better than I am. What's in my imagination is far worse than having seen it."

Her eyes were tearing up and she broke from Jack's clench to grab a tissue from her pocket. "I can't help thinking about what might have happened. I thought the worst things in the world were Jenny's rape and the trial, but this..." Her voice faltered as she choked back the tears. He leaned across the table to lay the backside of his curled fingers against her cheek. She reached up to gently cup his hand against her face.

"Everything's okay now. You know that, don't you?" Jack's voice was soft. He tried to sound reassuring. What Jack knew was that he was seeing the weeping heart of a mother — a mother whose son was alive while another woman's son lay cold. He took her hand in his once again.

She looked deeply into Jack's eyes. "How can I thank you? I can't say words for what it means, what you did. Things could have gone so differently. I could have lost him. Or — you. When I think that I kept Nick away from you for so long — thought that it was best...," her face contorted in deep, sorrowful pain.

"I did what any man does to protect someone he loves. I'd have done it for Sam. I'd have done it for you, Kate. It'll take time, but we'll get past this. We're gonna be okay."

They sat there holding hands, without speaking, for a very long time. The silence was healing.

* * *

It had taken more than a week to push through all the questioning and paperwork. Most of the time Nick had been numb. It was the first time someone close to him had died, and the terrible circumstances had left him with a feeling that he was somehow responsible. The story had made it to the papers, with a brief mention on the local news. The officer involved in the shooting was on routine suspension of duties during the investigation. Nick's name hadn't been publicly released, as a minor, but the neighborhood buzzed with the story, and it was hard to get away from it.

Nick joined Jack, Sam and Diggs on the porch one afternoon. Fall was approaching, bringing with it the return to school and the threat of Brandon's trial. He knew that opportunities to meet for midday jams would very soon be limited. Nick couldn't help the lingering heaviness that hovered over his thoughts and his music. He couldn't shake the sadness that Benny would never again pick a hard-driving bass beat to a song, and would never have the chance to grow older, or to laugh, or to love.

After their third song, Nick set aside his guitar and took a long drink from his glass of lemonade. The mood between them all was somber.

It was Sam who spoke first. "Some things we gotta go through is hard. They's so hard they take the soul right outta the heart an' the song."

Diggs moved away from the congas to sit on the porch railing and stare into the yard. Nick wondered if the same sort of thoughts were pressing on his mind. "How you holding up, Diggs?"

"I'm wondering how things changed so fast, man. I'm wondering if I can keep up. I'm angry, man. Angry that a few stupid moves can do so much. Dude, people think they can do anything at all, without any thinking, and somehow they'll just keep going on the way they were." He paused, then looked over at Nick. "You didn't deserve this. Neither did Jenny."

"Ev'r bad action has a price. The learnin' o' that is hard. They stay with us like a debt we owe and we pay and pay like it ain't never 'nough. Ya got it right, Diggs. Nick and Jenny be payin' fo' trouble they didn't invite." Sam noticed Jack's silence that day. He knew Jack, too, had paid more than his share for evils done.

Nick dug his nails into the bottom of his chair, as if he would fall if he didn't. "That may be true for Jenny, Sam, but I did my part to invite it. I thought I could keep on the sidelines around a lot of things I knew weren't right."

"I'm more to blame than you on that, Nick." Diggs countered. "Man, I knew a lot more about what Benny and Brandon were doing and just ignored it. I saw an uglier side of Benny than you even know." He turned toward Jack and Sam. "And I need to tell the truth. I was in that house when Brandon brought Jenny home. I was so used to ignoring his games with underage girls that I ignored it that day, too. He preyed on them, but I just kept believing they were all willing to put out, so who cares? I needed to care, man. But I didn't. You did, Nick. You had courage. He planned to get away with it, but you made sure he didn't."

"I wonder. If it hadn't been Jenny, would I have done anything? Does anyone else deserve that? I also wonder if, in some sick way, Brandon did what he did to get back at me for abandoning the band. He knew how I felt about Jenny."

Sam moved into their thoughts. "At yo' age ya spend time mostly findin' out what's right. That be what youth is fo' — book learnin' an' life learnin'. That don't never stop, but getting' older means ya learn to *do* what's right 'cause ya *know* it is. Ya learn the reasons. Ain't ever'body would say it like yo' sayin' it now. Some jus' don't never learn nothin'. Don't even try. But you done learnt somethin'. It ain't right to kick y'self fo' not doin' somethin' back then, 'cause ya didn't *learn* it 'till now." Sam's body was bent forward in the seriousness of his words. "But now ya know. Ya learnt it hard, too. Ya learnt that bein' on the sidelines ignorin' what's wrong ain't no good place t' be. We can avoid evil and we can fight evil, but when we ignore evil and jus' live with it, we be the sorriest souls on God's green earth. So, what that makes ya do in the future is gonna be yo' character shinin' up. And, Lord

248

knows, ya both got lotsa character."

Through all the talk, Jack said nothing. He thought that, just maybe, Sam was the wisest man he would ever know.

* * *

When Sam showed up later in the evening at Jack's door, with dobro case in hand, Jack needed no persuasion. There were things that were best worked out in song. They settled in across from each other on the porch, in the last of the day's light, but Sam didn't reach right away for his instrument.

"You was awful quiet this afternoon, Jack."

"You said it so well, Sam. There wasn't much for me to contribute."

Sam scratched his ear and looked at the ground. "They needed t' know what you was feelin', son."

"I'm not sure that knowing my feelings would've helped a whole lot."

"That mean ya don't know 'em y'self yet?"

Jack gave him a sideways look. "You never miss a beat, old man."

"They was a pow'rful lack o' soul in the song today. I know ya felt it, same as me. These young'uns done had too many things thrown in the road they ridin' on. Ya may not like it an' ya may not see it, Jack, but they look t' ya t' see how ya handle things. They respect you. What ya done here on this porch lately makes a diff'rence t' 'em. I ain't sayin' it t' push. It just be fact. They's feelin' a whole new song in 'em, an' I ain't jus' talkin' 'bout the music."

"There hasn't been a whole lot of time to put things in perspective, Sam." He felt uncomfortable at the idea that his influence was something more permanent than momentary, more important than casual, requiring a bigger part of him than he'd ever before been asked to give.

"Sometimes it ain't good t' let time shape how things look o' where they need t' go. It be like an open wound needin' balm t' keep it from festerin' an' goin' bad. When the feelin' is raw, the need t' change goes deep. Bad healed scars jus' get in the way and stay ugly."

"Where're you going with this, Sam?"

Sam looked him in the eye. "The things that be changin' here wouldn't o' been happenin' without ya, Jack. Yo' actin' like slidin' 'em under the carpet's gonna work. They's a whole lotta kids, jus' like Nick and Diggs right now, tryin' t' make sense o' it all. They was all hangin' out at the same place, an' now that place ain't there no mo'. It was a place t' belong. It weren't a good place, but it was there. Another'll come along by an' by but that ain't happened yet." Sam paused to pull his dobro from its case.

"You know what this here place done fo' ya back when yo' uncle took that on? Same as it's done fo' Nick and Diggs. Now, ya'll had a pow'rful lesson dealt t' ya. Maybe while things is still raw, you can make it count fo' them, an' some others, too. Maybe this be the place fo' that t' happen."

"You may not know what you're asking, Sam. The troubles of kids today run even darker and deeper than they did in my youth. It isn't as easy as it might seem."

"So, it ain't easy. That means you jus' give up without tryin'? I ain't sayin' ev'r kid's gonna take t' it. Most don't play music, but they all wanna hear it. They all wanna belong somewhere. They deserve a chance t' see things 'nother way, too. Then they got a choice. Maybe they jus' ain't had no choice b'fore."

"I need to think more about what you're saying, Sam. And I

promise I will. For now, let's play some music. We both need it." He knew he wasn't avoiding the subject. It was too important to ignore. Sam seemed to know that, too.

Jack lit the lantern on the porch as the gloom of twilight was fading to dark. The days were getting shorter now and the nights more brisk. Sam tuned his dobro to an open D, playing pieces of songs to set each string to pitch. There was something comforting to Jack about the moment, with just the two of them there. It had been a long time since they'd shared songs alone — since the first days after he'd arrived. With all that had happened and the heaviness in their hearts, they both needed to make a special time of simplicity and peace. He took up his guitar and they moved, yet again, into the gentle dance of deep-felt song. The moment turned into an hour, and then another. It was the chill of the night that eventually ended their song time.

"It won't be long before it's too cold for outdoor jams." Jack watched Sam put away his instrument. "If we wanted to continue this and invite more people, we'd need to move it somewhere warmer. You think maybe the old garage might work for that?"

Sam's gentle face raised toward Jack and his eyes were smiling. "That 'd do nice, Jack. Right nice."

'Tis the gift to be simple,

'Tis the gift to be free,

'Tis the gift to come down where we ought to be,

And when we find ourselves in the place just right,

It will be in the valley of love and delight.

When true simplicity is gained,

To bow and to bend, we will not be ashamed

To turn, turn, will be our delight,

'Til by turning, turning, we come round right.

— Simple Gifts (a traditional song)

ℬ 39 ℭ

It had been hard work to empty the detached garage that bordered the alley and had taken nearly a week. The contents Jack sifted through had been hauled to the dump, the local salvage store, or the basement of the house. What remained was an empty shell with a cement floor. It was a solid, 2x12 framed structure with a sturdy roof, but the inside walls needed to be gutted. He was glad he'd waited until the heat of late summer had passed to tackle it.

With sledgehammer and crowbar at hand, he surveyed sections of the interior that were rough-finished with old, wide boards, with some areas covered in plaster. The job had been crudely done over an extended period of time, with no planning other than to create wall spaces for the hanging of tools and utility shelves. None of it showed his uncle's workmanship. He decided to start on one side of the garage door and work his way to the other, piling the junk material in the middle of the floor for hauling while stacking the best boards to the side for reuse.

Toward the back of the building under a low shelf he discovered a shorter board near the floor, which wasn't attached to anything else. A small hole drilled to one side allowed it to be pulled back from the rest of the wall. Behind it was a metal box about eight inches deep and fifteen inches square. A small, ornate padlock hung from a hasp that secured it. It was locked. He shook the box gently and found that there were things inside. Someone had taken special care to keep the box hidden where no one

253

would think to look.

He was about to use the crowbar to pry open the hasp when he remembered the small key sitting in a jar in the windowsill of the breakfast nook. It, too, had been ornate and carefully hidden.

Jack took the box to the kitchen and sat down at the table. He picked up the jar, opened it, and dropped the key into his hand. It fit the lock, but it took some strength to twist open the old mechanism.

The box was filled with a variety of items that someone had undoubtedly kept as treasures. A ceramic-faced doll with a blue lace dress lay on top of the contents, covering items which he took out one by one: a small metal box containing a ball and jacks; wooden matchboxes full of beads, metal toys and old coins; several faded award ribbons from unknown events; a yellowed handkerchief wrapped around a lock of blond hair and six baby teeth; faded, black and white photos of people he didn't recognize, from the early 1900's; a book of poems; three carved wooden ponies; a silver baby spoon; and four small journals filled with writing.

He opened one of the journals and began to scan it, hoping to determine the owner of the box. It didn't take long to discover that all four journals had been written by his mother, as a young girl. He'd spent the remainder of the afternoon reading each of them. He'd read them twice.

The second time through, he'd wept.

ട 40 രു

Nick was half awake when the phone rang early on a Saturday morning. Now that his senior year had begun he wasn't as quick to rise on the weekend. It hadn't taken long for teachers to start piling on the homework, and he'd waited until Sunday morning to tackle his assignments. That morning he'd rolled over and decided to sleep for another hour.

A few minutes later his mother knocked at the bedroom door. Nick was tempted to ignore it and pretend to be asleep, but his stomach was beginning to grumble and he hoped she was thinking about making breakfast. He grunted his greeting and told her to come in, but didn't turn back over to face her. The bedside moved downward as she sat at the edge, and he felt her lay a warm hand on his back.

When nothing was said for a long moment, he turned over to look at her. There were tears in her eyes. He panicked. "What's wrong?"

"We have more bad news, baby."

He dreaded what might come next — the news was obviously very hard. His mother gathered herself to tell him, and the pause was unbearable. Was it Jenny? Jack? Sam?

"That was Jenny's parents on the phone." His heart sank to his stomach and his mind reeled. "They got a call from their lawyer earlier this morning. Brandon was found dead in his jail cell yesterday."

Nick was ashamed that he felt an emotionless sense of relief without sorrow. Nothing more had happened to Jenny. When the reality of what he'd heard hit him, he was surprised to remain so numb. "Why are you crying, mom? I didn't think you cared about him."

"I care about you, son. You've been through so much. I hated bringing you even more to deal with. It's true I didn't care for Brandon, but I didn't want him to die."

"How? What happened?"

She paused again. "He'd made a homemade knife of some sort. He slit his wrists."

Nick wasn't shocked. His mind went back to the last look he'd seen in Brandon's eyes, when Nick had told him that he lacked the courage to kill himself. That had somehow changed, but it'd been true enough on that day. Brandon had never learned how to face real consequences. Now he never would.

"Is Jenny okay?" He worried about the effect the news would have on her.

"She's fine, honey. There won't be a trial now. That could be the best thing, really, as bad as this is. Jenny's parents didn't want him to die, either, but there's still a sense of relief. They hated what she was about to go through. And I dreaded that you had to testify against a friend, as horrible as his actions were."

"Does it make me a monster if I say I'm glad it's over?"

"If it does, then we're both monsters, son."

256

෨ *41* ෫

Jack slid the stack of journals over to Kate. They sat across from each other in the breakfast nook — he was conscious again of that significance — drinking coffee on Sunday morning. She'd called to tell him of Brandon's death and he'd asked her to visit.

"What do we have here?" The way her eyebrows playfully furrowed as she asked was disarmingly lovely to Jack.

"The voice of a young girl. My mother."

"Your mother? How long have you had these?"

"I found them two days ago in a locked treasure box. It was hidden in the wall of the garage. Remember the key we found in the pantry? It fit."

Kate examined the books carefully, skimming through random pages. What she saw caused her to stop and look at Jack. "You've read them?"

Jack stared at the table for a long moment before nodding his head and looking up at her. "Several times. You can read them, too, if you want."

"Maybe. I'd like you to tell me about them."

Jack closed his eyes for a moment. "They start when she was ten. They're not daily diaries, just scattered entries." He paused in a long silence. Kate remained still, gazing calmly at his effort to gather his thoughts.

"She missed my grandfather after he died. He was special to her. She felt misunderstood by her mother — my grandmother.

She loved my Uncle Dan immensely. He'd come back to live at the house. The first entries are just the thoughts of the average young girl." Jack sipped his coffee as if he needed it to continue the story. "Then things changed. Each day when my uncle and grandmother went to work, they'd left my mom with the couple who lived next door — Lenny and Maggie. I knew Lenny when I was a boy. He played upright bass a lot, right here on the porch. We called him Laid-Back Lenny because he never worked hard at anything. Maggie was the breadwinner of the family. She left the house for her swing shift job each day at two." He stopped.

"And...?"

"Lenny began molesting my mother when she was twelve. By the time she was thirteen, he was having full intercourse with her regularly. He'd made her feel she was born to be a bad girl when eventually she began to enjoy what he did to her. He'd convinced her that her mother and brother would both have to die if they ever found out. She was scared to death something would happen. Her entries make it sound like she'd go home some days dreading that she'd find them dead."

"Dear God." Kate's eyes were moist with tears.

"It continued until she got pregnant at fifteen. That was when my uncle and grandmother sent her to a private home for unwed mothers in California. The baby would be born there and adopted out. Sam once told me it had cost them a lot to do that, but they were trying to save her reputation — what little remained by then. She wouldn't tell them who'd fathered the child. She was known to be loose with boys at school, so they assumed it was a result of that. They were worried."

"Lenny was the father, wasn't he?"

"Yes. My mom was a looker and at twelve she'd started developing. It's probably what prompted Lenny to take up with her eventually. Before the early molestations became full sex, she was also dealing with attention from older boys at school. She started acting on what she was learning to do and was caught a few times. My grandmother gave her a sex talk which, unfortunately, reinforced that only bad girls do the things she'd been doing, and only good girls got married. The talk had halted the activity with the young boys at school, but Lenny was cagey and seductive, and things got heavy. It seems, at least, that he'd used condoms, and it took a couple of years for that mode of protection to fail." He paused with pain in his eyes.

"When it did, they sent her away. Was the baby adopted out?" Kate was bracing herself to hear that the baby was Jack.

"That's what the staff at the home told Uncle Dan. By then my grandmother had died. My mother believed it was her fault. She didn't talk about the birth in her journals, so it's hard to say what actually happened to the baby. Mom didn't return immediately after that. She told Uncle Dan she'd been offered a job at the home and wanted to stay there."

Wasn't she a little too young to be living on her own in California?"

"The private home for unwed mothers was a front. They also ran a brothel on the side, for select girls. She describes the kind of things she was taught and what they made her do. It's where she learned to seduce men for money. She was very beautiful and alluring, so I'm sure she made a whole lot of money for them over the few years she was there. That's where I was conceived."

Tears rolled down Kate's cheeks. She stroked the fabric on the journals as if in some way it was comforting Jack's mother.

"It was her pregnancy with me that brought her back here. She didn't want to give me up for adoption or abort me. She didn't want to raise me in a whorehouse, either, so she ran away from the home. There are entries written directly to me before I was born, telling me that she would never give me up, wanting to keep me and love me. She knew if she'd ever told the truth about the home to Uncle Dan it would have destroyed him. She was right. It would have killed him to know what he'd sent her into."

"The last of the entries are from shortly after she arrived back home. Lenny had tried to take back up with her, and she'd at last called him the miserable son-of-a-bitch that he was and threatened to tell Maggie about the child. At the very least, the home had made her bold and given her a kind of power. Once she left this house, she vowed never to return to the neighborhood, and she never did. She lived off of the attention she'd learned to get from men. She must have left the journals behind. Maybe she even hoped that one day they'd be found and her voice would be heard."

Jack rose from his seat and went to the coffee pot with his mug, where he stood silently, motionlessly, as if trying to remember why he had walked there.

Kate got up and went to his side, placing her hand on his back. "And you found them."

"I found more than that. I heard the voice of a little girl as she struggled to make sense of confusing things happening to her. I found out why she became who she was. I found the true heart of my mother."

Jack turned toward Kate with tears in his eyes. She wrapped her arms around him as he began to sob. They held each other tightly for a long while, until slowly the embrace became a kiss. Not a kiss of passion, but one of deep longing and tenderness, of things unsaid yet desperately waited for, and needed, and desired.

* * *

Late one evening Sam sat in Jack's living room, talking over the finding of the journals. Sam was deeply disturbed to learn of the things that had happened and his complete ignorance of them during those days.

"All that time Lenny sat playin' his bass t' yo' uncle's fiddle, my dobro, yo' guitar. We never knowed. It weren't right that he kept his secret and watched what we all knowed you and yo' mama was goin' through. It weren't right. He done that like it was nothin'." Sam shook his head with great sorrow furrowing his brow.

"My mother never wanted to come to Uncle Dan's. She shunned it completely and I never thought about why. It was always some man she was with who dropped me off gladly at the doorstep. I'd always hated it, but I never questioned the reason. Uncle Dan probably thought she was avoiding Aunt Eva's condemnation. I guess I did, too."

"I seen the difference in yo' mama. I seen it when she come back. She took t' her ways, but she loved you the best she could know how, when you was born."

"I wish I'd known. You were right, Sam. Young girls don't choose to take on loose ways on their own." Jack said with remorse.

"The heart of a woman runs deep, Jack. It's meant for one man. In a way, you was that man for her. She gave up on all the others easy, like she was taught, but she kept you, Jack, the best way she knowed how, she kept t' one man."

"It seems so." Jack paused to gather his thoughts. He looked directly at Sam for a long, silent moment. "Sam, I have something to ask you."

Sam looked warily at Jack. "It's big?"

"It is. It looks like I'll be staying around for good. I know now that I want that. And I want Kate to be part of my life. Can you help me handle it? A long term relationship isn't something I know anything about, but I know that you do."

Sam's eyes flew wide open with surprise. He clapped his hands together and rocked back in his chair as he said, "Praise be, I ain't never heard such a grand question. It ain't one you even need t' ask me, Jack. It surely is my answer to prayer come at last."

Jack chuckled. "I guess God listens to old dobro players and fools, eh Sam?"

"He do, indeed. Does Nick know 'bout it?"

"Not yet. Do you think he'll be okay with it?"

"He'll be grinnin' that big grin o' his. Yo' the only daddy he's ever had. Might as well be with his mama. Are you plannin' t' tie the knot?"

"That's too big a leap to even think about yet. We need time to get past all that's happened and mend. It's a big step for me, you know. Her, too, in a way."

"I do know that, indeed." Sam's look became serious. "You done figured out yo' heart about Kate?"

"Well, Sam, I just told you I want to be with her. Doesn't that say a lot about how I feel?"

"Hear me out, son. I seen the struggle you been havin' over a woman's love. Kate's a woman that only got the heart t' give herself to one man. You seein' it that way now, son?"

"I've always seen it that way, Sam. That's why I ran."

"There ain't no room fo' doubt in you about this, Jack. Ain't no room for runnin' neither, not no mo'. This world ain't kind toward the nat'ral way a woman's heart bends."

Jack was uncomfortable. "What are you trying to say, Sam?"

"I ain't been one t' judge how folks take t' courtin' nowadays. I seen a lot o' changes in what goes on in my time, but I ain't never believed they was good fo' the soul. Not fo' a woman and not even fo' a man. That ain't pop'lar to say, but deep truth us'ally ain't these days. They's a pow'rful thing happens when love is set t' waitin', an' it don't happen no other way." Sam paused to let his words settle in. He saw that Jack looked puzzled.

"Let me say it plain. I'm asking if ya plan on takin' Kate t' yo' house and yo' bed b'fore ya take her t' the altar." Sam looked intently at Jack.

"That surely is plain, Sam." Jack was taken aback.

"In my youth that weren't even a question that needed t' be asked. Marriage weren't no piece o' paper that said yo' things and kids got shared legal-like and yo' wife got her a new name. A weddin' night was mo' than just a vacation from work. Folks knew they was makin' a deep change. A sacred change."

Jack hadn't given much thought to the real reasons for marriage. In fact, they had seemed obscure and rather perfunctory, being merely a legal promise to stay together. He intended to stay with Kate, but the question of how that commitment would be approached sexually or legally hadn't yet arose. He and Kate had only just reconciled and declared their feelings for each other. The idea of marriage was way too new for him. It made him uneasy.

Jack smiled. "Are you being my father here, Sam?"

Sam remained serious. "I s'pose I am, Jack. My daddy had the talk with me b'fore I married my Lucille. When we was married, our weddin' night was special. Real special. Yo' my friend, Jack, but you ain't never had no daddy to give you the talk. I know my ways is old, but you ain't never gonna convince me that they ain't fo' today no mo'. And that goes double fo' you mo' than most, Jack. A wife ain't never gonna be no whore in any man's eyes — not even fo' you. Ya feel what I'm sayin', son?"

"Yes, Sam. I feel it deep."

ℬ 42 ℭ

The work to convert the detached garage into a small music venue was progressing nicely. The soundproofing insulation had been covered with sheet rock and textured, and sound-deadening windows, high above eye level, had been installed and trimmed out. Jack had chosen a variety of deep, rich colors to give the place a festive mood, and a stage riser at one end covered a myriad of cables that allowed sound equipment and lighting to be controlled from the far corner of the room. Electrical outlets lined the walls and were recessed into the stage. A security system was also wired in.

Nick was helping Jack install a series of small stage lights that would be suspending from the ceiling by an adjustable support. Their conversation was light and filled with anticipation about the music that would be happening there.

"Will the porch jams move into here?" Nick's question was wistful. He'd come to love the activity being on the front porch.

"Not unless it's too cold to be out there. The porch jams are too important. The best way to get neighbors involved is to be out where people can see us. The garage will be for scheduled house concerts, winter weather or whenever it feels right to move the music here. We used to spread out onto the lawn years ago, when a group of listeners or jammers got too big, but the weather doesn't always cooperate in the northwest."

"House concerts? You mean like a band playing at a party?"

"Not like that at all. They're actual concerts. A lot of artists love to do house concerts, even some that are more widely known. About thirty or forty people buy tickets and show up, just like a concert held at a small commercial venue. The laws are okay on residential concerts as long as they don't happen too often and don't disturb the neighbors. If all the money goes to the performer, it keeps it non-commercial and legal for zoning laws. They're often done just for the love of supporting good music."

"That's so cool! I've never heard of them."

"They aren't widely promoted. It means we have to work on creating a community of folks who want to participate."

"Like how?"

"The word gets out. Festivals, porch jams, other concerts, a web site, social media. You'll be surprised how things can happen."

Jack frowned as he examined the rigging for the lights. "We need more mounting bolts. I thought I had enough." He looked at Nick. "You wanna take my van and fetch some at the hardware store?"

Nick was taken by surprise. "I'm not allowed to drive. I don't have insurance."

"You have a license?"

"Yeah. Got it last year, but the rates are too high for mom to put me on her policy."

"Hmm. It'd sure be nice for you to be able to drive. Now that you're getting a little stubble growing on your face you may just be old enough to drive, too." Jack took a friendly jab.

"Hey, whatya mean? The stubbles been there a long time, but I just quit shaving it. It takes forever for it to grow, but who cares? It's the look, you know?"

"Yeah, it is. Looks great on you, Nick. Tell you what, I'm gonna talk to your mom about helping to get you the insurance."

"Really?!"

The kid in Nick had poked through once again, right through his shadowy beard. Jack laughed. "Yes, really. I think I can talk her into it. I'm sure she could use the help with you driving."

Just then Jenny appeared at the open garage door, wearing a flowery dress and sandals and looking very pretty. When Nick looked up and saw her, his eyes gleefully widened, causing Jack to turn and welcome her. "Hello, Jenny. Don't you look lovely today. Glad you dropped by. Come in and see what Nick's helping me do to this place."

Jenny smiled and glanced around the room. "It looks great. I like the colors; they're so fun." Her expression became shy. "I was hoping to find you here, Nick."

Nick rose and moved across the room to where Jenny stood. "How are you doing?" he asked. "Your mom called mine a couple of times to say you're fine, but I was hoping to hear it from you. I'm glad you came over. I haven't seen you in school."

"I'll be there starting next week. My teachers have been sending assignments home the last couple of weeks — my folks thought I wasn't ready to go back. I guess that was true."

Jack continued working busily at the other side of the room. He knew this was a sweet moment for Nick and he remained quiet and inconspicuous in the background. Since they hadn't stepped outside to talk he tried to be respectful of their privacy, but they seemed unconcerned that he was able to hear their conversation.

"It's been tough but I'm doing better." Jenny paused as tears welled up in her eyes. "Now that everyone knows what happened it's been kind of embarrassing, but people have been nice." She shook off her emotions with a brief shudder, like shaking off water after a swim. Nick reached for her hand and squeezed it.

"Nick, I came to thank you. What's happened to you must be horrible, too. I know you've gone through a lot because of me."

"Not because of you, Jenny. *For* you. I did what I did for you because I care so much about you." Nick was amazed how easily the words came out. He'd told her he cared. "I hate what happened to you and I wish it hadn't, but you should never feel embarrassed by it. You didn't provoke it or choose it in any way. It was done to you against your will, and it was despicable."

Jack grinned inwardly. *Bravo, Nick. Bravo!*

"You've been so good to me, Nick. I've always had the feeling that you really were my friend and not just after me because you think I'm pretty. You proved it."

Nick laughed. "Don't make me sound too noble. I don't think you're pretty. I think you're absolutely gorgeous. I also think you're smart, funny and nice to be with. That's intimidating for a guy like me. You're my friend, Jenny, because I'll take anything I can get just to be around you, but don't think I wouldn't love for there to be more between us. I'm crazy about you." Jenny blushed and gave a sheepishly shy shrug.

Jack was really impressed. *Well said, son.*

"So would you allow a good friend to take you to lunch? The Vietnamese place has great noodle bowls." Nick was bold. He figured that as long as he was laying it on the line he might as well take the risk to get things going.

"Sure," Jenny said, "but aren't you working with Jack?"

"Oh, yeah." He gulped and turned toward Jack just in time to see him slipping out the side door. Nick smiled.

"Guess not. Let's go."

* * *

267

They had both ordered beef noodle bowls and giggled at their initial efforts to eat them politely. Nick finally gave up the pretense and exaggerated his troubles by picking up his noodles with chopsticks and slurping them down noisily, much to the chagrin of the proprietors. It caused Jenny to laugh until her eyes teared, which was the whole point for Nick. She, too, stopped trying not to slurp but managed a rather graceful way to shovel the noodles into her mouth.

"Not a good meal to order on a first date," she remarked.

"But this isn't a date, so no worries, right?"

She smiled at him as she used her napkin to dab her chin. "No worries, even if it was a date. Not with you."

Is she trying to say something?

"Seriously, have you dated much?" Nick wasn't sure he wanted to hear the answer, but he had to ask.

"Some. Mostly first dates."

"Trolling for keepers?" He threw it in with a devilish grin.

She chuckled. "I guess you could say that. In a sea of guys that are only about how they look, how I look with them, their status, the car they drive — and how far I'll let them get." The last came hesitantly and without a smile. She said, very seriously, "Never anything else."

"That's not what you're about."

"I don't think of how I look as a personal accomplishment that I had anything to do with. And I sure as *heck* don't think I'm entitled to things just because I exist. No one deserves respect simply because they were born. Respect is something we earn. It comes from hard work and doing things that count. Using the gifts you were given to do good things — things that count."

Nick smiled broadly but didn't say anything.

"What?" Jenny said with an uncomfortable giggle. "Am I being an idiot?"

"You're being wonderful, Jen. All this, and the ability to slurp noodles, too. I can't imagine a better first date. So, am I gonna be one of the lucky saps that gets a second chance? I promise to be a gentleman." Nick decided straightforward boldness would be his new way with Jenny. She deserved nothing less.

"No, Nick."

She paused a long moment to tease him and watch his disappointed reaction, before adding, "*I'll* be the lucky one."

❧ 43 ❧

"So. when do I get to meet Jack? You know I'm dying to." Sue had finished her sack lunch and now sat in the break room sipping her third cup of coffee. Her interrogation mode was on full power.

"Maybe we can all have lunch together next time we both have the same day off." Kate scooped the last spoonful of potato salad into her mouth.

"I have to wait that long?"

Kate laughed. Their shifts were definitely scattered lately. "Don't worry, Sue. You'll meet him soon enough."

"Okay. I guess it's still pretty new and you want his time all to yourself. I'll give you that much. So, does he take you on real dates now?"

"We went to dinner at *Jake's Fish House* the other night. That felt like a real date. It's not like he lives across town. I see him all the time."

"Hon, you need romancing. Sitting at the table eating mac and cheese with Jack and Nick is *not* romantic."

Kate dug into her lunch sack for the rice pudding and pulled out a folded piece of pastel blue paper. She opened it up, then smiled and handed it to Sue. "No, but this is."

Sue looked at the note. On it was a caricature of a man playing a guitar, circumscribed in a heart shape. The note read:

Katy make me a happy man

Tell me that your heart is true.

Say you love me every day

The way that I love you.

"That beats dinner at *Jake's* anytime. What a sweetheart!"

"He is. Once he stopped holding back he became a different man. I've found flowers on the coffee table, a picture of us on my dashboard, a string of pearls in the refrigerator and notes all over the place. I don't know where he comes up with this stuff, but I sure do like it."

"So, has he asked you to move in with him yet?"

Kate knew that Sue could never understand how things were between her and Jack. There would be no 'moving in' for them and they weren't having sex — not even around the blurry edges. With things the way they'd started, they had both agreed to approach their new romance the old fashioned way. As difficult as that was to do that, Kate had to admit that it also felt right. It sent a good message to her son that Jack was not spending the night with her.

"We're taking that slow, Sue. Trust me, things are moving just like they need to." She wasn't going to open up to Sue's relentless quest for juicy stories.

"Well, you sure look happy these days."

"Yes, Sue. I'm *very* happy these days."

ℬ 44 ℭ

Nick and Jenny sat at the dining room table on a late Saturday afternoon, studying for an economics exam. The table was strewn with books, papers and empty soda cans.

"Do you wonder if you're ever gonna need to know this stuff to get by in life?" Nick hated economics. To him, it was all about numbers and statistics and politics.

"Picking out toilet paper at the grocery store is an economic decision. So is buying a car." Jenny batted her eyes at Nick. She knew Jack had been car shopping with Nick earlier that day.

The aroma of roast garlic chicken filled the air as Kate bustled in the kitchen preparing an early dinner. She sprinkled dried cranberries to finish off the salad, then walked to the door of the dining room and stood quietly, watching Nick and Jenny discuss the controversies of normative economics while holding hands under the table. Her heart filled with love and pride.

"You're welcome to stay for dinner, Jenny. Why don't you call your folks and tell them."

"Thanks, Mrs. Weber. Do you need us to clear this stuff off and set the table?"

"We'll just do a casual meal in the living room so you can get back to studying when we finish. Don't worry about helping. I've got it all under control."

Jenny made the call. Jack arrived a few minutes later with a bottle of Chardonnay and a gallon of Rocky Road ice cream.

Looking at the disarray of papers covering the table, he chuckled. "School is for the young and the strong." They smiled their hellos and watched him walk into the kitchen, set his dinner offerings on the counter, and sidle up behind Kate to plant a lingering kiss on her neck.

Jenny whispered to Nick, "Are they in love?"

He answered her out loud, "Either that, or Jack's a vampire." He ducked as Jenny gave his hair a playful tussle.

"Hey, mom, did you make a lot of chicken?" Nick yelled into the kitchen.

"Enough for an army. Why, son? Were you planning on eating for ten?"

"Maybe we could call Sam and Diggs? We can make it a dinner party."

Kate looked out from the kitchen. "Good idea, babe. Give him a call and tell them dinner will be ready in twenty minutes. Tell Sam I made cornbread." Her eyes twinkled.

"Cornbread!?" Jenny's eyes lit up. "I *love* your mother's cornbread."

"I'll tell them to bring the dobro and djembe. We've done enough studying for today. We can have a Cornbread Reunion!"

Jenny cleared the table while Nick went to make the call.

* * *

The dinner was wonderful — full of laughter, enjoyment and jovial bantering. More than once during the meal, Jack had sat back quietly and taken in the happy faces of each of the people he'd come to love so much. It felt like family to him. His family.

The dinner made way for the songs. Time had done its work, and the music was once again full of feeling and soul. The sense of sharing breathed new life into their hearts, and the hope of their future was all about being together.

Jack had taken special notice of Diggs. In a few short weeks, Diggs had settled into a comfortable friendship with Sam, and the changes in him were remarkable. Jack supposed it had a lot to do with living a life that didn't need excuses — a lesson he'd also learned for himself. That night, Diggs had a good place to be, where he belonged. They all did.

As usual, Sam seemed to read his thoughts. As they finished a song, he spoke them out loud. "This be a perfect place t' shine tonight. Feels like a good worn shoe that fits the foot jus' right, don't it?" They all agreed.

"I like the feeling, too, Sam." Diggs looked around shyly as he spoke to them all. "I was looking for a place to rent the last few weeks, man, 'cause my business is starting to pick up a lot. Sam asked if I'd think about renting from him. I think I'm gonna do that — rent from Sam."

"Cool!" Nick voiced his typical abbreviated response to what they all felt.

Jenny added, "You're lucky, Diggs. Being part of all this seems like it'd be a great thing."

"You say that like you're not part of it, Jenny. You are." Jack knew it was important to answer her comment for Nick.

"Well, I guess I mean the music, too. All I do is listen."

"We're both in that boat, Jenny." Kate responded. "But it still means we're part of it."

"It ain't the playin'. It's the sharin'. They's gonna be a pow'rful lotta work t' get things goin' at the garage, and that be a way t' help, if yo' willin'. A heap mo' people gonna be sharin' by an' by. You jus' wait. A place t' hang out don't jus' happen, an' a lotta them folks will jus' be listenin', too."

Jack looked at Sam. "You may be surprised at what you're getting into, Sam. We all might."

"We be doin' what yo' Uncle Dan was doin'. Bringin' folks t'gether and makin' it feel like community. They may even be a few needin' what Diggs done found — a new kind o' Hanger. That be okay, too. My house is gonna be open thataway. Even after I pass, 'cause I be givin' it t' you, Jack.

Nick was stoked like a fire. "That's the coolest idea, Sam! I'll help, and probably Diggs, too." Diggs smiled his agreement.

Jack was concerned. Sam was taking on a lot for a man his age. "You know that it won't be smooth, don't you, Sam? This is a neighborhood that can breed trouble."

"Ain't I seen that a'ready, Jack? We done learnt it the hard way, too. But where they's discord, they's always the hope fo' harmony. We done found it here, an' we ain't special no mo' than others. We jus' practice it is all. All we gotta do is show up and try, with whatever the good Lord gives us."

"You're right, Sam. I think we've all learned that."

Even you, Jack. Even you.

Boda Wise is the pen name and Second Life avatar
of an author and musician who lives in the Pacific Northwest.

Finding Harmony is her first novel.